LOVER

LOVER

ANNA RAVERAT

SARAH CRICHTON BOOKS

FARRAR, STRAUS AND GIROUX   NEW YORK

Sarah Crichton Books
Farrar, Straus and Giroux
18 West 18th Street, New York 10011

Grateful acknowledgment is made for permission to
reprint the following material:
To the Easton Foundation for permission to reprint text from Louise
Bourgeois's *Untitled (I Have Been to Hell and Back)*, 1996. Embroidered
handkerchief; 49.5 × 45.7 cm. © The Easton Foundation/Licensed by
VAGA, New York, NY.
Excerpt from *We're Going on a Bear Hunt* reprinted in the United States with
the permission of Margaret K. McElderry Books, an imprint of
Simon & Schuster Children's Publishing Division, from *We're Going
on a Bear Hunt* by Michael Rosen. Copyright © 1989 by
Michael Rosen. All rights reserved.
Excerpt from *We're Going on a Bear Hunt*. Text © 1989 by
Michael Rosen. Illustrations copyright © 1989 by Helen Oxenbury.
Reproduced in Canada by permission of the publisher, Candlewick Press,
Somerville, MA, on behalf of Walker Books, London.
To *Crazyhorse* and Dave Smith for permission to reprint an
excerpt from Dave Smith's 1971 interview with William Stafford,
published in *Crazyhorse*, vol. 7.

Library of Congress Cataloging-in-Publication Data
Names: Raverat, Anna, author.
Title: Lover : a novel / Anna Raverat.
Description: First American edition. | New York : Sarah Crichton
Books/Farrar, Straus and Giroux, 2017.
Identifiers: LCCN 2016032803 | ISBN 9780374193652 (hardcover) |
ISBN 9780374715687 (e-book)
Subjects: LCSH: Self-realization in women—Fiction. | Life change
events—Fiction. | Married women—Fiction. | Adultery—Fiction. |
Domestic fiction. | BISAC: FICTION / Literary. | FICTION /
Family Life. | FICTION / Contemporary Women.
Classification: LCC PR6118.A387 L69 2017 | DDC 823/.92—dc23
LC record available at https://lccn.loc.gov/2016032803

Our books may be purchased in bulk for promotional, educational, or
business use. Please contact your local bookseller or the Macmillan Corporate
and Premium Sales Department at 1-800-221-7945, extension 5442,
or by e-mail at MacmillanSpecialMarkets@macmillan.com.

www.fsgbooks.com
www.twitter.com/fsgbooks • www.facebook.com/fsgbooks

1 3 5 7 9 10 8 6 4 2

For Lola, and Alfie, and Vince

This being human is a Guest House.
Every morning a new arrival.

A joy, a depression, a meanness,
some momentary awareness comes
as an unexpected visitor.

Welcome and entertain them all!
Even if they're a crowd of sorrows,
who violently sweep your house
empty of its furniture.
Still treat each guest honorably.
He may be clearing you out for some new delight.

—*Rumi*

PART ONE

1

Births:	9
Deaths:	64
Marriages:	12,167

"How many girls and how many boys?"

"Pardon me?"

"Of the births—how many girls, how many boys?" I say.

"We don't have the breakdown," says Trish.

"But isn't that the next question you'd naturally ask? If a country manager reports a baby born in one of our hotels in Shanghai, or Kiev, or Atlanta, wouldn't you want to know if it was a boy or a girl . . . ?"

"The number of boys and girls has no value, business-wise," says Trish.

". . . How he or she is doing? How the mother is? Where they live, or where they are going to live? Do we send a gift?"

"We don't collect that data, Kate."

"Why not, though? Guests of the future, those kids . . ."

"There are only nine of them. People are born in our hotels, people die in them, but those are not typical Guest Experiences. More people get married in hotels, and many more attend as guests of the wedding but also guests of the hotel."

"Double guests," I observe.

"Exactly. And we, or the hotel hosting the wedding, are also hosting the wedding guests," says Trish.

"Double hosts," I say.

I zone out of the meeting and doodle on my branded notepad. I didn't get any sleep because I found emails from another woman on Adam's computer last night. I haven't told him yet because I don't know exactly what I've discovered. Adam crashed out on the sofa but at least he actually slept. He's never had trouble sleeping. Before we got married, when shopping and cooking still felt like playing house, the first time we had a night in, Adam fell asleep in front of the television and I minded. Abandoned on the sofa. The same sofa he slept on last night while I lay awake in our bed, worrying.

I turn the hotel-corporation logo into a skull-faced totem pole with Trish's hairstyle, and it occurs to me that most of our double-concentrate wedding guests are themselves married, or have been, or will be, which means that all over the world, hotel rooms and corridors, bars, spas, restaurants, lifts, and lobbies are populated with brides and grooms of the past, present, and future and I'd guess, though we don't collect this data either, that quite a high percentage are also adulterers because the other thing that hotels are often used for, apart from weddings, is affairs.

"Loyalty is crucial," says Trish, and my attention snaps back into the room. "We talk a lot about brand preference and actually it's the same thing as brand loyalty, which grows out of the Guest Experience, so the key question is: What Do Guests Want?"

She pauses a moment for this to sink in.

"We need to work out what inspires brand loyalty and

apply it. Rigorously. We can't just do things and hope for the best. For example, adding hash browns to the hot items on the breakfast buffet in all the Palazzios, or reinstating concierges across all the Regals, or providing branded umbrellas in the Empire Express chain—are these going to make guests choose us again? Are they impacting the Guest Experience? I'm happy to sanction things we *know* drive brand preference, but if they're not then they are just a cost to the business."

Around the table, several costs to the business shrink visibly—Laura, who brought back concierges, a popular but expensive idea; Owen, who designed the "Empire Strikes Back" umbrellas, so well made that they bound open in their enthusiasm to protect you from the rain; and Sam, who masterminded the hash-browns initiative, which has been slated at head office even though I bet we'd all have hash browns were we staying in a Palazzio, which is unlikely because although Palazzio is our biggest and best-known brand, it's a little downmarket for most of the executives in the room.

Trish takes us through the figures for 2007, how we're performing relative to our main competitors. It's not good news. The main competition is, as always, Hilton and InterContinental Hotel Group, but now we also have to watch out for Novotel.

"We've got to steal market share," says Trish. The Senior Vice President for Sales and Marketing and my new boss, Trish is one of the most powerful people in Palazzio Hotel Corporation. Highly ambitious, a tall and broad bottle-blonde, a formidable presence in any situation, a handsome woman you'd have to say, and, on a good day, sexy. She goes on. "Our strategy to steal share is brand preference. We must win loyalty so that guests choose us. Not just once but every time they need a hotel." The whole room agrees with Trish. This is what we must do. I've only been here four months, but already I've heard what people say about her: you can dot the *i*'s but don't cross the *t*.

"The question we need to answer is: What Do Guests Want?" says Trish, and summons Nick from marketing. He is wearing a yellow cashmere golfing jumper. Trish stiffens her spine and leans in toward the screen. The rest of us slump and lean away.

"We know that finding a hotel at the end of a long day of meetings or travel can be stressful, so we want our Hardworking Heroes to start relaxing the moment they see the familiar Empire Express sign," Nick says. "We want them to start feeling at home when they walk over the branded welcome mat at the main entrance, and when they enter the registration area the background music should soothe their minds and reinforce their confidence that they've made a smart choice. It's not just visible things that make a difference—we need to leverage all the senses to build up a sense of familiarity and ease with our hotels. In many ways we're training guests just as much as we train staff."

Like dogs, I think—but don't say. There are fifteen people in this meeting, eight hundred in head office and six hundred and thirty-three thousand spread out over twelve thousand hotels in a hundred countries. We're all just single digits in a giant corporate machine and the idea, I've learned, is to blend into the bigger number.

Trish clears her throat. "Nick's point is that although you can see many aspects of branding in broad daylight, where it really works is subliminal. And we have to achieve consistency across *all* areas."

Nods of agreement in the half-dark room.

"We've been doing a lot of work on how to make the Guest Experience richer, and what we've come up with is Signature Scent." Nick clicks up a new slide:

Brand Standard 739

Scent Specifications
- Hotels must provide the brand-defined Signature Scent throughout reception and lobby areas
- The SS must have a strong presence in all public areas of the hotel
- The SS must be operational from 0700 to 2200 hours
- Scent machines must be located at regular intervals (the quantity of machines will vary according to lobby size)
- Scent cartridges must be replaced monthly to ensure consistent delivery of scent
- No other scented products in the lobby and registration areas of the hotel. (Staff wishing to wear perfume may wear the Signature Scent as body spray.)

"Do we really need that last point?" I say. "Surely nobody will opt to *wear* the Signature Scent?"

"They do," says Nick. "We piloted this in New Orleans and Singapore. People wanted the spray."

"It's a freebie," says Sam. "Try some!" She brings out a box from underneath the table with samples—"Diamond" for the Regal hotels, "Palazzio Pearl" for the Palazzios, and "Empire Amethyst" for the Empire Express chain.

"Look," says Trish. "There are more complaints than we can tolerate about hotels not being 'fresh' enough. Bad smells drifting into the lobby—burned food, fried breakfasts, even drains sometimes. This is how we're addressing it."

"But it's not just that," says Sam. "There's a positive side to this too! It's like the advice you get when you're selling your house—prepare warm bread or fresh coffee when people are looking round, because the delicious smell will make them more likely to buy. We go so much by our senses. It must go back to when we lived in caves and things like that."

"Right, I get it," I say, "though we might want to look at the acronym. The SS could be problematic in some places."

"Like where?" says Sam.

"Germany, France, and Great Britain for a start," I say. "Austria, Poland—"

"I really don't think it will make much difference, but you can check that when you go," says Trish.

I'd forgotten about my trip to Poland. I don't know how I'm going to get through it now.

I think back to yesterday—Sunday afternoon, pottering about at home. Adam is getting ready to go out for Christmas drinks with his friends. Our daughters are in the kitchen feeding chocolate cereal to Charlie the dog, a black Staff who's grown stout with age.

I want to check the gym schedule, because we're going

to Adam's parents for Christmas and the polite extra eating can only be mitigated by exercise before as well as after, so I go into the box room we use as a study to see if I can use Adam's computer. This is already strange because Adam always keeps his computer locked and, knowing this, why bother? But still. I wander in and waggle the mouse and BAM!—his emails. A woman's name I don't recognize. And her calling my husband Prince Charming.

I recoil from the screen, retreat from the room immediately. Dazed, I sit on our rumpled, unmade bed. Downstairs the children start squabbling. They sound so far away. Bubbles rather than voices rising up past my ears. I am a spent swimmer with no land in sight. If I ask him, he will fob me off. On some distant shore, Adam steps out of the shower.

He enters with dripping-wet hair and a towel wrapped around his middle. I can't look at him. "I'm going to run a bath for the girls," I say, and walk out. It is surprisingly easy to act normal, especially since normal already includes one or both of us being a bit pissed off.

Once the children are asleep and Adam out, I set up on the floor in the study with bags of presents, wrapping paper, tape, scissors, glass of wine. Adam's emails have been carefully put away again, the account locked. A little box is waiting for the correct password. I type in Adam's birthday, my fingers and nerves aflutter because I am stealing something, or attempting to. The numbers and letters I tap into the keyboard come up as dots on the screen, as if the computer is aiding and abetting me by hiding my break-in, but then it switches allegiance—it's Adam's computer after all: wrong password. I go back to sitting on the floor, swig the wine, and put the glass down too quickly so that some of it sloshes out onto the gift I am wrapping, a pale blue toweling dressing gown for his mother.

Aha—his mother's maiden name!

Password Incorrect.

I am relieved—I have failed to transgress—but then I remember why I am doing this. Who is Louise Phelps and why is she calling my husband Prince Charming?

Somewhere inside myself I already know. Often Adam doesn't come to bed until the small hours—he dozes in front of the television until I am asleep—and if knowing includes this feeling of heavy, unspecified dread, then I've known for ages, been working very hard at not knowing, at keeping that knowledge battened down, out of sight, out of earshot, in a locked chest where I can't feel it. Recently it has started seeping out. I bought a book called *The Happy Couple: How to Make Long-Term Relationships Last and Thrive*, the kind of book Adam scoffs at but hasn't noticed me reading because he doesn't come over to my side of the bed very often; or if he has noticed, he isn't commenting. And, a few weeks ago, when I woke and Adam wasn't there, I tiptoed into the study and surprised him at his computer—which he hurriedly closed, bundling me back to bed. Not a big thing, but clues don't have to be big—they just have to be spiky enough to poke through the membrane of usual awareness, like a splinter, or a thorn. The next morning, when I asked him what he'd been doing, he said, "Working." I did not question further.

I type more passwords, less hesitant now, as if finding the right word will avert rather than bring on disaster. It isn't our wedding anniversary, the place we met, the place we married. I continue wrapping presents. A train set and a pirate ship for the girls, a selection of handmade chocolates for my mother, a pair of beige cashmere socks for his father, and for my father a DVD boxed set of Laurel and Hardy.

Two hours later, my wineglass drained, I have a mini-epiphany. I tell his computer that I have forgotten the password and it replies with a security question to which I know the answer: his father's middle name.

I find Prince Charming straightaway. I still don't know who Louise Phelps is, but in her email she commends Adam on his impeccable courtesy, she agrees with him that they should no longer be in contact, and she is grateful to him for having had the good sense to stop this thing before it had got out of hand, because she doesn't want to threaten her marriage either. So that's odd. Instead of discovering an affair, I seem to have discovered the end of one.

I scroll through an exchange of chatty, flirty, witty emails, outraged at the sheer effort Adam made on Louise Phelps's behalf, and I hate reading how she lapped it all up. It is like watching a courtship, I think, then correct myself: not "like." My husband has been chasing another woman and here it is, right in front of me in one long chain of correspondence: the most compelling thing I've ever read.

There are eighty-four emails between Adam and Louise

Phelps, each one a cold, metal scoop taking something away from my insides. I was safe before; now I'm not. It wasn't perfect, our marriage, but it was solid with firm foundations, a good place to bring up a family. I read thirty-two of their emails, but I don't have time to read them all because it is 11:45 and Adam said he would be back by midnight.

At 11:59 I am in bed, long and rigid in the dark, eyes staring up at the ceiling, arms stiff by my sides. I hear the front door open at 12:14, some slumping about in the hall, which would be Adam taking off his coat and boots; some clunking, which would be him emptying his back pockets of wallet, keys, and phone onto the kitchen table; the suction sound of the fridge opening and a clink—more beer, maybe a glass of milk—the TV going on and the sitting-room door being pushed, by his foot probably, over the carpet and softly closing. The sounds rattle off me.

1:14. Adam by now passed out on the sofa. The house is quiet but I am not absorbing anything. The thoughts racing over my surface are brittle, less than a millimeter deep. I lie in the dark, a blinking stick.

At 3:20 I open *The Happy Couple* by Dr. Janis B. Rosenfeld and Dr. Michael Abrahams MD and turn to the chapter on infidelity. There are different sorts, apparently; listed in a handy chart and color-coded. Least threatening is when one-half of the couple gets a crush on a third party: sugar pink, not so bad, can even be invigorating for the main relationship. In the middle are active flirtations, bright coral, but if also a secret these turn into traffic-light red: Stop! Danger! At the far end of the spectrum, past chili pepper, beyond brick and beets, shrouded in burgundy lurks the darkest kind, but even this is not necessarily marriage-death. The important thing, say Rosenfeld and Abrahams, is to be able to talk about it.

We never talk about things like this. I trawl my memory. Once, in our twenties, Adam admitted admiration for Jennifer Lopez; it didn't blossom into an ongoing conversation, but there were other things we didn't mention. For example, we didn't talk properly about the fact that his work wasn't going very well. Adam quit his job three years ago to set up his own business. He keeps busy but doesn't earn enough for us to live on—we've barely been scraping by—which is why I'm back at work full-time as "Director of Business Innovation" at PHC. It's a new role and I'm only just getting to grips with it, but basically my job is to contribute to the financial growth of the company by generating new projects, products, and services. I was pleased to take this job; I had good years at home with the girls and they're both now in school, and anyway I like work. I love hotels—I've built my whole career in or around them and it's always an adventure, staying in one. Hospitality has always appealed to me; looking after people, making them feel at home.

The Guest Experience meeting isn't going too well and Trish's irritation is growing. "Look. If we all want to keep our jobs, and I assume we do, then we are going to have to do better than this. Our brands are not currently preferred by the market. Let me recap: we have made a promise to shareholders. Palazzio Hotel Corporation's profits will rise from three hundred and thirty million pounds to four hundred and forty-five million in the next twenty-four months. The City will not be kind if we don't deliver on it.

We have to open more hotels, we have to get guests in, and we have to keep them coming back: with transport links multiplying and everything becoming faster and more dig-ital, travelers' tastes and needs are evolving rapidly, forcing us to innovate constantly or lose out to the competition. This place badly needs some innovation—" She pauses and looks over at me, and for a moment I fear she's going to say that the future of the company depends on how well I do my job. Thankfully, she doesn't.

"The Guest Experience is what holds it all together, it's the key to brand loyalty. Gérard—could you capture this on the flip chart?"

I'm not the only one crazy with lack of sleep and strung out on coffee and adrenaline—Trish's hair is more firmly sprayed, her eyes more lavishly made up than usual, as if she needed to fix herself into place. I notice Trish's eyelashes made into long spiders' legs by thick coats of mascara, not quite hiding the puffy circles that betray a fair few night-caps of single malt, and the silk scarf side-knotted at her throat, a kind of faux-casual air-stewardess look. It's the faux you have to watch out for.

Gérard writes on the flip chart *What Guests Want*, and underlines it.

"We've done some market research on this," he says.

"And what does the market tell us?" says Trish.

"Location is important. Perhaps the most important—"

"We know that. What else?"

"Clean room, good price . . ."

"Yes, yes, of course—but those are basic. Granted, we have to get the basic things right, but every hotel has to, that's what the guest expects. Those are Guest Expecta-tions." Trish pauses while Gérard writes it on the flip chart.

"Beyond these, when they stay in our hotels, what experience can we give them that will make guests choose us again? What's going to inspire brand loyalty? What Do Guests Want?"

"What do guests want?" repeats Gérard thoughtfully.

The $443 million question. I look at Trish's tired skin, the shadows etched under her eyes that no amount of light-reflecting, skin-plumping, or radiance-bestowing Dior, Chanel, or L'Oréal could conceal.

"What do guests *want*?" says Nick from marketing, sounding desperate.

I feel my own eyes prickling. I didn't close them for more than twenty minutes last night. I have drunk so much coffee that my fingertips feel wrinkled, my tongue a used doormat.

"A good night's sleep," I say.

Nick lets out a little cry of relief; his shoulders drop.

Gérard breaks into a wide smile.

Trish practically hugs me.

2

As soon as I get out of the office, profit and guests and
their various experiences leave my mind. The cold evening
air is a door that closes on Palazzio, the outside another
room. Normally I'd be worrying about getting home in
time to read a bedtime story to the girls, but tonight all I
want to read is the rest of the emails between Adam and
Louise Phelps. I need to see for myself how it started,
and when, and where. I take the back way to the station, a
narrow forgotten street, little more than an alley, longer
but much quieter—just Peter and his junk shop, his friend
Ronnie and their parrot. Not many office workers venture
back here because there are no coffee shops or sandwich
bars, but I like to get away at lunchtime and I don't want to
go to Starbucks or Subway, because when you substitute
one corporate world for another you're breathing the
same stuff.

"Shop" is probably too grand a word for Peter's place;
it's more like a lockup with some shelf units and tables
outside. Or a drinking club for bedraggled pensioners;
Peter and his friends standing around in heavy overcoats
in winter, reclining on deck chairs in summer; smoking and
drinking whatever the weather, listening to crackly old
vinyl, the record player on a foldaway picnic table against
the wall. The other friends come and go but Ronnie is stal-
wart. Something awful must have happened to him once
because his nose looks as though it were bitten off at the
end, so what he's got now is a shortened snub with alarm-

ingly large nostrils. Ronnie is overweight and a bit thin on top, wears a flat cap to cover it, gathers the rest of his hair in a scant ponytail. He wears a gold earring and a gold signet ring and looks like he could have been a roadie touring with big bands, lifting and fighting his way around the country. Peter, a Greek-Cypriot, is as thin as a whippet with high cheekbones, lined olive skin, and a bony nose. Both of them dye their hair black and sometimes you can see white roots growing out.

"Hello, darling," says Peter.

"Hello, darling," says Ronnie.

"Hello, boys," I reply, and they chortle because they are long past boyhood.

"Whiskey for you, darling?" says Peter as usual, and as usual I decline, though tonight I am tempted.

"How's Toto? I bet parrots don't like the cold much," I say. Toto is quiet in his cage just inside the door.

"I give him whiskey," says Peter. I hope he's joking.

We first spoke when I bumped into him carrying a life-sized horse's head down the alley that he said was a bust of Shergar the kidnapped racehorse, but our acquaintance really came about because of Toto, who was left behind by a guest in the Palazzio, South Kensington, two months ago. The poor creature ended up in head office, but premises decreed that no animals could be kept on site so I took it round to Peter.

"Where you going to take it if I say no?"

"Battersea Dogs Home?" I said. "I've heard they take other animals. Well, cats anyway."

"Are you crazy—they will kill it!" said Peter.

"Or we could take him to a vet, they might be able to find a home for him."

"I will keep it," said Peter.
"Are you sure?"
"Yes, I like animals. Does it talk?"

I come out of the alley onto the busy main street by the Tube and am waiting to cross the road when I feel a rumbling underneath, a slight vibration in the soles of my feet. It must be an underground train, though I've never felt this shake here before, up through my heels and into my spine. I glance at the people standing next to me but they give no indication that they feel anything—eyes fixed on the red man on the pedestrian crossing. Everyone is on autopilot apart from a Japanese couple to my left who are pointing in a book. Everything looks so solid but it's just a layer and there's all this stuff underneath that I rarely think about.

Is Adam having an affair? The couple are showing me a map that they can't read and neither can I. The green man appears, people start to cross the road, and then comes the worst sound I ever heard, the sound of a person being hit by a car: THUdd. And a short squeal, wheels skidding.

The woman slaps her hand over her mouth and her partner clutches her arm. The crowd crossing the road freezes. Everyone's full attention is yanked to the spot. Everyone within hearing distance, a surprisingly wide radius, recognizes the sound instantly—one of our kind, down.

The car, a glossy black Audi, stands still on the road, fumes rising from the exhaust, white air curling up from under the front bumper like breath. For a quarter of a second, motion all around is suspended: all ears are on full alert, all bodies calibrate, and all brains send the message that there is no immediate threat, because there isn't a pack of rampaging Audis and this one is not about to strike again.

Two or three people huddle over a body of which I can only see the legs, bent awkwardly, and the bottom of a pair of shoes. It's a man, I think, judging by the soles. Perhaps the driver is one of those huddling over him, because the driver's door is open, and the car is empty. People are moving toward the accident, to get a better look. I cross the road in order to get farther away and as I do, I see the car is not empty after all—there's a boy of about five years old with curly hair strapped into a booster seat, wide-eyed and silent. I wonder if I should go over. Then again, it might freak him out completely to have a stranger approaching out of nowhere. I am not a doctor, I tell myself; I would probably just get in the way.

Drifts of music float up. There's a busker at the bottom of the escalator, strumming a guitar and singing in a sweet voice about love. A man's voice comes over the loudspeaker, announcing delays on other lines, the two of them in a strange, disconnected duet. The singer's very good. I'm glad to see lots of copper, silver, and gold coins lying on the black felt lining of her guitar case like so many wishes. I've got to do something about those emails. I wish I knew what. I reach into my purse and drop in a pound.

As I come up out of the underground, it is raining hard. Cars have their headlights on, pedestrians have their heads down, hoods and hats on. The rain-soaked road could almost be a river. A big ball of stress inside me rises and expands like dough. I have to pack for Poland but I'm upset and exhausted and I'm worried that Adam will notice and want me to explain so I detour via the bookshop, a slightly disheveled independent five minutes from our front door. I go in quite often. I've ordered some books to fill the holes in my Christmas gifts but there's a queue by the till. I flip through a book by Paul McKenna that's on display. The title shouts: *I CAN MAKE YOU THIN*. Great! I skim-read the chapter headings and the four Golden Rules. I look at Paul McKenna's photograph: bright eyes, a knowing smile verging on a smirk, a good suit with a posy of chest hair poking out the top of his shirt, and an expensive gold watch—a really lovely, solid gold watch. When I realize that the main thing I've noticed is the gold watch, I snap out of the reverie. Can you be hypnotized by a photograph?

The nice man on the till really is nice; he's courteous, he looks at people properly and listens. If I had a flirtation with someone like him, that would even things out. But I know this kind of tit-for-tat thinking won't solve our problems. I put Paul McKenna down; this is not the sort of thing I want to be seen looking at in public, especially not in my local bookshop and especially not by the nice man on the till. I am not going to buy this book.

Instead I pick up *Where in the World: The 100 Best Places to Stay*, go straight to the index and look up Palazzio Hotel Corporation. I'm pleased to see that we have eighteen entries; our highest-rated is the Regal on Park Lane, at number three. I've never stayed the night but I spent a week of my induction there and it was fascinating. I'm proud to work at PHC, though I still haven't got used to the corporate side of things; sometimes it feels as though I've joined an army by mistake.

The nicest hotel I ever stayed in was in Sweden, outside a village at the edge of a lake. White sails far out on the glittering water. People sitting outside a couple of busy restaurants, talking in the afternoon sunshine, boats rocking in the small harbor, masts and metal knocking against each other with a satisfyingly industrious sound.

Sigmaholm was the name of the village and the hotel. When I arrived, a large brown dog lay sleeping in the shade, and there was a woman reading a magazine on a lichen-covered bench, a small boy happily piling pebbles at her feet. Once a monastery, some of the peacefulness had carried over into its life as a hotel. The rooms were fairly bare—white floorboards, single bed, small desk with a lamp—and yet the feeling was not of austerity but of softness, and clarity. A quilted cushion on the wooden chair, a blue-and-white-checked blanket folded at the foot of the bed, a couple of old books on the shelf, both of them in Swedish but I looked through them anyway, charmed by the near and far: here was something I could hold, smell the mildew-dotted pages, run my fingers over the knots and grooves of the paper, sense the life of them, guess at their meaning, but still never really know them. A casement window opened out onto a walled garden. Growing between the bricks were mosses and daisies and other plants, some with tiny pink flowers, so that the walls themselves were living things, truly part of the garden.

I wanted to go back there for our honeymoon but instead we toured Ireland, staying in bed-and-breakfasts along the way. We ranked the guesthouses in our own league table; best bed award went to a place in Tralee, best breakfast in Tramore, the worst bed-and-breakfast was in a scuzzy place in Westport. Adam said it would be all right so we stayed, but the bed was a padded sinkhole. The sex that night was quick and he ended up sleeping on the floor. In the morning we were served pale sausages and eggs as lumpy as the mattress on damp toast. Adam arranged his into a cock and balls and we giggled like schoolchildren all through paying the bill, and went and had sex in the hire car. Ravenous afterward, I tormented Adam with descriptions of the breakfast at Sigmaholm: six different kinds of fresh juice and smoothie, homemade pancakes with berries and syrup, oak-smoked dry-cured bacon, organic eggs, rye toast—I love everything about hotels, but if I had to choose one thing it would be the breakfasts, Aladdin's caves of tempting foods you've got to try: acacia honey—translucent, the color of sunset; a soft white roll, warm, with farmhouse butter; a small bowl of fruit salad; a couple of spoonfuls of the bircher muesli because you've heard about it; just one madeleine with the second pot of coffee. "Just a little bit" has been my basic approach to eating and drinking since I was a teenager. Unfortunately a little bit of everything over twenty years adds up to quite a lot.

"Look at Mummy's big boobies!" said Hester the other morning as I was getting dressed, which wasn't even true—they're so small that I don't have to lift them to dry underneath—and "Mummy's got a great big floppy bottom!" said Milla, more accurately.

"Don't be cheeky," Adam told the girls. I would have liked him to say that he loved my bottom, thought it the best bottom in the world and that he wouldn't be without it, but inevitably things had changed a bit since the honey-moon; less sex, more bottom, two young children, my full-time job, him running his own business from home, a mortgage that seemed too big on a house that seemed too small: the distance between us was understandable. I'd noticed, just hadn't known what to do about it, and I knew Adam felt it too. We'd started a few projects. Last autumn I suggested we make the backyard nicer, so Adam heaved up slabs of paving and broke the ground with a pickax to make flower beds. Underneath was dense, wet clay—not crumbling earth full of goodness as I'd imag-ined, but anyway I planted bulbs for the spring. I didn't think daisies would grow out of our walls because they were only one brick wide and too new, too tightly packed.

In the middle of that walled garden at Sigmaholm was a round stone well filled with water, coins lying at the bottom. I dipped into my purse and found a penny—thought better of it and took out a gold pound instead; maybe the powers that be don't care whether the coin is copper or gold, but I wasn't sure about that. At dusk they lit candles all around the hotel; I could see the glow at the windows. The garden was full of birds darting down from the eaves, the hum of insects and distant cars. I made my wish. Hooves clattered past on the road outside, the unseen horses as tantalizing as a half-remembered dream.

3

We are arguing about what to call it. He disputes the use of "affair" because they didn't have sex and therefore it was not an affair but an "inappropriate friendship." I believe him about the sex but object to the wording. I think "affair" is more accurate because their "friendship" was a secret from me and from her own husband and from their normal perhaps boring but appropriate friends, and because they had kissed.

"Ah, but the kiss was chaste," said Adam. "Just a quick goodbye at Charing Cross station. Bob and Tim were there."

"Fleeting, maybe," I said, "but not chaste. I saw the emails, Adam. She called you Prince Charming."

"There were other people there. Bob and Tim."

"You wrote in one email that you couldn't stop thinking about her."

"It was a brief kiss goodbye at the station."

"On the lips."

"Yes, but brief."

"OK," I said, "you can have 'brief.' You can't have 'chaste.'"

The girls should be in bed by now. They usually have a book at bedtime but tonight they are watching a DVD of *Diego and Rosita* and Adam tells me his story.

Once upon a time, there was a man named Adam who

was a director of a small to medium-sized business. He was good at his job; his staff and clients and board of directors all loved him, but he himself wasn't happy. He couldn't get excited about finding new ways to sell toothpaste, or orange squash, or processed cheese. It was making him die inside. And so, one day, he left that company and struck out on his own, to do some honest, more satisfying work. A year after he left, there was a leaving party for an old colleague, which Adam attended, and lo and behold he wound up sitting next to his former administrator, Louise Armstrong, an extremely pretty girl ten years his junior. They talked all night. She had married and was now Louise Phelps, had a baby, had stopped work, left London and gone to live in rural East Kent, where she was bored and lonely. (She didn't actually say she was bored and lonely but that's what came across.) Adam listened. He felt sorry for her. Plus she was still extremely pretty, even if she had not yet lost the baby weight. And so a correspondence began, which was innocuous, and although they did meet for a drink once—with Bob and Tim—it was no big deal and not worth mentioning to their respective spouses because, although he sees that, from another point of view, mine for example, it could look quite different, they really were just good friends.

I go up to our bedroom, not to sleep—to growl, and chew over Adam's account, unpalatable, but the bones of it might be true. Half an hour later I make a demand: Louise Phelps's phone number.

"What are you going to say to her?" he asks.

"I don't know," I snap back.

*

We are curt in the kitchen. The children have noticed that something is wrong and they are watching us closely. Charlie the dog, a barometer for tension in our household, looks miserable and doesn't have to be told to stay in his basket. He has a coughing fit, and Hester, who is four, goes and puts her arms around him and says, "Poor Charlie."

"Yes, poor Charlie," I say, lifting Hester out of the dog basket.

Adam sends the girls upstairs to brush their teeth. When they have left the room he hands me a folded piece of paper. I open it. On the top half of the paper, placed centrally, tilting upward, is her name and number, written in pencil. This knocks the breath out of me—something about the clean white sheet, seeing her name in his hand.

Louise Phelps answers her phone straightaway.

"This is Kate. Adam's wife."

"Hello," she replies, sounding nervous.

"I found the emails between you and my husband. I want to know what's going on."

"Nothing," she says. "Nothing is going on. We were emailing, and I suppose the emails did get a bit flirty, but nothing apart from that."

"But you did see each other," I assert.

"Yes, just once—"

"Did you have sex with him?"

"No! No! I promise you, no. Nothing like that at all."

"Does *your* husband know about this?"

"No. He doesn't and if he found out he would never forgive me. Please don't tell him. It was stupid and I am really, really sorry."

She sounds wretched, and young. I feel suddenly very tired and very bored. Maybe this isn't a crisis. Maybe it is just a colossal pain in the arse, something we have to get through, like admin—a big pile of marriage admin.

The emails brought back memories of us fighting, years ago, over another work colleague. Before the children were born, when Adam worked at an advertising agency in Soho, there was a group who used to do lunch and after-work drinks together—innocuous, until I started to hear the name Sara a bit too often and with a bit too much enthusiasm, which in itself would have been OK, but one weekend when I was away one of the group invited the rest to lunch at a country pub and Adam took Sara on the back of his motorbike. We had a huge row and it was uncomfortable between us for a while, but a few months later he moved jobs and the motorbike ride faded into the horizon. I try to remember the last time he took me out on the back of his motorbike.

"Are you in touch with Sara?"

"Who? Oh, her. No. Not at all. Look, Kate, it was just a stupid email flirtation and that one drink—"

"—with Bob and Tim," I supplied.

Adam nodded.

"So where were Bob and Tim sitting?" I asked.

"They were sitting next to each other and we were sitting next to each other."

"And did you stay like that or did you move around?"

"Stayed like that, pretty much."

"So basically you were talking to her the whole night."

"Basically, yes."

"And what did you talk about?"

"Work, mainly. She's not working now, since she had the baby, and she's been quite down—postnatal depression."

"You want me to feel sorry for her?"

"No, I'm just saying—"

"Because I DON'T feel sorry for her—"

"I know."

"She knows you're married."

"Yes."

"She's married too."

"Yes," says Adam quietly. He'd told me about that motorbike ride with Sara years ago, but he had hidden this thing with Louise Phelps and I had uncovered it and was he now being sincere? Tone is important. Also, it's important to call things correctly, but in this case it was difficult—not quite an affair but more than a flirtation; possibly Adam's term "inappropriate friendship" was the nearest, but it sounded so silly that I couldn't bring myself to say it. Adam had always teased me about being a pedant, and I would correct him: not pedantic but precise, and although this was part of the joke it really did feel important, because finding the right word can be very settling—like telling, or being told, the truth.

"You kissed her."

"Very briefly, just a peck."

"Yes, but on the lips. She's postnatally depressed and she lives in rural East Kent, Adam. Of course she thought you were Prince Charming—the big boss in the big city making big eyes at her."

Fury balloons up inside me and just as quickly the air escapes, my anger shrivels, and I stop shouting because in fact I *do* feel a bit sorry for Louise and because Adam isn't the big boss anymore and actually it's possible that he is depressed too. He didn't leave his well-paid, secure job to satisfy a burning desire to set up on his own; he left because he couldn't stand it. He started to complain about his work more and more. "It's bullshit," he would say, frustrated, and his situation gradually worsened until he came home from work one day and lay down on the sitting-room floor in his mac and suit and tie and cuff links and shiny shoes—it was a collapse, really—his leather briefcase beside him like a brick. I knelt down and stroked his hair, helped him up off the floor, hung up his coat, unlaced his shoes and loosened his tie, sat him on the sofa and held him. I told him he didn't have to do that job anymore; we could sell the house, leave London, and live differently, because nothing was worth him feeling that way.

His despair, him being lost in it, was frightening. After Hester was born, I stopped work to look after the girls, so we relied on his salary. We talked about what we could do, where we could go. We discussed moving to Cornwall, but when we thought about actually living there all we could imagine was closed fudge shops in February, so we decided to stay in London. My parents are still in Yorkshire in the home my brother and I grew up in; Adam's live in Nottingham. We couldn't imagine setting up in those places either; relocating and starting again anywhere would take a whole lot of energy that we just didn't have.

Three months later he left his job and we set out on a new life—except it was the same as the old one, with far less money. Adam didn't get happier and things between us became harder—instead of plotting his escape together we argued more and more, which was understandable given the pressures of having a young family, not enough money, and getting his business up and running. I told myself that it would take a while to adjust. That was three years ago.

In *The Happy Couple: How to Make Long-Term Relationships Last and Thrive*, Dr. Janis B. Rosenfeld and Dr. Michael Abrahams MD say any crisis can be weathered if the relationship is strong enough. I believe them. Their top three indicators of a fit and healthy relationship are talking, spending time together, and satisfying sex. I want a marriage like they describe, but ours is limping along badly and I can't blame it all on a pretty ex-colleague from rural East Kent. Drs. Rosenfeld and Abrahams say that sometimes it takes a crisis to bring about change. Unfortunately, they don't define "crisis." I'm not sure Louise qualifies, though Adam's collapse on the sitting-room floor probably does. In any case, according to their criteria, we're in trouble.

"We don't talk and we don't spend time together," I say.

"We are now," says Adam.

"And we hardly ever have sex."

He sighs. We are both quiet.

"You know that book I'm reading?" I ask.

"Which one?"

"The one about long-term relationships—in that, they say that something like this can actually be good."

"*How?*" The incredulity in his voice makes me smile. If he thinks things are terrible, then maybe he's not hiding anything. Maybe it was a simple fuck-up, an error of judgment caught just in time, a problem that can be fixed.

A noise comes from the children's bedroom—a sleepy whimper that we both know will grow into a cross child if it is not attended to immediately.

"I'll go," says Adam.

While he's upstairs, I just sit. I am hollowed out by exhaustion, ready to collapse inward. I feel myself give up the fight. I see the spines of our photograph albums, wedged in on the shelf above the TV. Not long ago I finally got round to adding snaps from a fortnight in Crete we'd had when Milla was eighteen months old and I was pregnant with Hester, our best family holiday. We'd booked last minute and found a one-bedroom villa in a lemon grove, set apart from a network of larger villas around a swimming pool. From the shade of the trees we watched the world go by. The owner was a tall, strong man in his sixties with a deep tan and long, thick white hair and beard. He would water the plants, taking his time, trimming the grass where needed and, with the sharp side of his shovel, cutting away the rogue branches sprouting out of tree trunks. The courtyard was lined with large terra-cotta pots and raised beds: more lemon trees, roses, geraniums, jasmine, and camellias. The cleaning lady worked quietly; all you could hear was the creak of her sandals. Early each morning she would sweep the dropped blossom into scented heaps.

Our tiny cottage was the cheap option but we loved it—or I thought we had. That's when Adam first started to complain about his job; was he unhappy even then? He would take Milla to buy bread for breakfast; I'd set the table with orange juice and coffee, butter and honey, and they'd come back with Milla carrying a warm loaf, proud and delighted. Most days we'd take a siesta after lunch, snoozing together on the big bed in the sunlit room.

Nowadays we go to bed separately. I try to remember when that started and when we began having arguments about money, which I would like to write off as surface but which go deep into who we are and how we live. Most nights I go upstairs first, Adam waiting until he assumes I am asleep. Often, very late, he folds laundry and hangs up washing. He moves carefully on the landing, but there's a creaky floorboard in front of the airing cupboard that always wakes me up. I lie in bed listening, waiting, but when he's finished folding clothes he goes into the study and quietly closes the door.

In the mornings I catch him in the kitchen as he's busying about refilling Charlie's water or getting out cereal or taking things over to the dishwasher. Sleep-softened, I put my arms around him, nuzzle and kiss him, and he'll squeeze me. "Hug me with *both* hands," I say, and sometimes then he will put down the bowl or the box or whatever he's carrying and hold me properly.

Upstairs the toilet flushes, and I hear the familiar weight and timing of Adam's footfall as he comes back down.

"It was Hester, she kicked her duvet off again. Maybe we should get her one of those sleeping-bag things you told me about."

I nod.

"You look knackered," says Adam.

"Thanks," I say, but I can't muster any real pique because I know he doesn't mean it like that.

"I don't mean it like that," he says gently. "Shall I make you a cup of tea?"

I listen to Adam moving around the kitchen, the soft pad of his socks on the tiles. He's unpacking the groceries— I can hear the tall corner cupboard open, tins knocking against bottles, fat bags of pasta rustling as he shoves them onto the shelf, the cupboard closing and now the rush of the tap. I imagine the amber light as I hear the click of the kettle being switched on. The cupboard door creaks as it opens because the bottom screw needs tightening, the lid clatters on the work surface as he takes a tea bag from the old gold tin that I like. A little tap of wood on wood as the door closes again, a spoon clinks in a cup and the background noise of the kettle—a sort of air-shuffle—gradually loudens and obscures other sounds. The steam will be rising up past the pile of paper on top of the fridge, which includes shopping lists, bills and bank statements, and a letter from the school about a trip to the Museum of London with a permission slip that needs signing. I can be in the room without being in the room. I switch on the TV; it's the news. There's a story about a would-be terrorist whose dastardly plot was sniffed out by a dog at Heathrow and not a police dog either but a lay-dog owned by a member of the public, and now this dog is a hero.

Adam comes in with the tea in my favorite cup, a gesture that is not lost on me but I don't acknowledge it. From the kitchen I hear the low, comforting thrum of the dishwasher. He sits down on the sofa at a strange new proximity— usually when we are in the middle of a row there's at least a meter between us, but tonight Adam puts himself only half a meter away. It's another gesture, and this time I do respond, because if he is prepared to sit in the gulf between us then the least I can do is throw him a line.

"Have you heard about this dog?" I ask.

"Yeah, brilliant, isn't it?"

"The girls will love that story," I say.

"I told them about it today, they did love it. Milla wants to train Charlie."

"To do what?"

"Anything. I said we could try getting him to beg."

"I should try getting you to beg. For forgiveness."

"I will—I am," he says, faltering—he thought we'd left the war zone.

"Charlie's a bit old for training, isn't he?" I say, instantly regretting the forgiveness comment. Maybe I should just give the guy a break. If we can manage to talk to each other, to show some affection, things will be all right.

"Oh, I don't know," says Adam. "He used to fetch a stick and walk to heel, remember?"

"Not really," I say, because Charlie has always been unbiddable. When I met Adam, Charlie was young and sleek. They came as a pair. Adam used to bring him to work, where he would bound through the office, knocking over wastepaper bins and eating food from unattended desks, which some people found endearing and others found annoying. I was in the second group, but it wasn't enough to put me off Adam, and over the years I'd grown fond of Charlie.

"I'm taking Charlie into Hester's class this week," says Adam.

"That's good," I say.

The newsreader announces another item: "*A hotel in Yorkshire has been used as a camping ground by a group of Eastern Europeans . . .*"

Hearing the word "hotel," I perk up and lean forward.

The TV shows a hotel room, emptied of bed and other furniture, full of one-man tents, the kind you see on footage of mountain expeditions, low, neat, and narrow; eight little tents in two straight lines.

"The hotel manager told reporters that he thought nothing of it when a couple asked for an extended stay and insisted on a ground-floor room. Little did he know that at least eight people were living in the room using the sash window to come and go, conveniently screened from view by a large rhododendron. By day, the migrants roamed around the area seeking casual work, picking up shifts in the mills, traveling in an old van from factory to factory."

The television shows the van, a white Leyland DAF with no windows at the back.

"Blimey," says Adam, "they don't make those anymore."

"But what really shocked local people is what happened at night."

The camera shot changes to show the moors, wide and bleak in the December rain. The hairs on the back of my neck rise.

"Uh-oh," I say, "if this is about murders I don't think I want to hear it," but I don't turn off the TV.

"At night, the group came here above the industrialized outskirts of the city to hunt sheep. Local farmers say at least fifteen sheep were killed."

We see the interior of a large warehouse. There's a close-up of a mattress knifed open, foam fluffing out like sheep's wool, springs like spilled innards. "Wow," I say, "they gutted the bed as well."

"Police came close to catching the gang but at the last minute the hunters dropped everything and disappeared."

There's a shot of the old white DAF, parked and abandoned on the edge of the moors.

I sink back into the sofa, unsure whether I am horrified or impressed. I turn to Adam to see what he made of it. He's fallen asleep. I should not be surprised but I am, and disappointed. The sofa feels like moorland.

But no, I say to myself, come on—he's had a stupid midlife-crisis-flirtation kind of thing but he finished it of his own accord without going really badly astray. He hasn't been knocked over by a car, we haven't had to leave our country or hunt for food in the wild. Here he is, asleep on the sofa, our two daughters safe in their beds. I don't want to lose him, or rather—I want to find him again, to wake up and find him there, really there.

I rouse him. He struggles to wake, but he does—I can see the effort he is putting into bringing himself back.

"I am really, really sorry," he says, and I know he is not talking about dropping off.

"I know," I say.

He pulls me closer, puts his arm around me, kisses my head.

"I love you," he says, and a bit of hope rises inside me—maybe we can find some shelter after all.

"Come on," says Adam, "let's go to bed."

4

Milla is building a wall of cereal boxes around her bowl, a barricade against my breakfast, which she says is smelly and disgusting. I am not actually having yogurt and banana this morning, but either she hasn't noticed or she likes her fortress anyway. Possibly I overused yogurt and bananas when she was a baby. And avocados. And I should never have mashed them together, despite what it said in *Your Beautiful Baby and Toddler—Food for the Foundation Years.* We all have different things for breakfast, which my own mother thinks is crazy. "It's the only meal of the day that could be really simple and no work at all—everyone could have the same thing out of the same box." Although I don't remember breakfast being this simple in my childhood. Milla, who is six, is fond of cereal. What she really likes is chocolate cereal, but I only allow that on Saturdays. Hester, who is four, prefers porridge, so I make a tiny pan every morning. Adam, who is forty-two, has tea and toast. I watch Adam butter his toast and wonder if the thing with Louise Phelps came about because he is unhappy. Maybe he really is having a midlife crisis. I don't get a chance to follow this thought and see where it leads because the doorbell rings. Family time in our household is characterized by many things begun, few finished—not just thoughts but fights, films, sandwiches, games, drawings—and we don't seem to be able to put anything away either. Adam answers the door, thanks someone, and now there's a ripping noise.

"What's that?" I call from the kitchen.

Hester jumps down from her chair and runs through to the hallway.

"It's my new brochures and business cards," Adam calls.

Hester runs back in with a glossy brochure for Adam's business.

"Look—there's Daddy!" She points at a photograph of Adam on the back. He's wearing a blue checked shirt, no tie, his thick brown hair slightly in need of a cut. He looks glamorous and confident.

"Gosh," I say.

"And here's the card." Adam hands me one.

"They look great," I say, and I mean it, but then I see the four large cardboard boxes in the narrow hallway.

"Thanks," says Adam, and following my gaze, he adds, "It was practically the same price for two thousand as five hundred."

"But what are you going to *do* with two thousand?" I say, and instantly wish I hadn't because now we're into an old area of disagreement.

"Send them out. Try and drum up a bit of business, Kate." Adam turns his back on me and stacks the boxes against the wall.

It's not fair to say that we don't put anything away—I am the untidy one. Adam does put things away, but he never throws anything out. There's a pile of magazines in the bathroom that keeps slipping over because it's too tall, more magazines in the box room, files full of old bank statements, photographs that didn't make it into the album, utility bills from previous addresses. Adam is a collector by nature. He has a jacket for every possible type of weather.

He seldom wears a tie but he has kept every tie he's ever bought or received, even those he dislikes, in a thick forest in the wardrobe.

"Sorry," I say, "I shouldn't have said that. They do look great."

"Thanks. I'll keep them under my desk," he replies. We're both really trying and it almost makes me cry, how hard it is to keep out of a row.

"I don't want to be called Hester anymore," says Hester. "I want to be called Diego."

"Diego is a boy's name," says Milla scornfully, and then she says, "Mummy, why were you and Daddy fighting last night?"

"Oh! I thought you were asleep."

"I stayed in bed but I was awake. You were shouting."

"Yes, I'm sorry about that."

"What were you fighting about?"

"Well—" I scramble for something to tell her.

"We were just having an argument, nothing for you two girls to worry about," Adam says.

"I saw someone get run over yesterday," I say, changing tack.

"Ohhh!" say the girls.

"Did you?" says Adam. "You didn't mention it last night."

"Not everything gets mentioned," I reply.

"Were they killed?" asks Milla, and I regret having brought this up.

"No, sweetheart. The car had slowed down to turn a corner—it wasn't going fast enough to kill anyone."

"Was there blood?" she asks.

"I didn't see any."

"They might have had all their teeth knocked out," she says.

"Will the tooth fairy come?" Hester pipes up.

"No, Hester—the tooth fairy isn't real," says Milla.

"She is!" Hester protests. They go to collect their reading books from their bedroom, bickering all the way up the stairs.

"There was a little boy in the back of the car," I say to Adam.

"Oh, no," he says, and I feel a surge of love toward him for understanding. "Was he hurt?"

"He was very quiet. I did wonder if I should have gone to check on him. He must have been in shock. I should have gone over."

"But what could you have done?"

"I *should* have gone over and waited with him," I say, flooded with regret.

"I didn't mean to make you cry," says Adam, putting his arm around me.

"You haven't. I've made myself cry." I pull away to wipe my eyes as the girls come back downstairs.

"Let's make Mummy a nice cup of coffee," says Adam.

"I want to do it!"

"No, I want to!"

"We can *all* do it," says Adam.

"Actually, I'd better go."

"Are you friends again?" asks Milla. I hesitate, even though we made love last night for the first time in ages.

"Yes," says Adam firmly. "Go and find your shoes."

Milla stays exactly where she is, watching my face for confirmation, which I try to give through a reassuring smile. I check the time. Adam follows me into the hall and

I put on my coat and scarf. From the kitchen I hear Hester say, "Poor Charlie," and Milla shouts, "Hester, you're not allowed! Get out!"

"We need to talk about it some more," I tell Adam.

"Mummy! Hester is in Charlie's basket again!"

"We will," he says, and calls into the kitchen, "Mummy's going to Poland today, come and say goodbye."

The girls run to hug me. The leave-taking is always more intense when there's been a row, and today both girls follow me over the threshold in their socks into the drizzly cold morning and venture onto the damp pavement. We wave goodbye until I get to the corner and then Adam shepherds them back inside and I hope he notices their socks and changes them.

5

The temperature is minus fifteen, apparently not too bad for Poland in December. So far the longest I have been outside is ten minutes; we disembarked from the plane but the doors of the bus would not open so we stood on the runway while it was fixed. My teeth began to ache and the air felt sharp in my nose, which was because little icicles had formed in my nostrils. By the time I got into the passport queue I could hardly move my face, and when the border guard pleasantly inquired whether the trip was business or pleasure I could only reply in slow motion, "Bisn-nis."

I've come to visit a small hotel in Silesia staffed by people recovering from mental illness; they heal themselves through good work and community, and the reviews, especially ones about guests' experiences, are amazing. I think there's potential for a strategic partnership of some kind, or at the very least some inspiration for PHC. Trish doesn't seem very interested, probably because it's nonprofit, but Richard Robertson is. The much-loved president of PHC, Richard is known in the industry as a brilliant businessman and an inspiring leader. He's one of the main reasons I joined PHC. "We have a duty to care," says Richard—the same thing you hear from a lot of corporate leaders, but the difference is, Richard actually does care. He shares my view that if PHC is going to be truly successful it has to be a great place to work, because if you want happy guests, first you need happy staff.

The taxi is as warm as a nest. Soft voices from the radio curl around each other; a dashboard statuette of the Virgin Mary gazes out over the backseat, her sky-blue robes faded around the hem; there is holy water in a plastic vial next to a box of tissues; three cushions and a blanket that I wrap around my legs.

In the outskirts of Poznań we pass row upon row of accommodation blocks. Some of the paint is cracked and peeling and there's very little variation in the color of doors and windows. Set too far apart with nothing growing in between, the blocks look as though they came off a factory assembly line a long, long time ago.

We pass a church and the driver crosses himself and bows to the figurine of Mary. Out in the countryside we see roadside shrines: tall metal crosses, statues of saints on pillars, or tiny chapels with open doors, a jar of fresh-cut flowers inside, a freshly lit candle. I begin to watch for them; they remind me of the ones we saw in Crete.

We need another holiday like that. I decide to suggest it to Adam. He'll probably say we can't afford it, but now that I'm bringing in a regular salary maybe, by summertime, we could.

I look out of the taxi. We're on a straight road through flat farmland, a sprinkling of snow in the dips and furrows, an unending forest to our left. The landscape looks drained, all life retracted into the earth; even the trees are pale. Tall grasses at the edge of the road bend gracefully, translucent seed-heads made golden by the winter sun. The emptiness is soothing and I like moving through this new, strange country in the warm taxi, Mary serene on the dashboard.

Ahead, suddenly, a dark shape is barreling across the vast field—a large animal, fast-moving, low to the ground. "Look!" I say. The boar reaches the edge of the forest and plows in. As we pass that spot the driver slows the car. We crane round, but there's no sign of him now.

"Wah!" says the driver, exhilarated.

"A wild boar! He was moving so fast!" I say.

"Fast," agrees the driver, and adds something in Polish.

Nestled deep inside the town through old, crooked streets is Hotel Logica. I should have laid down a trail of crumbs to find my way back. Even though I am stiff from the car, after two and a half hours of looking through the window and daydreaming I am reluctant to come to the surface.

"Welcome," says the receptionist warmly. "We have been expecting you, Kate," and maybe because she uses my name, I feel I have come to the right place. The driver converses with the receptionist as I sort out the fare and a good tip. "Have a safe trip back," I say. The wrinkles at the corners of his eyes deepen as he smiles. We shake hands and I feel I'm losing a companion even though we barely spoke.

"He tells me you saw a wild boar," says the receptionist. "It's unusual, to see them out in the open like that. You're very lucky. Where you saw him, this is the

Lower Silesian Forest—you also have wolves inside. They nearly died away, but now they are protected, they come back."

"Do you ever see the wolves?"

"They stay in the forest. If you want to see them you have to go there."

"So! You want to find out something about our hotel?" says the manager, whose name is Marcin, a lean man with salt-and-pepper hair, a rock-star smile, and tobacco-stained teeth. His voice is very low, no doubt seasoned by years of smoking. "But first, I will show you your room and we will make sure you are comfortable."

It's a small hotel, twenty-seven rooms. There's no lift. Marcin carries my bag and leads the way. On the third floor we walk along the corridor to a narrower staircase, which goes up one more flight. He unlocks the wooden door with a proper key and sets my bag inside.

"This is your room, we hope you like it."

"It's very nice, thank you."

"You can settle in now and I will send you some tea perhaps, or some coffee?"

"Tea, please."

"Ah, yes! You are English! Of course!" He laughs.

"Does this mean I can make jokes about Poles?" I say.

"Of course!" Marcin says. "But there aren't any!"

The room has very little in it, just the necessary. I wouldn't have chosen any of it, but it's a relief not to have to choose.

One of the great things about staying in a hotel is that real life is someone else's job: someone else takes the decisions; someone else does the shopping, cooking, cleaning, laundry. It's like being a child again.

Tea arrives. On the tray is a round, brown teapot full of good strong tea in a knitted cozy, a jug of milk and a saucer with slices of lemon, a bowl of sugar, and a big slice of homemade cake: my favorite. I know that cake is not supposed to feature in the diet of someone who wants to lose three or four pounds, but cake is good for the soul.

There are two windows in my room. One has a view across the street to the tall painted buildings opposite and the other is in a nook jutting out from the roof that's barely high enough to stand in but wide enough for an armchair and low table. I pull this table closer to the chair and put the tea things there. The window has small panes and a low sill, perfect to sit by. It looks over cascading rooftops and gives a glimpse of the countryside and forests beyond the town. It has started snowing and large flakes drift slowly past the window. I pour the tea, piping hot and a little bit too strong, which I use as an excuse to add a spoonful of soft brown sugar. I give it a good stir and while the tea is still whirling I pull up my legs onto the chair and shift the cushion so it's in just the right place. I sip the hot, bittersweet tea and gaze out over the rooftops and chimneys toward the Silesian Forest, thinking of the wolves.

The evening meeting has a pace unfamiliar to me. Two of the twelve staff cover reception, but all the others are present, and for my benefit they are running the meeting as much as possible in English.

"People need to work," says Marcin. "It is important for a person to feel useful. But the work must be meaningful, and people need other things. It's easy to forget this and trudge along and so to help us remember we ask everyone here to name what's most important to them. So, who will speak next?"

"I need time. I like to work slow," says a woman, smiling at me.

"I need sunshine," says the woman next to her, and the rest of us laugh since it is dark and snowing outside.

"I need family," says one man, and starts to cry. His neighbor places an arm around his shoulder to comfort him.

Marcin leans closer and whispers, "He lost his family." I want to ask how, what happened to them, but the meeting moves on.

"I need clear skies," someone else says. "Nights when I can see the stars."

"I need to love what I do."

"I need rules."

"I need to break rules! I need freedom!" says a painfully thin young woman, rather angrily.

"What do you need, Kate?" asks Marcin, for which I am completely unprepared.

"I need cake!" I say, realizing immediately that this is too flip after what others have said, so I look for something to say on that level. "And I need—" I continue, but don't know what to say. "I need . . ." Something is working its way up. I am aware of being watched and closely listened to. "I need to believe." To my surprise, this brings up a sob. The man who needs family passes me the box of tissues. When I look up, several people are smiling at me and their faces are kind.

When I return to my room, housekeeping has been. The tea tray is gone, the duvet turned back, the curtains closed, my pajamas folded and placed on the pillow; just like the turndown service in any other good hotel. At PHC it's policy for the head of housekeeping to leave handwritten notes on branded notepaper with gifts of chocolate to welcome guests. The notes always say the same thing, but the chocolate varies; once, I found three Mars bars piled like logs on my pillow, another time there was a single Ferrero Rocher and a bath towel twisted into a large white swan. All this is supposed to make you feel welcome and special, but in fact I was filled with self-loathing after gorging on two and a half of the Mars bars and guilt when I dropped the half-eaten one out of the window, and the towel origami was unnerving because I had to wring the swan's neck to undo it.

Here, someone has given more than the few minutes per room allocated at PHC: the earrings I left by the side of the sink are paired and lying in a saucer; the knotted cord of my headphones has been untangled and loosely coiled next to my phone; my hat, scarf, and gloves are warming on a radiator; the papers I'd left strewn over the table are in a neat pile; my shoes straightened. These little attentions are touching, and make me cry again—just a little bit.

I call Adam and resolve not to bring up Louise Phelps. If I mention her we will argue again, and the structure already feels shaky: another blasting row could bring the whole thing down. I decide I won't even mention her name. I ask how the girls are, what they had for breakfast. The subject of the inappropriate friendship rises in my throat. I force it back down and ask what the weather's like, but it bursts out anyway.

"*Was* it an affair, though?" I hear myself say.

"You saw the emails! I ended it before you even found out!"

"Yes, I know, but—"

"NOTHING HAPPENED," says Adam, slowly and emphatically.

"Maybe it was an infatuation," I say.

"What difference does it make? Stop banging on about it, Kate, *please*—it's driving me mad." And then he says, more patiently, "Maybe it *was* an infatuation, but it's over now and we have to concentrate on us."

He's right. An infatuation is just a crush; everyone gets them. Like flu or the common cold, they pass. I had one once, for a long time, on my art teacher. He took our class to the National Gallery, asked me what my favorite work of art was: there I was in uniform, thirteen, with bare knees; I couldn't tell him it was him. I liked the Rubens and Rembrandts, so I said that. He told me he liked John Singer Sargent, that his favorite was Van Gogh. He also told me that Van Gogh only became famous after his death and that during his lifetime the only person who liked his work was his brother. Van Gogh died penniless and unrecognized, which is how I felt around the art teacher. I was just a girl then, had never loved any other man; for I thought this *was* love. It survived my first kiss with a lad from town, the boyfriends with bikes and then mopeds and then cars. I wonder what he's doing now, the art teacher, what he's done with his life. And what have I done? I married an executive who hated his job so much he quit and, perhaps feeling penniless and unrecognized, had an infatuation with a girl from the office. It's not so very different.

6

I arrive home and open the front door to the sound of splashing and the smell of food cooking—a rich, meaty, garlicky smell. I drop my bag in the hallway, rush to Adam as if I've been overboard all this time and he's the lifeboat; he stops stirring the bolognese, puts both arms around me, and pulls me out of the sea of worry. I crumple into his shoulder; he kisses my hair.

"The girls are dying to see you," he says. "They're having a squabble-bath." We call them that because they always fight over who has the most bubbles and try to divide them into equal soap-mountains.

"Mummy, guess what?" says Hester as they get into their pajamas.

"Daddy took Charlie to her class," says Milla.

"*I* was going to tell her!" shouts Hester.

"Milla, let Hester tell Mummy, all right?" says Adam.

"Well, Daddy brought Charlie and we all hugged him," Hester continues.

"Who did you all hug—Daddy or Charlie?" I say.

"Charlie, of course! And guess what Daddy did?"

"What did Daddy do?"

"He brought Charlie's toothpaste and toothbrush to show us and guess what?"

"I don't know," I say.

"Guess what flavor Charlie's toothpaste is?" says Hester.

"Chicken," says Milla dryly.

"Milla! *I* wanted to tell her!"

"Urgh, chicken-flavored toothpaste, yuk!" I say.

"Yes, but Charlie likes it," says Hester.

"Because he's a dog," says Milla.

"Actually, it's chicken-*liver* flavored," says Adam.

"Eww," I say.

"What's chicken liver?" asks Hester.

"It's a part of a chicken that you can eat," says Adam. "You can get chicken-liver pâté. In fact, I think you've both had some."

"Did I like it?" asks Hester.

"I didn't," says Milla.

"Do you remember eating it?" Adam asks her.

"No."

"How do you know you didn't like it, then? I think there's some in the fridge, actually. Shall I go and get it and you can brush your teeth with that?"

"Oh, nooo! Yuk! We're not dogs!" squeals Hester, delighted.

"Daddy, that's disgusting," says Milla.

"How do you know it's disgusting? Try it," says Adam.

"No way, I'm using my normal toothpaste," says Milla.

"Yeah, me too," agrees Hester, and they rush off to brush their teeth.

"You are brilliant," I say to Adam.

"Thank you," he replies.

*

Later, when the girls are asleep and we are drinking wine in the kitchen I ask Adam if he has called Louise since I found the emails and he says not. He looks at me fair and square and says, "No. I didn't and I won't. I promise. Nothing happened with Louise."

"Adam," I say, "I believe you didn't have a proper affair or anything like that with her, but I'm not totally sure what—"

"Listen," he says calmly. "This has gone far enough. I know it must have been horrible for you finding those emails, and I was a complete idiot about the whole thing, but it was nothing."

"I just want it to go away," I say, although what I really want is for it never to have happened at all.

"So do I," he says. "Come on, Kate—I'm sorry. I'll say sorry as many times as you like."

He hugs me and I do feel better. I sink farther into his arms and he kisses me. We kiss the way we used to, and everything feels simple again. Maybe that was the problem; we just stopped kissing. I remember what I read in *The Happy Couple*: it's not necessarily a calamity if your partner has an affair that makes them feel more youthful, exciting, and attractive. It can even be a wake-up call for the main relationship. The crucial thing is that you are able to discuss it.

"You know that book, the long-term relationship one?"

"Mmm?" says Adam, pouring the rest of the wine.

"Remember I told you it said something like this can actually be a good thing and you said 'How'?"

"Yeah."

"Well, the reason is—they say it can be a wake-up call."

"Exactly," says Adam. "That's exactly what this is—a wake-up call."

We clink glasses, agree to get a babysitter more often and go out just the two of us, and when we go to bed we have sex—for the second time in a week, which hasn't happened in a long time. Not the lovemaking kind; more like rutting, more like something coming into season. But anyway, afterward both of us sleep really well. Many marriages survive affairs, and some may even thrive on them—or so say Rosenfeld and Abrahams, and maybe they are right. And maybe Adam is right, maybe this isn't even an affair, or wasn't, because whatever we eventually agree to call it, it's over.

7

The day we leave for our Christmas trip to Adam's parents', I get up early to make a chicken-and-leek pie. I made one two years ago when they were staying with us and it was a hit. His dad had triple helpings and afterward dozed in front of the evening news; his mum asked me for the recipe and I remember Adam cozying up to me, pleased as a cat.

A story comes on the radio about a Frenchman living in Manhattan who gave up his job as an advertising executive to start his own fashion line after seeing a picture of a pair of shoes.

"What was it about the shoes that so inspired you?" asks the reporter.

"They were embroidered—these shoes were made in 1690 and they were embroidered in the most wonderful way—they looked so contemporary, the embroidery was so free! The way the cobbler—or artist, really—let the stitching roam all over the shoe, I wouldn't have expected that and I saw these shoes and straightaway I knew what to do. I went out and I bought myself a pair of shoes—just a pair of white tennis shoes—and some thread and I started to embroider them and I loved it. And when I finished the shoes, I started on my jeans, and after, my T-shirt, and my jacket, and that's how it started."

"What color thread did use on your shoes?"

"White. The white silk thread is very luxe, very generous

with the plain white canvas and the two whites are not the same, you know? But they talk to each other."

"And what did you do while you were sewing—what music did you listen to?"

"Nothing. No music. I just sit in my small room, a hundred feet above the ground, and I can see the river from my window, and the bridge going over it, and all day long I sew, and I look at the weather forecast and if they say it will be sunshine, I say, 'Perfect! I can have the window open while I sew and I can feel the breeze come inside the room,' and if they say it will be rain, I say, 'Perfect! I can sew even more today.'"

I wish for things to be simple and good and true, like the Frenchman in his tower embroidering white silk thread on a pair of white canvas shoes. It feels good to be quietly moving around the kitchen rolling pastry from the packet, weighing and chopping and stirring with Charlie watching from his basket, nose raised to the smell of the chicken. Poor Charlie; he trembles when spoken to. Hester thinks he's excited because it's Christmas, Milla thinks he's cold and keeps covering him with a blanket. Charlie totters between kitchen and front room, several minutes behind whomever he is following. If someone else comes in the other direction he'll start following the more recent person, which about-turns make him look confused, but he isn't, only forgetful.

Packing the car later that morning, frost melting from the windscreen, sun bright, I buckle the girls into their booster seats and they arrange selected teddies and toys around them, arguing over space. Charlie lowers himself to a cushion on the floor, Adam loads up suitcases and bags of presents. The car is too full. Adam is wedging things down the sides. I bring the pie out, hand it to him, and go back inside to check the windows and doors are locked. I hear a smash and run outside to see Adam with his arms raised in exasperation over the pie broken on the ground, steam rising.

"Oh, no!" I exclaim.

"I didn't do it on purpose!"

"I know, I'm just saying!"

He swears as he lifts pieces of crockery out of the warm gloop. Charlie sniffs the chicken, heaves himself out of the car, and waddles round the back, eager to get a bite. Adam pushes him back. "He'll cut himself! Can you get him away, Kate, please!" I bundle Charlie into the front and shut the door, but he jumps onto the backseat, disturbing the carefully placed toys and sending up a wail from both girls. I tell Adam to mind his head and slam the boot shut and move the car to the end of the street so that Charlie is away from the enticement. The girls unbuckle themselves and argue all over again about whose toy goes where.

"Why do you have to fight about it again? Can't you just put them back where they were before?" I snap. The girls resume their bickering in whispers. I look in the rearview mirror and watch Adam shovel pie remains into a plastic bag with the dustpan. He dances back as some spatters on his jeans and I see him swear and fume. He strides into the house; shoulders up, head down—a familiar sight. It's just a pie, I tell myself. My disappointment isn't all about the pie, but if I mention it there's danger of sparking off a bigger row or causing a sulk to set in like fog.

I take out my phone and look at the picture Adam sent a couple of days ago of a really horrible sofa. Soon after we got together, I walked past a store on Fulham Palace Road and took a photo of a bed with an enameled black headboard inlaid with mother-of-pearl hearts, diamonds, clubs, and spades. We enjoyed being appalled and had a lot of fun speculating who would buy such a monstrosity and, even worse, who could design one and think it was all right. The game evolved and we played it happily for years. Looking back, I can't remember when it faded. So it lifted me to receive this picture of a superbly ugly sofa made up of three different colors of leather, all rolled around each other at the ends like a gigantic Licorice Allsort.

Adam comes back out in a pair of fresh jeans and apologizes for breaking the pie.

"It's OK, it was an accident," I say.

"I'm cold," says Milla, grumpy because we've been in the car for fifteen minutes.

"So am I, and so is Charlie," says Hester.

"Right, hang on." Adam opens the back door, tucks a blanket round each of the girls, and drapes a towel over Charlie, who lifts his head momentarily and goes back to his doze.

"What about these guys? I bet they're cold too, aren't they?" says Adam, meaning their toys.

"Yes!" shout the girls, delighted.

"Right," says Adam. "I think they need a blanket too, don't you?" He pulls a tissue out of the box and lays it over Winnie-the-Pooh, another one for Piglet, one each for all their toys.

"Is that better?" he says, and kisses the girls.

"Yes, Daddy," they chime, happy again. Adam puts on a CD of Christmas carols. As we set off, he starts singing along to "Jingle Bells," and the girls and I join in.

On Christmas Eve we go out with Adam's parents. The party is a small gathering of friends and relatives Adam has known all his life, including his Aunty Vera and Aunty June, who send Christmas cards every year, which I fail to reciprocate, always hoping Adam will do it.

This time, to appease my guilt, I've brought cards that the girls have made and written. There's a holly wreath on Vera and Stan's front door, a bunch of mistletoe hanging in the hall, walls decked with dozens of Christmas cards in hanging loops. Perhaps they didn't miss not getting one from us.

Vera greets us. "How are your parents, Kate? How's your mother, still teaching? Headmistress at a large school, wasn't she?"

"Yes, she's still there," I say, my daughters weighing down each leg so that I enter with giant, slow steps, walking on the moon. My mother is the head of the school I went to; at home she worked all the time and in school there were six hundred other girls competing for her attention. I only saw her from afar—across the assembly hall, at the end of a corridor, disappearing into the staff room. Just after I started that school, when I was eleven, my father had an affair—but they got through that and are still together.

"It was a grammar school, Vera," says Aunty June.

"That's right, for the clever ones—like our dear Kate," Vera says warmly, "and like these little ones—" She goes to kiss the girls but they shrink back.

"Shy," says Aunty June. The girls slide their heads and shoulders under my coat.

"That's right," says Aunty Vera. Vera and June don't seem to mind, in fact they seem to think it's just as it should be. They have the luxury of time and they're generous with it. Perhaps the girls hear the warm welcome in Vera's and June's voices, perhaps their natural curiosity gets the better of them, or perhaps it's too hot under all those layers of coat, because they begin to peep out, one after the other.

"Come on, girls, say hello!" says Adam, reaching down and prizing them off.

A buffet is laid out. People are loading plates and going to eat in the lounge where the Christmas tree is. I find myself in the kitchen with Adam's mother, perusing the food.

"Do you think Adam would like a sausage roll?" she says.

"I don't know, why don't you ask him?" I reply, and instantly feel mean—she'd only been thinking of her son; his appetite, what he might like.

"No, wait—I'm sure he would. I'll take him one," I say, grabbing a sausage roll and heading for the lounge.

Adam is on a sumptuous couch in the bay window, but before I reach him Aunty Vera touches my elbow. "Wouldn't you like a plate for that, dear?" she says. She's wearing a low-necked peach pullover, a white tissue bunched up and tucked into her bra strap like a rosette. "Here, take mine—it's only got a few crumbs on it."

"Thanks," I say, battling on so she won't see the tears spring to my eyes. I am a terrible wife—I don't send Christmas cards and I can't even remember a plate for the sausage roll I hadn't wanted to provide for my husband. No *wonder* he'd— Well, that was over now.

I make my way to Adam, bearing the sausage roll like an offering. He eats it in one bite, licks his fingers, and looks around for more. I return to the kitchen. I may as well ferry sausage rolls between kitchen and lounge, mother-in-law and husband, since I don't have it in me to make polite conversation.

"You were right, he did want one, and now he wants another!" I say, and maybe she hears the forced brightness in my voice because she says, "Oh, darling, you sit down and have a rest. You must be exhausted with your busy life. I'll take them and you have a little sit. And have something to eat yourself!"

"I want to lose weight," I say as she disappears out of the kitchen with the plate of sausage rolls. I look down—those bulges aren't folds of fabric, they are midriff. "Spare tire," I say to myself, pinching a roll of belly between fingers and thumb.

The house is horribly overheated. Damp patches bloom under my armpits. I don't want to sit next to the chicken wings and drumsticks, mince pies, Twiglets, crisps, and quiche. I go out through the back door with my phone. My parents have been leaving messages; they want to say goodbye before they go to America to stay with my brother.

They're flying on Christmas Day because my mother is unsentimental about such things. I can phone them back and get some fresh air at the same time.

Dad answers straightaway and I hear a click: the second handset being picked up. My mother often does that, and sometimes she rings off again without even saying hello. I don't know if she realizes how obvious it is to the caller.

"It's Kate," I say.

"Hello," says my mother; evidently she's decided to join the conversation today.

"Hello, sweetheart," says my father. "Where are you?"

"I'm at Vera and Stan's house, you remember them from our wedding."

"No, I don't think I do," says my mother. "Should I?"

"It doesn't matter," I say.

"Anyway," says my father. "How are you doing? How are the girls?"

"They're fine, thanks. How are you both? All ready for your trip? I bet you can't wait to see Greg and Susannah."

"You sound exhausted," says Dad.

"Yes, you do," says Mum.

"I am." I feel suddenly defeated and let out a little sob. I dab my lower eyelashes with my finger, a gesture that catapults me into the form of my mother, who does exactly the same move. Experiencing my mother from the inside is disconcerting since we're not that close.

"Oh, dear," says Mum.

"And Adam nearly had an affair," I blurt.

"Oh, Kate," she says, sounding concerned now.

"I haven't told anybody."

My dad lets out a deep sigh. "Oh, sweetheart."

"He didn't—I mean, he hasn't actually had an affair. He ended it before it turned into anything. It was more like an inappropriate friendship."

"A what?" says my mother.

"A near miss," says my dad.

"Yeah, kind of," I say.

"Are you all right? Do you want us to come and help?"

"No, thanks, Dad. Anyway, you're going to Boston. I'm OK. I didn't really mean to tell you—it just kind of blurted out."

"That's perfectly natural," says Dad.

"Yes," agrees Mum. "I didn't tell anybody when your father had his affair."

"You told me," I say.

"Apart from you. Anyway. Once you get past it, you have to *really* get past it. I remember reading something very useful, it was Elizabeth Taylor. She said, don't serve it up every day for breakfast."

Adam is nowhere to be seen. I look for the children, needing to locate them like coordinates on a map before I can know my own position. Hester is lying on the sitting-room floor with her arms around Charlie; Milla is explaining something to Aunties Vera and June on the sumptuous couch.

Adam comes up behind me, takes hold of my waist, slides his hands down to my hips. "Where have you been?" he says, nuzzling behind my ear.

"Can we go home?" I say.

"Sure."

"I mean home-home. Not today obviously, but maybe on Boxing Day? We need to spend time together," I say.

"Mum will be disappointed," Adam says. "I told her we'd stay until Wednesday."

"I know, I'm sorry, but can we anyway?"

"Yes, we can," says Adam, steering me along and kissing me under the mistletoe.

"That's what we like to see!" calls Adam's mum from the kitchen.

The night after Christmas we pack up our daughters and aged dog, bags and presents, and set off for London. There are not many other cars on the motorway.

"It's so *empty*," I say.

"Yes, but we'll get home quicker, and the girls are asleep. We can have a peaceful journey," says Adam.

"I talk underneath and you talk on top," I say into the dark space in front of me.

"I didn't talk over you!"

"That's not what I meant. What I'm trying to say is that you'll often say things and mean them literally, and I'll often say things and mean them—well, *not* literally."

"Ri-ight . . ."

"When you say you want a peaceful journey, I think you mean you don't want to talk."

"Well, what is it that you want to say?" he asks, sounding frustrated.

"It's not that I want to say something in particular, it's that we need to be able to talk, and we're not."

"But we've been getting on much better, haven't we?"

"Yes, and that's good, but . . ."

"You're going to have to help me out here, Kate, because I don't understand—I don't know what you want."

"I'm sorry," I say, scrambling about for whatever it was I'd intended. "I don't know either."

Adam switches on the radio. We each retreat. I cast around for reassurance that returning to London is the right thing. Three indicators of a healthy relationship: talking, satisfying sex, time together. These seem right, but Rosenfeld and Abrahams meant that a couple should do all three and I couldn't help feeling that the sex was filling up the time we might otherwise have had in bed together, talking. Daytime is the missing piece. We need some time when I'm not at work and we're not with Adam's family. Going home *is* the right thing. A song comes on that we both like and Adam reaches out and puts his hand on my leg and gives me a reassuring squeeze. "I do love you, you know," he says.

"I know," I say. "And I love you."

8

We come home from his parents' laden with goods and not just Christmas presents: two rugs they don't want anymore, his mother's old food processor in a big plastic box, six matching Marks & Spencer mugs, a set of power tools that his dad no longer uses. There's no floor space so Adam lays the rugs down on top of other rugs and rams the mugs into the cupboard so that it's as tightly packed as honeycomb.

I take Hester and Milla to the bookshop to spend their book tokens from Aunties Vera and June. The woman there greets us warmly and asks the girls about their favorite Christmas presents. The nice man comes in with two Starbucks and I suddenly feel more awake, as if I've just downed a double espresso myself. I hope this isn't apparent, especially to the girls, but they've already made themselves cozy in the armchairs at the back of the shop, reading. I study the shelves. In the Philosophy/Self-Help section, Paul McKenna is still promising that he can make me thin and presents evidence by way of before-and-after photographs. They are all fairly drastic cases. It shouldn't be too hard to lose three or four pounds, maybe four or five, if I follow his golden rules, but before I get to them the girls start bickering and lasso me in.

"I found it first!" says Hester, holding on tight to one of the *Wimpy Kid* books.

"But, Mummy, she's not reading these ones!" says Milla, making a grab for it.

"I can if I want!" Hester squeals. Hester's too young for *Wimpy Kid* so I distract her with a whole new series, the *Jewel Fairies*, and tell her she can afford four. She fetches the whole lot down off the shelf and makes three piles: most wanted; nearly most wanted; wanted. Milla sits on the *Wimpy Kid* to hide it from her sister and starts reading *Flat Stanley*. Seconds later, the fight forgotten, she's absorbed, transported by the book.

I'd like a new book but I'm too exhausted to pick one. Next to me is a stand of *Mr. Men* titles, which reminds me of our wedding. The best man structured his whole speech around them, holding up each book as he extolled Adam's virtues: Mr. Tall, Mr. Strong, Mr. Clever, Mr. Busy, Mr. Grumpy. He invented a new one to describe Adam's finest quality: Mr. Loyal. Hester asks me to help her choose which *Jewel Fairies* to take home and I join her cross-legged on the floor. The books are now in two piles, almost equal in height: "the ones I want most," and "the ones I really, really want as well." Her criteria seem to be the name of the fairy and the picture on the front cover, and the help she needs is really just a witness to the minute calibrations of her own process. She goes through them in pairs and eventually whittles it down to *Diamond*, *Garnet*, *Sapphire*, and *Topaz*. Milla buys *Flat Stanley*, *The BFG*, and the *Wimpy Kid* book.

At home, Charlie is coughing in his basket. Adam is using the power tools to put up shelves so that we have somewhere to put the power tools, which seems like a double negative, but then I've had other moments lately where things warp like this: I heard a woman say "some affairs" when actually she'd meant "summer fairs," and the other day

a man in the office complained loudly, "My wife is broken."
I looked around, shocked, only to realize he'd said "Wi-Fi."

I start making turkey soup from the leftovers wrapped
in tinfoil that his mum sent us home with. Her old food
processor is in the corner; there's nowhere to put it and
I know I'll never use it, but declining wasn't an option.
Adam's parents needed us to take it so they could justify
their purchase of a brand-new one. The new shelves are
going on the back wall of the side return where Adam keeps
his Ducati. Over them he's putting a makeshift roof of cor-
rugated plastic, completely absorbed in his own world.

The turkey soup bubbles on the hob. I sit on the kitchen
table with my feet on a chair and watch Adam through the
window drilling in the dusk. He doesn't look in. The radio
is on outside and I can hear muffled voices through the wall.

PART TWO

I have been to hell and back.
And let me tell you, it was wonderful.

—*Louise Bourgeois*

9

When I get back to work in the New Year there's something to distract me from my marriage: Trish has got together with Don Mitchell, the Executive Vice President for HR and Legal, to hire consultants to facilitate both their teams on a "back-to-the-floor" day. We are packed off in minibuses and parceled out to various PHC London hotels.

I am sent to the Regal on Park Lane and given some brand-new navy blue overalls with the company logo stitched in gold thread on the breast pocket. As I'm getting changed I think about the Frenchman embroidering his white shoes high above the Hudson River; how simple things can be when you just do something you love, or spend time with someone you love.

I make my way up to the twenty-seventh floor as instructed, carrying my real clothes in a carrier bag. The consultants didn't think about footwear so I'm wearing tights and tan slingbacks with a kitten heel; stupid shoes for January but I like them. Waiting by the lifts is one other person in box-fresh overalls like me and I'm delighted to discover that it's Richard Robertson—six feet four inches tall, seventy but still trim, his bearing upright, his hair silver and smooth. Before he moved into the corporate side of the company and became president, Richard had been general manager of the Regal on Park Lane and, among other famous guests, once welcomed Princess

Grace of Monaco, who reportedly developed a crush on him.

"Hello, Richard. I didn't expect to see you here," I say.

Richard smiles. "Why ever not?" he replies. "Trish and Don invited me along. Things like this are wonderful; any day spent in one of our hotels is a good day, especially this one."

Park Lane, as the old hotel was affectionately called by all who knew her, was the world's first five-star hotel, the hotel that set the standard that others aspired to, the hotel that inspired the game of Monopoly, PHC's best-known and best-loved hotel, and Richard's favorite.

People say that he would have been happy to stay on as general manager there and that he only took the job as president of PHC because the company had started to fail; the incumbent had made a mess of it and set the organization on a very bad course. A couple of months in, PHC hit an iceberg. Shareholders summoned Richard to the City and instructed him to make immediate savings on expenditure by reducing the workforce: seventy-five mid-level managers were to go from head office and if things did not drastically improve there would be another hundred. Richard refused: "This is not of their making. Sell a hotel."

At that time, the shareholders hoarded hotels the way dragons protect treasure. They rose up against him in their boardroom lair. Gone was their etiquette and old-school charm. Money was being lost hand over fist, *their* money. Do it or we'll have your head on a platter, they breathed. It's them or you.

Richard shut himself in his office. A man in his prime, he didn't deserve to be cut down like this and finished.

Neither did seventy-five of the people under his care, but if he didn't do it, the shareholders would. He sat at his big oak desk, head in his hands at the thought of those seventy-five people, their seventy-five families, their seventy-five homes.

Every hour his secretary, Valerie, brought tea—picking up the previous cup, cold and untouched, and setting down a fresh one. She did this five times. He drank the fifth cup and started to pace. He drank the sixth and demolished the sandwiches she'd provided, asked for his senior team and discussed his idea with them for an hour. When she brought the seventh cup he asked Valerie to arrange an all-staff briefing, immediately.

People were nervous and skittish. At the back two young bucks jostled, one tipped over a chair, an older manager made him pick it up again. With his senior advisors standing around him, Richard explained the situation; set it out clearly and proposed this: instead of sacking seventy-five people, he would sack everyone and rehire them the next morning on slightly lower salaries. When things improved, salaries would go up again. If they turned things around, everyone would receive a bonus to cover the amount they had forfeited. Anyone could opt out, but only a handful did. The highest paid took the greatest pay cuts; Richard halved his.

The effect was startling: the atmosphere in the company went from doom to determination; petty differences were put aside as people took heart and aligned behind a single purpose. Eight months later PHC was full sail to the wind and after another five months the bonuses were paid in full. People say it wasn't the plan that inspired them, though it was bold and brave; Richard's openness and honesty mattered more. That was the beginning of the glory years for PHC, the era of Richard's rule. The shareholders were pleased about the profit return and they had to admit that Richard had done something extraordinary, but they never forgave him for standing up to them nor for seeing them as they really were.

A slightly officious woman who must be one of the facilitators exits the lift and interrupts us to explain that we are going to be working with Mel, one of the guys from the maintenance and engineering team. We will be descaling showerheads. Mel's late, so the facilitator lady informs us that every single shower in the PHC estate has to be descaled four times a year. In all the larger hotels, any with seven hundred or more rooms, descaling showerheads is a full-time job, and in the Regal on Park Lane this job belongs to Mel from Barnsley. Richard smiles benignly through her short lecture.

"You knew all that, didn't you?" I say to him when she leaves us.

"Yep," he replies.

Under Mel's supervision, we unscrew the first showerhead and dismantle it, soak the component parts in a solution of chlorinates, then clean and rinse each piece before putting the showerhead back together and reattaching it.

"I'm very methodical," Mel tells us. Floor by floor he works his way around the 812 bedrooms, and when he's finished at the top he starts again at the bottom. "Like painting the Forth Bridge," he says.

Elevenses is instant coffee and a Penguin. I tell Richard and Mel that I'm worried about spilling bleach on my nice shoes and that I'd like to nip back to the office to pick up the trainers I keep under my desk, for the lunchtime sport I rarely do. Richard says he's been thinking the same thing about his brogues and would I be so kind as to collect his tennis shoes, which makes me feel all right about having raised it. Mel shakes his head at us and goes on with his work.

I find my trainers, pull them on, and go up to fetch Richard's shoes. It's unusually quiet upstairs; the secretaries must be on "Back to the Floor" as well since it's too early for lunch. As I walk from the lift to Richard's office, I see into the boardroom: Don at the head of the table, Trish by his side, and twelve other very smartly dressed people. That's odd, I think, recognizing several as shareholders. Why are they meeting without Richard? Perhaps they're planning a surprise for his retirement, but that's a whole year away. Since I can't very well go in and ask, I open the closet in Richard's office and find his white leather Reeboks. As I make my way back to the lift, Trish comes quietly out of the boardroom.

"How's it going?" she asks brightly.

"Surprisingly good fun, actually," I reply. Then I add, "You're busy here then?"

"Yes—an emergency board meeting."

"What's the emergency?" I ask.

"Oh," says Trish, "not a *real* emergency—nothing to worry about. But it is confidential. For now, anyway. And, um . . ." She hesitates. "I hope you'll respect that. Completely. Don and I are dealing with this."

"Oh," I say, "right."

"Thank you, Kate. I knew I could rely on you," she says, patting my arm. She calls the lift, and when it arrives she turns and walks back to the boardroom. I keep my finger on the doors-open button and watch as she reenters the room.

In the short cab ride back to the hotel, I go over what just happened. It doesn't feel quite right, but on the other hand, neither does running to Richard after Trish asked me not to. Telling him what, anyway? I push it to the back of my mind—there's enough other stuff in there to bury it.

Over the next few hours Richard, Mel, and I disassemble and reassemble showerheads and do other jobs in between; changing lightbulbs, fixing TV aerials, nailing down the long red carpets where they have curled up or bunched along the corridors. Because we have actually been helpful—unlike most people from head office, Mel says—he gives us each a small bottle of the chlorinates to use at home: "Industrial strength, can't buy it in the shops—it'll make your shower run like a monsoon," he says.

I learn three other things from Mel:

1) Dirty linen put into the laundry chute on the twenty-seventh floor reaches a speed of 100 mph by the time it bursts out in the basement. If housekeeping gets a plate or a whiskey glass wrapped up in the sheets by mistake the resulting force is enough to take someone's hand off. Because

LOVER

of an accident in which a cleaner's thumb was broken by a wet towel, the maintenance team constructed a caged area around the bottom of the chute.

2) Maintenance and engineering run something called Window Bingo, an annual sweepstake on what the window cleaners have seen throughout the year: couples having sex, naked or half-naked people, men dressed in women's underwear, that kind of thing. Mel tells me this while Richard is on a loo break and later I ask Richard, delicately, how much he thinks he is aware of what goes on.

"I've worked in hotels for fifty-two years, Kate," he says. "Started as the bellboy in the Queen's Hotel in Leeds city center and worked my way up and around from there—I think I have a fairly good idea of most things that go on. It's not all good, I know that, but what's the alternative? I don't want to police people."

3) In addition to back of house, the official area for staff in a hotel, there are unofficial places too: internal, unseen, like the dips and hollows, tubes and cavities inside a body, vital space needed for expansion and contraction, for the lungs to breathe, the heart to beat. Maintenance and engineering have a sort of den shared with housekeeping behind the clean linen store in the basement. They've got a three-piece suite down there, a fridge and a dartboard. Upstairs in the reception area the concierges have transformed their poky little office no bigger than a broom cupboard into a refuge decked with plastic flowers and pictures of bright blue seas and skies. This is mainly the work of Ernesto, the head concierge from Cuba, but his colleagues—Jockey from Sri Lanka and Benjamin from

Newcastle-upon-Tyne—wholly approve and regularly add to the collage so that it covers the walls and ceiling entirely. They keep it private, but sometimes, if you're standing in just the right place when the door opens, you glimpse a flash of cobalt like a kingfisher darting down a riverbank.

10

"Hello, Kate! Hello, Gérard!" says Sam, coming over to our desks.

"Hello, Sam, how are you?" I say.

"I'm walking the world," she says, marching on the spot, "with the global marketing team—we're doing the whole world in four months, and the brand team are walking from LA to Las Vegas in two months. It's an idea to get people moving more, and to build team spirit. We each have to take ten thousand steps a day. It gets a bit obsessive, we're checking our pedometers all the time—" Still marching, she looks down at hers, clipped on to her belt. "If you're interested, they do one where you climb mountains—you could get a group together and climb K2 if you like, or Everest. Something in the Himalayas might be nice."

"Hmm," I say, "I've never really fancied that. Bit cold."

"Kilimanjaro then!"

"I'd rather sail the seven seas," says Gérard. Gérard is not handsome but he's got presence, which is partly due to the fact that he's tall, with a great bulk of a body—not fat, just big: big hands, big feet, and a big face with crumples that deepen when he laughs.

"I don't know if they do boat ones," says Sam. "How would you measure it, in a boat?"

"Couldn't we just sit at our desks and pretend it was a boat?" I say, doing a rowing movement. It feels quite nice to stretch my arms out and I remember that I never actually checked the gym schedule. "I'd quite like to cross the Atlantic."

"They might think you're a bit weird if you do that," says Sam, nodding over to Trish's office, where she and Don are close in conversation, door closed.

"We should get them to do it. Stick them both in a boat," I say. I've heard a rumor that Trish and Don are together, so I'm testing it. Sam looks uncomfortable.

"You should check the website," she says, reorienting the conversation. "There's a map that shows where you are in the world. I'm in Belgium at the moment." She pauses. "It's a bit boring."

"What is—Belgium?" I ask, wondering how you can be bored by a country you're not actually visiting.

"No—the steps. It sounds great, walking round the world with your team, but actually, you do it on your own."

Later, Gérard, Don, and I are waiting for Trish in her office, and Don mentions that routine checks of CCTV footage have revealed that one of the night cleaners in the Belgravia Palazzio has been playing the grand piano at 5:00 in the morning. He's been doing this for months; taught himself to play using YouTube.

"Very innovative! What's his name?" I ask.

"We don't care what his name is, Kate. We just need to know whether or not he is legal in this country. If so, we can sack him outright. If not, we might have to think more carefully about how to get rid of him, since we shouldn't really have been employing him in the first place," says Don.

Trish arrives late but not rushing, an empty white cup hooked round her index finger, dangling like an oversized charm on a bracelet.

"Sorry I'm a bit late," she says as she takes her place at the head of the table. "Gérard, please could you get the door?" I've noticed this with Trish—she's always asking people, graciously, to do things she could just as easily have done herself. And nobody ever complains; they just do her bidding. As Gérard gets up, Trish leans over to Don and speaks quietly, something brief. Don's eyebrows go up and he smiles at her. It's a private moment between the two of them and witnessing it slightly wrong-foots me. They do make a good couple—if, that is, they are a couple. Trish is divorced and lives with her teenage daughter. Don's married with two children, but you don't hear much about his wife. I wonder whether Adam and Louise ever had moments like this at work, whether anyone ever clocked it the way I am now; seeing them close, swapping office gossip—perhaps they were the office gossip, and knew it and didn't care.

Trish looks fantastic today in tight blue pin-striped trousers, a shapely pink shirt with jeweled cuff links, and red heels. A woman in a man's world, she does corporate sexy very well. But it's not just her clothes—there's something else. She seems powered from the inside and she glows.

"Instead of sacking him, couldn't we reward his dedication?" says Gérard. "I have a piano, and I know from personal experience that it takes a lot of discipline to practice every day the way he does. This cleaner comes in early to play—it's not on our time. Those fifteen minutes are his."

"Maybe—but the piano isn't," says Don. "The piano belongs to us and he does not have permission to play it, nor would we grant permission—what if a guest were to come downstairs and see a cleaner in his overalls playing the Steinway?"

Later, Stanley, the head of security, tells me that the pianist's name is Jean, that he's a widower from Brazil who has a seven-year-old son and they live in Stockwell with Jean's aunt. Six days a week, Jean starts work at 5:00 a.m., finishing at 2:00 p.m. to collect his son from school. He does have a valid work visa, which means he's in danger of summary dismissal. I watch the CCTV footage, looking for something to use in his defense.

At the beginning, the films show Jean passing the piano as he washes the floor at 5:00 a.m., pausing, mop in hand, to look at it. One day he touches the piano and apparently finds it dusty, because he looks at his fingers and wipes them on his overalls. The following day he polishes the dark wood and dusts the keys, and after that, for several weeks, he cleans the piano thoroughly, right down to its curled feet, which is maybe how he discovers the practice pedal that dims the sound down to almost nothing, because one day he puts on the practice pedal and sits down on the velvet seat and has a go at the keys. Just for a few minutes. The next day he sets up his mobile phone where the sheet music goes and takes a YouTube lesson. After that, he comes in early and practices every single day—fifteen minutes—

and even though there's no sound on the CCTV footage, you can tell he's making progress because he goes from using one hand to both and then both at the same time, and his range extends—his hands move farther up and down the keys and he introduces sharps and flats.

I seek out Richard. Valerie is at her post outside his office, still his devoted secretary, or maybe more of a PA/guard dog/bouncer combo. Richard is at his desk; he stands to invite me in. I tell him everything; the secret meeting that Trish asked me to keep from him and how lousy I've felt about that for the last two days, and about Jean the night cleaner in the Belgravia Palazzio who is at risk of being sacked. He listens closely to everything I say and I can tell from the way he jostles the change in his pocket that he's perturbed.

"That's odd," he says, of the secret meeting, "I did wonder if they were up to something. But never mind about Trish and Don; it's *marvelous* that this Jean is teaching himself to play—simply wonderful—I always thought that piano should be used more. There's no reason we shouldn't encourage it, as a company. Music is good for people—staff and guests. Don't you worry, I'll take care of Jean."

Something in the way he assures Jean's safety makes my bottom lip tremble.

"Whatever is the matter, Kate?" he asks. I want Adam to take care of me. That's what I thought marriage was, someone to keep you safe, somewhere to look after each other. I shouldn't cry in the president's office, but I can't help it.

A memory swims up to the surface of the moment I first set eyes on Adam. He was sitting in the director's office at my work, leaning forward, jacket on the back of the chair, shirtsleeves rolled up, forearms resting on his knees, hands lolling, back upright but relaxed, looking straight ahead. I was passing and stopped. Adam didn't see me but I saw him, and I knew. And maybe I sensed there would be some kind of trouble, because the thought that ran through my mind was "Oh, shit." But I liked his arms and I liked his face. I only saw him from the side, but that was enough— just the dip between his cheekbone and jaw, the proportions of his body, and his dark, dark hair. I knew before he even turned around. Recognition is simultaneous celebration and comedown; the sides go up but the middle goes down. I knew I was going to be with this man.

Unflustered, Richard passes tissues; doesn't hurry me, doesn't pry. Across his seventy years, over his glasses, he eyes me kindly.

11

It's hard to explain why I looked. Or perhaps it isn't.

I reach up to the shelf in the box room and take down the pink cardboard file labeled MOBILE, small block capitals in Adam's handwriting. Here they are in a thick stack, his mobile phone bills. This is silly, I tell myself; if he had anything to hide, he'd have thrown them away. Nevertheless, I close the door, and look.

I have Louise's number, in Adam's handwriting, to cross-reference with the bills. It is like trying to see a green insect on a green leaf, a gecko on a rock, a transparent jelly-fish in the Mediterranean Sea. At the end of the first page I turn over: row upon row of digits to trawl. What am I going to find in here anyhow? Nothing nourishing or life-affirming. Nothing marriage-affirming either. This is a shitty thing to do and I should abandon it now. Except that in all those numbers perhaps I will find the combination to unlock the clarity I need, an end to the subtle doubts that slip away each time I think I've caught one like a bar of soap in the bath.

I have a fluorescent-yellow pen, and with its help a pattern begins to emerge: yellow lines of Louise's number, mainly texts but some calls also. More than I expected. I highlight a flurry of communication leading up to the night of the drink with Bob and Tim, not much after it. What is it that I'm looking for, scouring these records? Him, I realize, because he's not with us, not properly. He is missing from his own life. Or he has another, elsewhere.

OK, I think, rallying myself—let's see when it started. I work back through time with the meticulousness I applied when the girls got nits from school. I combed their hair with an incredibly fine-toothed metal comb. It was remarkable how very many there were and, once I'd got over my initial disgust, how satisfying it was to get them out.

The frequency of Louise's number dwindles, though it is not entirely absent, but something else becomes apparent: three or four other numbers keep cropping up, one in particular, and I begin to look for these now too. I jot them down. I don't recognize these numbers, but they're most likely friends of his or colleagues. Except this one number keeps recurring over and over again: more than Louise's and much, much more than mine. I realize how scarcely my own number features in Adam's bills; how little, in fact, we speak to each other when one of us is away, or even during the course of a normal day—no nudges, jokes, hellos.

I keep wading through, by now waist-deep. Occasional sightings of Louise, this other number persistent. I go back about three years, and maybe I am in a kind of number-induced trance by now or maybe this submerged feeling is the one I need in order to do what I do next about this one recurring number. Like a sleepwalker, I dial it.

*

A woman answers and in the background I hear a TV. I imagine her in an armchair with her feet up, on her own. Maybe a cat.

"Hello?" she says cautiously—I suppose because she doesn't recognize the caller's number on her screen.

"Hello, is that . . . Laura?" I ask, plucking a name from the sky.

"Yes," she replies. Well, this throws me.

"This is Adam Pedley's wife," I say.

"Adam who?" she says.

"Oh. I think perhaps I've got the wrong number," I say, and hang up.

Instantly I spin a thought as fragile as blown glass: maybe this number actually belongs to a friend or a colleague he has a lot to do with and maybe it's that person's girlfriend who has just answered the phone and maybe she doesn't know Adam. I carry the thought with both hands to the sitting room, where Adam is watching TV, oblivious to the fact that I have been studying his phone bills.

"What's up?" he says, clocking my face, which I suppose doesn't look quite as it does normally, owing to the fact that I'm not feeling quite as I do normally.

"I've been looking at your phone bills," I say. "Who's Laura?"

"I don't know a Laura." He comes straight back—no blinking, no hesitation.

"Who's this then? I dialed this number and a woman picked up and I said, 'Hello, is that Laura?' and she said, 'Yes.'"

"Let's have a look," he says, holding his hand out for the paper. I pass it over.

"It was a woman," I say. "Who is she?"

I drop the glass thought, but Adam has sharp reflexes and catches it.

"Oh, her," he says. "It's just someone I was introduced to at football. She's a football person. Same team. There's a load of texts that go round about that." He looks casual, unflustered.

"But then why didn't she know your surname? And how come there are SO many texts to that number? And how come I didn't know about her? And whose are these other numbers anyway?"

"You're asking too many questions!" says Adam. "I don't know! You have to give me a chance to answer! That one is George," he says, pointing at one. "And I think that one is Bob. Or Tim. But I'd have to check."

"How come I didn't even know she existed, this foot-ball woman?"

"Because it's just football!"

"Well, I want to know who all these numbers belong to by the end of the night," I say, and stomp away. It's already late—past 11:30—but there's no possibility of sleep. I am a ball of electricity, a crazed magnetic field; thoughts simultaneously pull me toward them and push me away. Why would he keep four years' worth of item-ized phone bills if they were incriminating? He wouldn't. Unless he was relying on the fact that I never look at things like that; unless force of habit was stronger than conscious awareness of what might happen as a result; he never threw anything away so why would he, in fact, dispose of the phone bills? He wouldn't. He would keep them, stuffed into a pink cardboard folder on a shelf among other folders similarly stuffed. And since he had kept them, surely there couldn't be anything too hideous in there. Unless there was a part of him, subconscious perhaps, that wanted to be caught? But why?

I can't fathom his motivation, and in a way I don't really need to, except for my own growing need to get to the bottom of it, whatever that means. I go back to the box room and the bills. They have served their purpose, but I don't know what else I should do. I look in the drawer and find a blue fluorescent pen. Blue is their team's color, so that's fitting. I start to highlight the football woman's number. Blocks, not lines.

Just before the clock strikes twelve I hear a muffled slam. I get up from the desk and go to check the front door. It is locked. The lights are out and the house is quiet. I go upstairs; both girls are fast asleep in their beds, but Adam has gone.

I look around the house, calling softly so as not to wake the children, but he is gone. I dial his number, half expecting to hear his phone ring in the house somewhere, or just outside at least. Maybe he has gone out to get some air.

I unlock the door and walk out into the night. Halfway over the street I hear crunching underfoot, look down, and see that the road is strewn with broken glass. My spun-glass thought, smashed into a thousand tiny pieces.

Something shifts in me then. The empty street is a fact, like the number I didn't recognize and the woman who answered it. I don't need the specifics to know that I have opened the door onto a palatial disappointment. Inside myself I feel a departure and it isn't his. Fragments of glass lie sharp and twinkling in the streetlight. There's a widening, deepening gap between me and myself. This street where we've lived together for ten years is suddenly foreign. The house facing me doesn't look like home, but the door is open and my two daughters are asleep inside.

I cross the threshold again. Was the hallway always this narrow? Twice I drop the keys trying to relock the door, fumbling as if my fingers are grossly swollen and the keys too tiny to handle, or is it that my hands are shaking? The central heating is off and so are the lights, but I don't want to acknowledge myself by switching anything on. The secondhand glow of streetlights seeps in through uncurtained windows. Frozen in mind and in body I sit—not thinking; waiting. I call him several times through the night but he doesn't answer.

12

I am suspended in an emotional Grand Canyon, wide-eyed with shock, feeling nauseous. The canyon stretches in all directions: up, down, round, and about. The kitchen is cold. Shadows move across the floor. There are psychic edges and outcrops, thought processes in strata like layers of rock of different ages. Limestone, sandstone, granite, schist, and shale: I remember the incantation from school and I remember something called the Great Unconformity, a gap where huge mountains were eroded utterly, no sediments remain; a non-layer that exists yet does not exist. Like this night, which has eroded into a vast chasm: implacable, each hour quiet as a cathedral, deep as a vault. If I ever get out, I never want to come here again.

He answers the next morning at 7:00. He is at George's house. But he walked for a long time before going there. He walked and walked until 2:00 in the morning. He said he could have walked all night long.

"Did you have an affair with Laura?"

"It's Lorna. I don't know a Laura."

"Did you have an affair with Lorna?"

"Yes."

"Did you have an affair with Louise?"

"No."

"When did it start, with Lorna?"

"Three years ago."

"But her number first appears on your bill three and a half years ago."

"Well, I suppose it could have been three and a half years."

13

Call someone. The thought comes unbidden, like a shout from high up on the canyon ridge, and echoes like a bird cawing: caw, caw, caw, but there's no condor soaring above, the tips of its wings spread like fingers. I am wedged between my own thoughts, externalized like buttes and crevices, composed of sediment, interbedded with old beliefs. Mr. Loyal. Adam was devoted to me and the kids.

Call someone. Call, call, call.

Yes, I think, but who?

The answer swims up: a friend. It takes a moment to work out what this means; to locate images that go with this word. David, who now lives five doors down; Yvette; Jo; they are the main friends and can be dated from the same era. We formed friendships at university, an age ago. Yvette would want me to call her first but she lives in Brighton. Jo is on the other side of London, always busy, never without an answer.

I call Jo. My voice sounds dead to me and it must to her too because she says she can be with me in under an hour. It is 7:15 on Saturday morning.

At 8:00 a.m. Jo knocks on the door, with a bagful of warm croissants. The girls are just waking.

"What will I tell them when they ask, 'Where's Daddy?'"
I say.

"Tell them he's at George's house. I'll look after them
if you want to go and meet him," she says.

I don't want to go and meet him, but there is a conversation to be had or at least an exchange of facts, and it
would be better if the girls didn't hear it. The coffee Jo
prepares washes down my throat without warming my
insides. I can't eat the croissant. The girls chatter to Jo in
their pajamas, thinking it a treat that she is here, asking
about her children. Perhaps something in them has already
sensed my detached state and decided not to question it,
because when I say that I'm going to meet Daddy they
accept it without asking why he's not here.

"Jo's taking us to the swimming pool later," says Milla
cheerfully. "And she says we can have crisps after."

"And hot chocolate," says Hester.

"That's nice," I say.

I haven't changed my clothes since last night. There
seems little point in doing so, but I wash perfunctorily and
put on deodorant and a clean T-shirt. All my movements
are stiff, which has something, but not everything, to do
with sitting all night in a canyon.

Adam is waiting by the Victorian bandstand in the park;
hunched shoulders, fists shoved deep in his two front pockets, fugitive eyes. He too is wearing the same clothes as last
night and he hasn't shaved. It's too cold to sit.

"Let's walk," I say, and he falls in beside me. "There are
some things I need to know."

"OK. No more bullshit from me—I'll tell you the truth."

"How did you meet her?"

"Online," he says, "on a kind of dating website."

"What do you mean?"

"It's for people who want to meet and have sex, no strings attached."

"But you had strings."

"I told her I was single and I used a different surname."

"So that's why she didn't recognize your name—when I said, 'I'm Adam Pedley's wife,' she said, 'Adam who?'"

"Yeah."

"So what was it, your new name?"

"Does it matter? Look, Kate—I barely saw her. It was just a few times. I know it was wrong and you probably think I'm a complete asshole—"

"You *are* a complete asshole."

"OK, I deserve that. But listen, Kate, it wasn't a relationship, it was just sex—"

"How many times?"

"I don't know exactly, around six times—six to eight times—each year."

I fall silent, trying to recall six to eight times he could have seen her without me noticing.

"I wasn't in love with her, if that's what you're thinking," he offers.

"That's not what I was thinking. It hadn't occurred to me that you might be."

"Oh," he says, "sorry."

This makes me laugh a little. I feel as though I'm in a play. *The worst is not, so long as we can say "This is the worst."*

"What?"

And worse I may be yet. This is happening apart from me. It's all quite distant.

"You being in love with her would be worse. Although maybe a bit less cold-blooded. How did you manage to see her without my even noticing?"

"She works for herself so I saw her in the daytimes, usually."

"Jesus, Adam—*Why?*" I cry, and in the instant I close down again, push it out and away, muttering, "Stupid question . . ."

"It's not a stupid question, Kate. I'd ask it. There's no good reason—it is stupid. *I'm* stupid. I read an article one weekend about married people using this website and it sounded kind of exciting, and that night when you were in bed I went online and signed up. I didn't think I'd go through with anything, I was just doing it to see what happened, out of curiosity really, and a few people got in touch with me and this one, well, I met her one day after work and we had a drink—just a drink—and I swore to myself that would be it, but then—it wasn't."

I'd read that article too. It was in one of the supplements of the Sunday papers and we'd just got home from Cornwall. He was still working but we both knew the situation was untenable, that he couldn't go on. The Cornish holiday was meant to be an oasis, but getting to the beach was like planning an expedition because we needed so much stuff, and as soon as we hit sand Milla would chase seagulls or make off with other children's buckets or toddle out to sea, so Adam had his hands full following her while I set up base camp and stayed on the blanket with Hester, trying to protect her from the sand and wind and, occasionally, the sun. Looking back, a British beach holiday with two infants wasn't the brightest idea. I was trying to wean Hester but she was refusing to take a bottle and waking twice every night for a feed. The holiday cottage had terribly steep stairs, lethal with a heavy baby in the middle of the night, so I was feeding Hester in the bedroom. After a few nights Adam took up his familiar pattern— watching TV until the small hours, dozing off in front of the set, and coming to bed at 1:00 or 2:00 in the morning, whereas I'd been asleep since 10:00. We barely saw each other. I'd feed Hester around 5:00 a.m. and watch him comatose in bed and wish we'd stayed at home, spent the money on babysitters and a few good nights out together. We arrived home late on a Saturday night after two weeks, exhausted. The Sunday papers the next day carried that article. I'm not sure whether I read it before or after Adam and we didn't discuss it, but I remember thinking, God, that's awful. Now I imagine Adam reading it and what was his reaction—God, that's great?

"Did you ever stay the night?" I ask.

"Three or four times—when you were away with the girls."

"Which was it? Three times or four times?" I say. Again I push it out.

"I'm not sure, maybe four or five. I'd have to check."

"Where were we?"

"At your parents', or at my parents'."

"So those times you sent us on ahead in the car and said you were staying to lock up and set off early on your Ducati the next day, that's when you'd stay with her?"

"Yes," he says quietly.

It's a frosty morning, the grass white and crunchy under-foot, puddles glazed with ice. If there is a river at the bottom of the canyon, will it be frozen over? I don't know what time it is, but families are coming out, with buggies and toddler bikes, and there are dog walkers and runners.

"I don't want this," I say, looking at the canvas trainers I'm wearing—stupid choice; my feet are very cold.

"Neither do I," he says.

"But you *chose* it!" I burst out. "I *asked* whether you were having an affair. Why didn't you tell me?"

He pauses, looking at his feet, shaking his head. "I don't know. There's no good answer to that. I suppose . . . I just wasn't ready. I'm so sorry, Kate. I really am sorry."

No wonder now about Adam's late-night laundry, the one-armed hugs in the morning.

"So she didn't know about us," I say, meaning me and the girls.

"No."

"What did you do with your wedding ring?"

"I put it in my wallet." I picture his brown leather wallet stuffed with old receipts and loyalty cards; one for every shop he's ever been to. Nine stamps for a free coffee, ten for an ice cream; loyalty is cheap these days.

"Did she know about Charlie?"

"Yes, I told her about Charlie."

The distance holds and then it doesn't hold. Outwardly I am upright, stiff and cold. Inwardly something is being dislodged. A mountain of faith is being eroded into a non-layer, my own Great Unconformity—something that should have been there but wasn't. Or, more accurately, something that was once there and now was not. Like my husband, who, I now realize, left long before he was gone.

14

Jo makes me call my parents when all I want to do is sit and stare. I'm falling slowly—round and round, down and down; the chasm hasn't finished opening, which is OK as long as it eventually swallows me whole. I don't want to be crushed and broken into a thousand tiny pieces.

My parents are still with my brother and his family in Boston. Their transatlantic voices can't believe my news. Except they can. They can and do believe it; it is me who can't quite. Not yet. Not entirely. As long as I can hold it off I won't feel its full force. When I talk to Dad he says he's coming to London right now. No, Dad, it's OK, I'll be OK. Well, who's going to look after the kids when you go to work, then? he says. Jo can't stay indefinitely, she has her own job to go to, her own family to look after. I hadn't thought of that. My lovely neighbor Noreen, a retired childminder, might be able to help out, but that would mean telling her what happened. Then do please come, I say.

I am lagging behind: two hours after I put the phone down to Mum and Dad and my brother I suddenly feel aggrieved by their ready acceptance of what I told them. Why don't they disbelieve it, at least for a little while? Is it so easy to understand? Adam was devoted to me and the kids. That was the whole thing. Devoted. Adam had his difficulties, and don't we all, but he was committed to his family and this balanced it all out. First there was Louise, and now I have to factor in the woman on the other end of the phone. They mess it up. The sum won't work anymore.

There's a strange new taste in my mouth, vaguely chemical. I catch an unpleasant odor rising from my collar and feel embarrassed, even though there's nobody else in the room. I decide to take a shower, a task that I can do.

Our good friend and near neighbor, David, comes round. My neighbor now, not Adam's. I tell him the news, which he receives solemnly. We both recall a moment at a dinner party a year or so ago: Yvette and Saul and their two children were staying with us and I invited Jo and her husband, and David and his boyfriend, Edward. I made lamb-and-apricot tagine and couscous and a plum crumble and lit candles all around the kitchen, tall and short, thick and thin. Everyone looks beautiful by candlelight. Adam was on good form, pouring wine and making jokes. In the after-dinner talk our guests discovered that they had music in common and David went to collect his and Edward's instruments and played us a zippy jig on the violin and then something mournful, which Edward accompanied on the flute. Yvette played an aria, Saul borrowed the guitar and sang, Jo strummed something and sang along, but I didn't dare to and Adam never would.

I realized that night that the point of learning an instrument is to enjoy making music and maybe to play with other people. It doesn't have to be perfect. You don't even have to be very good. If you can play, you can make something alive. I had a heart-piercing moment of regret about the piano and wished I'd stayed with it. My mother used to drive me into town for weekly lessons with the vicar's wife. She stayed in the car rather than wait in the vicarage and I always wished she'd come in with me. The vicar's wife didn't seem to enjoy the lessons any more than I did, had me trudging up and down scales like a chore. Enjoyment didn't come into it.

At home the piano was upright against a wall in a cold room nobody used, gray damp mottled across the wallpaper. I rarely practiced and was eventually allowed to give up. After that, still wanting to learn an instrument, I tried the flute at school, but the music teacher kept saying he wanted to feel my diaphragm. I wasn't exactly sure what that was, only that it was dangerously close to my developing breasts and it seemed safer to cancel the flute.

At the end of the dinner party, while Edward and Saul smoked cigars in the garden and the others were in an argument about the next mayor of London and I was making mint tea and coffee, David confided that Edward had found a younger man and was spending a lot of time with him.

"He won't leave me, but he won't leave him either," said David.

"But you two seem so—*together*," I said. "I can't believe it, why would he do that to you?"

"He can't help it if he's fallen for someone," said David.

After having been motionless for a great part of the day, some connection fizzes and suddenly I can't bear to be still for a moment longer. The girls are cuddled up with Jo, watching a movie; they've been steering clear of me all day and I've let them because I don't know what to say or how to say it. I begin to whirr around the house, folding laundry and putting it in drawers, emptying wastepaper bins, sorting toys into the right boxes, straightening books on shelves. David follows a short distance behind, picking up the socks I drop, small plastic animals I don't notice, balled-up tissues I spill, the books I knock off the shelf. He doesn't talk and neither do I until I catch a whiff that brings me up short.

"Do I smell?" I ask David.

"Oh, honey," he says kindly.

"Do I, though?"

"A little bit."

After another shower I call Adam.

"How old is she?" I say, no preamble.

"The same age as me," Adam says.

"She's forty-two?"

"Yeah."

"Does she have children?"

"No."

"Why not? Doesn't she want them? Did she want them with you?"

"I don't know, Kate. We never talked about that."

"Well, at least she's not younger than me," I say, but quickly see this gives me no advantage, makes no difference: the number of times he saw her does not become greater than or lesser than. I can't stop doing the maths.

"She would have been thirty-eight when you met her and I was thirty-four. You were seeing her all through my thirty-fifth year, and all through my thirty-sixth year, and all through my thirty-seventh year."

I flick through those years as with a photo album. Each had been long and full of memories, but now they become flat and flimsy. The years fold like cards.

When I call Yvette, the first thing she says is "Why didn't you call?" with a slightly injured tone.

"I am calling," I say. "I'm calling you now."

Three months ago we were invited to stay with Yvette and Saul in Brighton. Adam said he couldn't come because we'd already agreed that he could have a full day on his motorbike and he didn't want to change it.

"You don't have to change it," I'd said. "Come with us on Saturday and go from Brighton on Sunday morning. It'll be great—you'll already be out of London. I bet the roads are beautiful."

"But I'm going with that group that I sometimes ride with."

"Can't you go from Brighton? We always get on so well with Yvette and Saul, it's a shame if you're not there."

"They're leaving through North London—it's the opposite direction."

"What if you get up a bit earlier?"

He didn't want to get up so early on a Sunday morning.

There was a late-afternoon walk on Brighton beach, Saul chasing all the children up ahead to wear them out, Yvette making supper at home, and me walking alone close to the shoreline, wondering where Adam was and wishing he were here. When we got back Yvette had made sausages, cheesy pasta, and green beans with butter and garlic. "Could I have a couple of fried eggs with mine?" said Saul, and "Me too!" "And me!" "I want eggs!" "So do I!" went the children, and a pan of eggs was duly prepared. Everyone tucked in happily, red-cheeked and tousled from the walk, but later, when the meal was eaten and I started to clear away the plates, Yvette said, "Let *him* wash up. I hate it when he does that and he does it all the time."

"Does what?" I said.

"I make a lovely meal and he always asks for more before we've even sat down to eat it—fried eggs, or a bit of ham or bacon, or 'Can we get that pâté out?' Whatever I produce, it's never enough for him. It's never enough." I realized I'd stumbled into a marital minefield, but instead of making me feel better about Adam and my problems it only made me miss him more.

He was late collecting us from the station the next day, said he'd just got back from the bike ride, said he'd needed a wash before coming to get us.

I call Adam a third time and ask if he stayed the night while we'd been in Brighton.

"Yes," he sighs. "That was the last time I saw her."

"And was that one of the four or five times or was that additional?"

"It might have been six or seven, I'd have to check."

"Check, then. Did you even go out on your bike?"

"Yes, I did."

"And when you picked us up from the station on Sunday

afternoon, you'd been with her all that day. And the night before."

Of course he'd needed a wash.

Downstairs, David is ironing the girls' school uniform, a thing I never do, and Jo is cooking, though I can't imagine what. After a while I hear them bring the children upstairs, a bath running. I hear Milla shout, "Hester, we're having a bubble bath and David's put LOADS in!"

The main sum still doesn't work out but I am solving other equations quite quickly. I kiss the girls good night and call him back. He is still at George's, sounds weary. To my mind he has no right to be weary even though it's Sunday evening and I suppose, like me, he hasn't slept since Friday night.

"Did you take her out on your Ducati when we were in Brighton?"

"Yes."

"You didn't go on a ride with the North London group."

"No."

"So you had a plan with her. All along the plan was with her and not the group." Our marriage is lying broken on the floor and I am putting the pieces together as if it's a jigsaw puzzle, only the picture I am building up is not the same as the picture on the box.

"And you took my helmet. She used my helmet, I suppose."

Adam is silent.

"This doesn't sound like 'just sex,' Adam. This sounds like you had a girlfriend."

I haven't yet reached the bottom. On some level I know that the shock is protecting me from pain but the knowledge feels ancient. I have vacated myself—I feel so removed that I briefly wonder if I'm having a stroke, but the thought floats away.

Jo looks up from the pan she is stirring; alarm registers in her face. Have I startled her? I make no sound at all, I am not conscious of taking steps; it's more like I am floating forward. I pass David, who has a glass of wine in his hand, and Jo, who is looking at me, concerned, wooden spoon held aloft.

The back door is open to let out steam from the cooking. I pick up the iron; not quite cold to the touch, cord neatly wrapped and tucked in around its base. I glide outside with perfect knowledge of what I am about to do. I raise the iron high above the Ducati and bring it down hard. The bike is covered with a green tarpaulin so I can't see what part I'm hitting, but it buckles and crunches under the cover and on the third blow there's the satisfying sound of glass shattering and tinkling to the ground.

15

Arriving at work on Monday, I am astonished to be able to go through the motions. I greet coworkers, hang my coat, go to my desk. Gérard sees the bandage where I cut my hand on the broken windscreen and frowns. "Are you OK? You look a bit pale."

"Do I?" I say, and look down at my shoes so that I am not lying to his face. "Rough weekend—the girls have been unwell," I say.

"I'm sorry to hear that," says Gérard. "Who's looking after them—Adam?"

At the mention of Adam a sob escapes. I hide my face in a man-sized tissue and blow.

"I imagine it must be very worrying when they fall ill," says Gérard, who doesn't have children. "Would you like a cup of coffee?"

"Yes, please," I sniff, already regretting the lie.

Gérard shuffles off to get coffee. His walk is very low to the ground for such a tall man; nothing seems to actually lift, and he has that small hunch around the shoulders that very tall people sometimes have. It strikes me that I know next to nothing about Gérard, just that he eats three pieces of fruit each day, takes his coffee black with no sugar, comes from a town near Bordeaux, and wears jumpers over his shoulders in the European style. There's a framed photograph on his desk of him with his cousin, who has the same overgrown shaggy hair but much darker than Gérard's. In the photo, Gérard's eyes are shut. The cousin is looking at him and they're both grinning.

He comes back with two mugs of coffee.

"You're very kind," I say. "I don't just mean the coffee, but thanks for that too. I haven't been sleeping very well recently."

"Maybe you should try the swim team," he says, and we both snicker. Lunchtime exercise is officially encouraged—there's a swimming coach who takes forty-five-minute training sessions and lunchtime yoga twice a week, but woe betide anyone on Trish's team who has the temerity to actually go. Yoga is too slow for Trish. She tried the swimming once but came out of the pool early because the lanes were congested, saying, "I can *float* faster than those people."

We used to go swimming as a family. The last time we went Adam told me that my swimming costume wasn't flattering.

At lunchtime I wander in and out of shops. In the chemist's I pick out some fruity-zesty shampoo and conditioner for the girls, but as I go up to pay I see the condom display and fear crashes through me like a bolt of lightning. How did he—? What if—? I text him: *Did you use condoms?* The answer comes back straightaway: *Yes. You don't need to worry about that.* Adam calls but I don't answer. I throw my sandwich in a bin after two bites.

In the afternoon everybody gathers in the lobby for a viewing of the new company film. It opens with uplifting music and aerial shots of PHC's biggest and best-known hotels around the globe, a collection of palaces in a corporate kingdom. We're all expecting Richard but it's Don who appears, his title emblazoned across the bottom of the screen: *Mr. Don Mitchell Esquire, Executive Vice President for HR and Legal, Palazzio Hotel Corporation.* I'm glad I told Richard about Don and Trish's secret meeting with the shareholders—only a week ago, though it feels more like a month—but it looks as though Don and Trish are advancing on several fronts. I'm not the only one to have noticed: in the darkened hall, there are mutterings.

" 'Esquire'—what's that about?"

"Where's Richard?"

"Being pushed out by this muppet, looks like." Don looms large from the screen. "Welcome to Our House," he says, and the camera swoops inside a hotel and pans around the smiling faces of uniformed staff. The rest of the short film is all pictures so that it can be shown to all 360,000 employees around the world. Don is the gracious host to people of all nationalities having model Guest Experiences. Queenly and benign in a wide-skirted blue dress, Trish is seen presiding over a meeting of impeccably turned-out junior staff.

"I bet they're actors," says someone nearby.

"Yeah. Nobody that good-looking works here," says the person next to him.

"Speak for yourself!" says the first person.

Toward the end of the film the music becomes solemn and stately as if a new country is being introduced to the world and there are shots of PHC's logo, as heraldic as a coat of arms. The music is all it takes: hot tears bubble up and out and I bend my head slightly to hide them. My sobs are inaudible but my shoulders shake. Even as I hope nobody notices, Trish appears at my elbow, leans in close, and whispers, "I know—exciting, isn't it?"

After the film I gather my things and get ready to go home. I've held it together through the day but I'm not sure I can keep it up. Ordinarily Adam would have done the school run, but today Jo did the morning and Yvette came up from Brighton to collect them. She's going to stay a couple of days until my parents get back from Boston.

"I hope they get better soon," says Gérard as I'm leaving.

"Who?" I say, then catch myself. "Oh—the girls. Thank you."

I'm leaving a couple of hours earlier than usual, so even though the cars have their lights on it's not yet fully dark. Deep pink mottles the sky behind the tall office buildings and the last rays of the sun are reflected in the windows. As I head for the Tube I feel an internal tug. I know this feeling and I know it won't go away until I act on it, so I turn and go back inside, back up the silver escalator and back to my desk. Gérard looks up and says, "Forgot something?"

"Yes. I forgot to tell you the truth. The girls aren't ill. I lied, I'm sorry, but we did have a rough weekend—Adam left. Or ran away. And I don't know if he's coming back. I don't know if I even want him to. I didn't see it coming— oh, maybe in a way I did, but it was still a shock. I had a feeling something wasn't right and when I finally looked it exploded in my face. So that's kind of it, really." I sprint through two-thirds of this and then wobble. Gérard rises, takes me by the elbow, and sits me down, pulls another chair close.

"Kate, I am so sorry to hear this. How are you?"

I shrug. I can't answer.

He nods, as if he understands. "How are the girls taking it?"

"We haven't really talked. It's only just happened—Friday night, and today's only Monday. They know something's up, but they haven't asked and I haven't said anything. Yet." I suddenly feel guilty that I haven't explained the situation.

"You might still be in shock, you know. It's like a sudden bereavement. You think you can carry on but—"

"It happened to you?"

"A bereavement, yes. My partner."

"Oh, I'm sorry."

"It's OK. It was years ago. It was difficult—really difficult—for a long time, but things are better now."

"How do you—I mean, if you don't mind me asking—how do you get over something like that?"

Gérard thinks for a moment. "You don't, really. The hurt doesn't go away completely, it becomes part of you."

This is the opposite of what I want to hear. I must look appalled because Gérard smiles and says, "I needed that time. It was like a passage and at the end I was really . . ." There's a pause while he looks for the right words. "At my place."

"'At my place'?" I repeat, not understanding.

"*Bien dans ta peau*—when you feel happy in your

skin, you are at home inside yourself. You are in your own place."

Leaving the office for the second time that night, I'm glad I told Gérard the truth. In the alley, Peter is outside his shop in a big black overcoat, rearranging a display of ornaments on a slightly wonky shelf unit. The busy high street is up ahead, winking with lights, purring with traffic, but here the air is still. It's very nearly dark. The pink clouds have faded into dark blue dusk.

"Hello, darling—do you like these? They are from Buckingham Palace. Gifts from the Queen. An old servant, she sold them to me, she doesn't want them anymore." A flattened roll-up cigarette stuck to his bottom lip moves up and down when he talks. I stop for a moment to admire the miniatures of Westminster Palace, Kensington Palace, St. James's Palace, Balmoral Castle, Windsor Castle.

"Where's Buckingham Palace?" I ask.

"She kept it. Take one, I give it to you," he says, cigarette wagging.

"Well, all right," I say. "It's not every day a man offers me a castle." I select Balmoral, set on a greenish mound with painted yellow and brown dots that I assume to be gorse and bracken on the heath.

16

"Oh, your big sad eyes," says Yvette when I get home, but I think Gérard was right; my eyes are wide with shock. Walking in the front door feels strange; there's a different hue, like someone's swapped our normal lightbulbs and made the hallway brighter, harsher. The girls rush forward and almost take me down, Hester at the knees, Milla at the hips. I manage to stay on my feet and work my arms out of my coat with both of them hanging on tight, pushing me back down the hall until we crash against the door. I slide down to the floor and they pile on top.

"Poor Mummy!" says Yvette. "She's just got home from work!"

"It's OK," I call from the bottom of the scrum, "this is normal!"

"Oh, right," says Yvette, and retreats into the kitchen. I tickle the girls before shoving them off, by which time Hester's little red tights are round her knees and everything I'm wearing is ridden up or out of place and static is making my hair rise like a ghoul.

"Thank you for coming." I hug Yvette, daughters at my side. Milla is watchful and attentive.

"I'll always come, whenever you need me," Yvette replies.

I lift Hester onto the kitchen table to pull up her tights, but she wants them off. The sight of her dimpled knees and sturdy little legs almost makes me cry—she's so young—

but I don't want to collapse in front of them and I still
don't know what to tell them, so I quash it.

At bedtime after I've read a story I tell them that Yvette
will take them to school and collect them and that they
will see Daddy again soon.

"Where *is* Daddy?" asks Hester.

"Why isn't he here?" says Milla.

"Daddy's gone to stay at George's house for a while.
We had an argument."

"I heard it," says Milla.

"Did you?"

"Yes. You were arguing about his phone. He wanted
you to give it back but you wouldn't."

"Well, that's not quite all of it, but—"

"That's not very nice, Mummy. You should have given
him his phone."

"It wasn't really about his actual phone."

"Yes, it was! I heard the words!"

"Don't lie, Mummy!"

"If you say sorry, he'll come home."

"You should say sorry, Mummy."

Say you've been married for a long time and there's always been a certain tension between you, something you
took for passion at the start and later explained away,
and say this tension grew, but so slowly that you didn't
notice until it was bigger than the house and even then
you had so many explanations—the children were young

and you were both exhausted, money was a worry because there wasn't enough, his job made him feel he was being buried alive so no wonder he was snappy and distant, and no wonder you didn't have sex anymore or even really talk. Say all these things are true, and say you thought you loved each other and so you waited, and waited, and waited for things to improve. How big an idiot are you?

"You're not an idiot, Kate. Adam deceived you," says Yvette.

"He did, but—how did I not see?"

"You were being lied to! You trusted him!"

"I suppose so," I say. But it's easier to chastise yourself for being a fool than to admit, even to your closest friend, the terrifying plummet of your humiliating failure to see. The fear is not that you will hit the bottom; the fear is that there is no bottom to hit.

I go to bed at 10:00 and turn out the light, feeling sure that I will sleep because I haven't for three nights, but I'm so wired I levitate above the mattress. After fifteen minutes I accept that sleep is not going to happen. I get up and check my emails. Jo has sent numbers: solicitors, barristers, mediators, family therapists, counselors, surveyors, and estate agents. A psychiatrist in Harley Street.

It looks as though it's going to be a full-time job sorting out the mess, so I may as well start. I email everyone on Jo's list, asking for appointments, and after that I respond to the emails Trish has sent in the last half hour. She wants to know how I'm going to solve the mystery of the Guest Experience; she's glad I thought the film was exciting and she wants to know what everyone else thought of her and Don in it; she wants me to go to Belgium on Wednesday to sign the contract on a 1930s palace for a new concept hotel we're piloting, an immersive experience where a particular moment in history is re-created in full. It's awkward timing, but maybe it will be good to get away for a couple of days, help me regain some perspective. My parents are coming to us straight from Boston and they can look after the girls so I tell her I will go. I look around. The bedroom looks exactly as it did last week—the book Adam had been reading, *The Curious Incident of the Dog in the Night-Time*, the latest Q magazine, and half a glass of water that has stood by his side of the bed for three days. The sheets are the ones we last made love in. I wonder if we'll ever do that again. The flurry of sex just before I found out seems desperate now. His pajamas are still under his pillow. I root them out and gather them to my face for a moment to breathe in his scent. The smell conjures him up so powerfully and yet his absence is so complete.

It's no wonder I can't sleep, I tell myself briskly. As quietly as possible, so as not to wake Yvette and the girls, I strip the bed and bundle his pajamas and the old sheets into the laundry basket, make up the bed with fresh linen. It's a joyless act that I regret instantly. I run a bath and steep in it for thirty minutes, but that feeling doesn't go away. Three and a half years. A thousand and one nights when he knew and I didn't. All those birthdays, Easters, Christmases, the summer holidays, the ordinary days. All that life. All those lies. And yet he was with us then, and now he's gone. My skin pink and porous from the hot bath, I retrieve the bundle and spread the old sheets on top of the clean ones, sip his old water, turn out the light, and hide in the dark with Adam's pajamas against my cheek, breathing in the smell of him.

17

At 3:00 a.m. I wake up and wonder why I am clutching Adam's pajamas, remember everything in a rush like a cold shower, and throw them across the room, which is unsatisfying since they are not heavy enough to hurl. I get up to make tea, wishing there was something stronger in the house. While the kettle's boiling I start a new shopping list and put *whiskey* at the top, then notice that the red wine Yvette and I shared last night isn't completely finished. I drain the bottle. The dribble of wine has sediment in it. For a flash, it's funny and I add to the shopping list: *vodka, gin, red wine, white wine, beer, advocaat, Bailey's, sherry, cognac, cherry brandy*. There's some relief in knowing that tea and biscuits are more my style. I rinse my mouth and find a digestive to go with the tea.

I reread Rosenfeld and Abrahams on infidelity, a chapter I know well by now. *It is entirely normal to have many questions*. This reassures me somewhat and I write them in a pad of A4, each on a new line and numbered in the margin. I have forty-six questions.

In the morning, I come down from the shower to find Yvette and the girls in the kitchen in their pajamas. The children are drawing. Yvette's made coffee, soft-boiled eggs, and toast. My shopping list is by the kettle with a few more items in Yvette's handwriting: *Paracetamol, ibuprofen, aspirin, coffee*.

"Thanks," I say, grateful that she got the joke.

"I love you," Yvette says, giving me a hug.

"Do you want to see our list?" says Milla, holding out the paper they've been huddled over. Their list says: *Haribo Gummi Bears (big bag), Haribo Starmix (big bag), Coke, Fanta, Sprite, Crisps, Ice cream, Shoklet Butuns, Pupi.*

"Wow, that's a good list! You'll have no teeth left!" I say. It's all in Milla's writing with the exception of *shoklet butuns* and *pupi*, in Hester's.

"What's 'pupi'?" I say.

"*Puppy*, Mummy!" say the girls.

"Oh, *puppy*—but we've got Charlie!"

We look at Charlie, wheezing in his basket.

18

Peter is laying out the stall outside his shop early. Along-side the miniature castles are two gold carriage clocks, a small yellow pillbox clock, two gilded oval photograph frames, an iron, a kettle. I notice a tea caddy and silver spoon decorated with the royal coat of arms and then other items with the lion and unicorn; three ashtrays in varying condition, a bone-china teapot, a used bath mat in thick white cotton with the emblem embroidered in faded gold thread, a white soap dish with gold edges and the royal emblem.

"Twenty-two-carat gold on that," says Peter as I pick up the soap dish and turn it over. On the underside is written *Buckingham Palace* in gold lettering.

"She got a lot of presents from the Queen, this old servant," I remark.

"Maybe she work there a long time. I don't know." Peter shrugs.

"I didn't know the Queen smoked," I say, picking up a slightly chipped ashtray.

"Secret," says Peter, and winks. I smile at the idea of the Queen being a secret smoker, and seeing this, Peter offers me anything I want from the royal selection. I'd quite like one of Her Majesty's soap dishes because they look so quaint—little porcelain tugboats—but I can't help feeling I'd be stealing if I said yes. PHC phased out soap dishes long ago because they lost so many. In fact today, Peter's whole stall is like a display of things most often taken from hotels. Clocks, picture frames, phones, irons, kettles, towels, sheets, and bath linen fit easily in suitcases, but people also manage to steal flat-screen TVs, rugs, curtains, minibar fridges, ironing boards. It's hard to imagine how, or even why, but if people are determined, they'll find a way.

I call our City law firm, Wells-Ash & Wade. Branton Kemp-Jones comes, a knight in navy blue. Before I go to Belgium, I have to sign various papers to make me a legal signatory for PHC. I hand him my passport.

"Not bad!" says Branton, looking at my photograph. "I look like a junkie convict in mine—I'm surprised they let me in anywhere. Yours is actually quite nice."

It would be impossible for Branton Kemp-Jones to look like a drug addict—a rugby addict or a cricket addict, perhaps. "But you're so preppy and healthy-looking," I say. "Obnoxiously so, if you don't mind me saying."

A slight droop of his head suggests that maybe he does mind. "One of the bulbs in the photo booth was out, so, you know, there were lots of shadows," he says.

"Don't get me wrong—you look great! I mean, it's great to look healthy, is what I mean."

"Thanks, Kate," he says, bouncing back to his imperturbable self. Branton rolls up the papers and ties them with a pink ribbon.

"It's quite old-fashioned, isn't it—signing actual parchment with an ink pen. You'd think nowadays we could just scan and email," I say.

"The old ways are sometimes the best," he says, sounding much older than he actually is. "Righto, that's done!

You are now a legal signatory for Palazzio Hotel Corporation, one of only five in this country and twelve worldwide."

The therapist emails me with her phone number and says she's available for the next half hour. I need somewhere private to make the call. I could leave the building, but that gets noted. Empty stairwells or emergency fire exits are sometimes OK, but not for this. Apart from the eleventh floor, all the rooms are glass, and although other people can't hear you if the door's closed, they can see you. Sometimes people sit in dark corners to make personal calls, but this is high risk as at any moment other people could barge in, slam the lights on, and find you crouching on the floor.

I take the scroll from my desk and head up to the eleventh floor, where the offices have real walls. I drop the scroll with Valerie and ask if there's an office I can use for ten minutes. She says the boardroom is empty and there's no reason I couldn't use that.

I close the door and sit down in one of the big leather chairs. It's a relief to be away from the bright lights and buzz of open-plan.

Elisabeth Quintrelle sounds deliciously posh and kind. I make an appointment to see her, and just before she rings off I say, "Wait! What do I say to the children? What should I tell them?"

"The main thing is to make sure they know it's not their fault. You could tell them that Mummy and Daddy are having a hard time right now and that's why Daddy is not at home, but that you both love them just the same as you did before and that it's not their fault this happened."

"OK," I say, writing it down word for word.

At the end of the day, I walk past Peter's shop. The shelves and tables outside are bare; almost everything has gone.

"You've had a good day," I say.

"No, not really," says Peter, taking a long draft from his can.

"It was eventful," says Ronnie. "The police raided him. Took the lot, and he won't get compensation."

"The royal servant is in prison and they say they like to arrest me too. Handling stolen goods, but I didn't know. She told me they were gifts from the Queen. I believe her, but she lied to me. Terrible," says Peter, shaking his head.

"She lied to you, Peter," says Ronnie. "You're innocent, you done nothing wrong, mate."

"I didn't know," says Peter. "I didn't know."

"Oh, dear," I say. "What about Balmoral? Should I take it to a police station?"

"No, darling—keep it. You didn't know—you're innocent. I'm innocent, you're innocent, we're all innocent!"

When the girls are in their pajamas, I sit on the rug in their bedroom and ask them to join me.

"The last few days have been really difficult and weird for our family," I say. They are sitting on their heels, alert. I've never seen them pay so much attention to anything and it gives me stage fright. "Mummy and Daddy had a big fight," I say.

"We know," says Hester.

"Because you took his phone," says Milla.

"Not exactly," I say. "One day when you're old enough to understand I'll tell you more, but for now, the most important thing for you both to know is that it isn't your fault."

"We *know* it's not our fault!" says Milla, as if this is the stupidest thing she's ever heard.

"It's your fault, Mummy, for taking Daddy's phone," says Hester.

"But we still love you," says Milla.

"Yes, and we love Daddy too," says Hester.

"We love you both the same," says Milla, and Hester nods.

"Oh," I say, completely thrown.

I talk with Yvette in the sitting room with the doors closed.

"There's so much I don't know," I say. "It's keeping me awake at night, wondering about everything."

"It's all so new and strange," she says sensibly.

I check the time. "I am going to call Lorna," I say. "Now."

"Are you sure that's a good idea?" Yvette clearly doesn't think it is. "What are you going to say to her?"

"I have a list of questions." I show the two pages I wrote last night.

"She'll never answer all those!" says Yvette, dismayed.

"She bloody will," I say. I know Lorna will talk to me because I've already arranged it with her via text, although

I realize she may not be expecting forty-six interview-style questions. I have a sudden attack of nerves as I realize my models are celebrity chat shows and police dramas, but I'm hoping I can make it sound natural.

"Hello," I say.

"Hello," she replies.

"So, I just wanted to talk to you because, well—you know why," I say, wishing I'd scripted the beginning as well.

"Yes," she says, sounding a little nervous.

In order to put her at ease, I skip questions one through eleven, which are about sex. I want to know what kind of sex they had and if it was the same—or basically the same—as the sex I had with him, or whether there were things I didn't know about, a fetish or something, or a lot of anal sex, but I can't start with that so I ask her how they met. She confirms that they met through the website three and a half years ago, and that he never told her about me and the kids.

"But you knew about Charlie," I say.

"The dog, yes. Is that important?"

"Not really," I say lightly, though it is.

I move on to the section that deals with how often they saw each other, how they arranged it, how many times he spent the night.

"About seven times this year, I think. Maybe eight. Nine or ten times the previous years. I wanted him to stay more often but he was always busy—with work, he said."

She confirms that the last time he stayed the night was

three months ago when I had been in Brighton. She'd been asking him for ages to take her out on his Ducati.

"The helmet he brought for you to wear, that was mine," I say, wistful, then rouse myself—still a fair few questions to get through.

"So that was the last time you saw each other?"

"No. We went out for a drink two nights ago. He had a lot of explaining to do. Three and a half years and now suddenly a wife and two kids!"

I am shocked that he saw her again so recently and instantly feel foolish for being surprised. "So, did you—?"

"No. No way. I just wanted to get some answers and tell him what I thought of him. Left him sitting in the pub with his stupid pint, never want to see him again."

"Oh," I say. "Can I ask a few questions about you?"

"What do you want to know?" she says.

Everything, I think but don't say. Instead I ask, "What do you look like?"

"I'm about five eight, quite curvy I suppose, wavy brown hair. People say I look a bit like Judy Garland. Adam used to say that, sometimes."

"Oh, well," I say, smarting. Judy Garland, for goodness' sake! I wasn't prepared for a film star.

"And what do you look like?" she asks.

"The Wicked Witch of the West," I say. She doesn't laugh.

The call ends soon after this, rather awkwardly:

"Thanks for talking to me," I say.

"I'm not sure what good it's done. Why are you asking me anyway? Why don't you ask him all these questions?" she says.

"I have."

"I probably shouldn't have answered any of it. Except that you have children, and I didn't know that. He took advantage of me as well, you know. It wasn't just you he lied to."

"Didn't you suspect *something*? I mean, he hardly ever stayed with you, didn't see you regularly, no birthdays or weekends or holidays. I mean, *hello*—alarm bells?"

"Frankly, if you have to ask me all these questions, that should tell you something. That should tell you all you need to know." She ends the call.

"Judy Garland!" says Yvette.

"I know—who says that? Who actually says, 'I look like Judy Garland'?"

"Maybe someone who actually does," suggests Yvette gently.

"I should've said I look like Scarlett Johansson," I say.

"But you don—" says Yvette.

"Not the point," I interrupt.

"Anyway. Do you feel better, having spoken to her?"

"Not really."

A couple of hours later I receive a text from Judy Garland: *You took advantage asking me all those intrusive questions. I didn't know he was married. Leave me alone and don't call me again. I'm innocent.*

"*Intrusive?* I didn't even get to the sex questions," I complain to Yvette.

19

In the middle of the night I rifle through my jewelry boxes quickly and quietly like a thief, stealing from myself. This pair of gold hoop earrings; this string of Russian River pearls; this silver bracelet with pendant heart, all presents from a fine jeweler in Soho. He took me to the shop once and, when I looked through the stock, the things I liked best were things he'd already given me. Whenever I bought new clothes or shoes I asked his opinion before cutting off the labels. His taste was impeccable, which is why his comment about the swimsuit stung. But he did choose lovely things.

My heart aches as I pick them out. I tip the jewelry into a stray sock and push it to the back of the drawer. My wedding ring is already back in its box and I'd never had an engagement ring—Adam couldn't afford one.

I'm still wearing the necklace he gave me last birthday, a sweet little diamond on a gold chain. At the time, I'd worried about such an expensive present. "But now it makes sense," I snarl down the phone. It's 6:00 a.m. I've woken him. I inform him that I spoke to Lorna, that I know he saw her two nights ago, and ask him why he didn't think to mention that. He had to finish it properly, he says, she was angry. Lots of angry women in your life, I point out, adding his mother and his sister to the list since they now know. She was demanding an explanation, he says, and since he had lied to her too he felt he owed her one. He will never speak to her or see her again, wishes he never had. It's all very well to wish, I say, and ask again, why? Why did he start, why did he carry on, and why did he start something with Louise on top of what he had going with Lorna? I set the trap, although I'm already in it myself, and we both watch as he stumbles toward it. I zone out. There's pain in my throat, as if it's being constricted. So this is how it feels to strangle a sob—it's strange when a cliché comes to life. And surprising how much it physically hurts to choke an utterance. This feels bigger than both of us—the pain I feel, the pain he feels: an age-old story. There he is in the position of the betrayer. Old as the hills. Here I am in the position of the betrayed. I try to concentrate as he lists all the usual reasons that people give for their treachery.

20

Everything has unraveled; my whole life has come apart. Trying to stitch something back together, I go through his phone bills, cross-referencing with my diary: dates that I was away coincide with peaks of activity. I work my way back through the year; last April, during the school holidays, we went to his parents', but Adam said he had work to finish and besides he wanted to ride his Ducati, so I went ahead with the girls and he stayed in London for a couple of nights. Adam's parents and I took the girls to Chester Zoo and Hester spilled a carton of Ribena all over the backseat of Grandpa's Mercedes. She cried and cried and I had a surge of irritation with Adam for not being there. It was cloudy at the zoo, all the animals inside or asleep, apart from the giraffes who walked slowly around their enclosure.

"Adam—"

"Yes?" he says, wary.

"Are there other things you haven't told me?"

"Such as what, exactly?" he snaps. "What do you want to know—sexual positions and degrees of pleasurability?"

I hang up, flustered. We are both exhausted by my ceaseless interrogation. I hound him until he goes to ground and throws out mean or one-word answers. If I could ease off, maybe he would be more forthcoming. He rings back and apologizes.

"There might be details you don't know," he says, "but why do you need them? Can't you leave it alone?"

I need the details to make it real. I need to know how wide and how deep: when and where. The precise coordinates of the betrayal are necessary in order to locate its exact position in my life because it feels surreal; a theory that I need to prove, over and over, until I can finally accept it. I know I'm obsessing, but the phone bills are the only solid thing, the only sure answer to all my questions. I do want to know sexual positions and degrees of pleasurability. I want to know everything. Or perhaps what I really want is for him to answer fully and honestly instead of going from one foot to the other, dodging blows.

I call every number I don't know. A few recorded answerphone messages, a few live. It's like discovering Bluebeard's chamber: the disembodied voices of women left hanging.

"Who?" asks one.

I describe the scene. "You may have met him online," I say.

"Ohhhh," she says, "I did dabble in that a few years ago. I may have spoken to him but I never met him in person."

"We exchanged photographs—we never actually met," says another woman.

One number is answered by a man. My belly drops, but it turns out he's only had the phone for a couple of months, bought it in a pub, didn't realize he'd bought a backstory.

One of the numbers belongs to Bob. "Hello, Kate!

How are you all?" he says. "How's Adam? It's been ages."

"But you saw Adam," I say. "You went out for that drink before Christmas, with Tim. And Louise."

"I'm sorry, Kate," says Bob, sounding confused. "When did you say this was? I haven't seen Adam for nearly a year. We must catch up next time I'm in London."

I find Tim's number.

"I haven't seen Adam in months. Do give him my best," says Tim.

It hurts to be in our home. It hurts even to be seated. I grab my coat, rush outside and onto the common. I come to the pond. On the water a pair of geese slowly cruise. I watch them for a while. A noticeboard informs me of something I already know about geese: loyal, faithful, they stay with their mate for life. That's how it's supposed to be with humans too, but I've lost my mate and the shame is brutal.

I call Adam to scream at him.

"Are these what you call details?" I shout. "Five more women and some guy who bought a phone in a pub?"

"But that was years ago—when I first signed up to the website! I forgot about them. A few phone calls, that's it. I didn't meet any of them!"

"And I spoke to Bob and Tim—they weren't there that night with Louise, so why do you keep on saying they were?"

"What difference does that really make now?"

"It makes a world of difference!" I yell.

"Kate—" he starts, but I end the call. It's raining lightly.

Traffic is dense and slow; drivers look out with envy at pedestrians who are moving faster. My hands, shaking a bit, go to the birthday necklace. I swivel the chain round and after a small struggle with the catch, take it off. Sitting in my palm, the gold chain furls over like a rope, diamond glinting underneath. It doesn't weigh very much. Avoiding eye contact with stalled motorists, I walk to the edge of the pavement and drop the diamond necklace down a drain.

21

When Yvette leaves we both cry a little. I'm not sure why she's crying, but it's been pretty intense so maybe they are tears of relief, or exhaustion.

The girls won't get out of bed, refuse even the offer of chocolate cereal for breakfast, and both of them are floppy and hot to the touch. I call the school. The fact that they are ill is actually easier because my parents arrive from Boston today. They'll look after the girls while I'm in Belgium and then stay on for a while when I get back.

I give them watered-down orange juice in their old baby bottles, which they still love to drink from, and Hester asks me to put on the CD of nursery rhymes they used to fall asleep to, which I do, and then she asks, "Does Daddy know we're ill?"

"I'll tell him," I say, soothing her hair back, noticing they've outgrown their pajamas.

"And will you tell him that Charlie is ill?" says Milla.

"He knows that—Charlie's been ill for a while—but I'll tell him again and he'll come and visit while I'm away. It's only for one night—I'll be home before you go to sleep tomorrow."

I call Adam, tell him the girls are unwell, and ask him to take Charlie to the vet again. "The medication doesn't seem to be helping. If anything, he's getting worse," I say.

"Should I have him?" says Adam.

"No," I say. "The girls can't lose their dad and their dog in the same week."

"They haven't lost their dad," he says.

I pack to the tune of "Humpty Dumpty" and "London Bridge Is Falling Down," and hear the girls giggle and I'm relieved—not *that* ill. I make them some jam toast and hot chocolate and take it up on a tray.

"I'm feeling better!" says Hester, gobbling hers all up.

"I'm not," says Milla, pushing hers away. I'm impressed with Hester's lack of duplicity and with Milla's cleverness. Whatever happens with me and Adam, at least I have my brilliant kids.

My parents arrive from the airport. Mum stands in the hall in her coat while I run outside into the rain to help Dad and the driver with their bags. Her stiffness seems more than can be attributed to the overnight journey. I realize they've had a row because it's "Your Father" and "Your Mother" instead of Mum and Dad, as in: "Your Father needs to pay the taxi," and "Your Mother didn't sleep on the flight."

"Sweetheart," my dad says, pulling me in for a big hug.

"That's right," says Mum, patting my shoulder while Dad is still hugging me.

"It's really awful, what's happened," she says. Dad releases me and Mum swoops in for a quick embrace. "But you'll be all right, won't you?"

"Of course we will," I say, including the girls in my answer, who I see waiting shyly at the top of the stairs in their too-short pajamas and unbrushed hair.

I make tea and give the girls more watered-down juice in their baby bottles.

"Aren't they too old for those?" says my mother.

"Yes, but they like them," I say firmly.

I ask Hester to put some biscuits on a plate and she and Milla open a family pack of digestives and pile the whole lot out. There must be about thirty McVitie's there. They each take six. "I think you'll be well enough to go to school tomorrow," I say.

Hester sits on Grandpa's lap and Milla sits next to the biscuits and my mother, who doesn't have a lap as such.

I ask about my brother Greg and his family.

"Oh, they're fine," says my mother. "We had a good visit, didn't we?" My dad nods in agreement. "Apart from your phone call, of course, which was awful. We felt we should come straightaway but the flights were all booked because of New Year. Greg and Susannah tried so hard to find us an earlier flight back." Dad nods again.

"But we want to hear about you, darling," Mum goes on. "What *happened*? What's going on?"

"Adam is staying with his friend George for the time being. He's going to come and see the girls while you're here and take Charlie to the vet." Everyone looks at Charlie, who trembles in response. Hester climbs down and goes to hug Charlie.

"Don't get in the basket," I warn. "I can't really talk about it right now," I say, meaning because the girls are in the room, but my mother thinks it's because I have to leave for the Eurostar and bustles me into my coat. In fact I have another hour before I need to go and two-thirds of a cup of tea left, but their formality has eased up and I don't want to jinx it, so after several clammy hugs with the girls, I say goodbye to my parents, pat Charlie, and head for the Eurostar.

22

I watch the flat fields of rural East Kent from the train and think bitterly of Louise, and of Lorna. I never understood what people see in Judy Garland and I have no idea what or who Louise looks like, but I know she lives somewhere in this pale expanse where puddles are acres wide.

On my way back from the buffet with a large white coffee I notice it's not just me; almost everyone is holding these long white cardboard cups or has one in front of them. I wonder what we all did before it became normal to be giant babies sipping on big bottles of milk; from where did everyone derive their comfort before Starbucks answered the problem with latte? Perhaps there was none. Perhaps that's why my mother is so buttoned up.

We reach the tunnel. Across the table, a young woman is reading intently. Her book is called *Magnetism: How to Attract the Life You Want*, about the cosmic law of attraction, which I've heard about from Sam, who told me it's the reason she made the large collage she keeps on her desk. It's quite eye-catching; center-page is a rainbow and at the end of it, a photograph of a woman's extremely toned stomach, although I think there's a pot of gold elsewhere on the board. Rosenfeld and Abrahams are in my bag but I wouldn't read them in public, just as I wouldn't purchase *I Can Make You Thin* from the bookshop even though I too want an extremely toned stomach. There were four golden rules in *I Can Make You Thin* but I can't remember them so I resolve to call into the bookshop when I'm back and have a sneaky peek.

The rhythm of the train is a lullaby but still I can't sleep. Instead, I work. I answer emails from Trish, who keeps up a relentless stream. Trish and Don favor hotels that are highly efficient; Valerie, Richard's secretary, has been heard to mutter that what Trish and Don seem to want is a kingdom of covered car parks. Richard is opposed to this type of hotel because they are highly impersonal; guests come and go, never interacting with each other or with staff. "There's no reason a man should creep into a hole and watch TV alone," he says. "A good hotel is like an old-fashioned travelers' inn, a place of conviviality where stories are shared and adventures happen." It's a difference not just in style, but in values. Richard wants hotels with life and soul and the Belgian palace has potential for that.

Despite the mess my marriage is in, I've really started to enjoy my job, to see how I can contribute: it's not just about innovation for income generation—though that seems to be Trish's focus—it's also about the reputation of PHC as a market leader and place of excellence. I'm supposed to build an "entrepreneurial culture" that shores up long-term success and sustainability. I've been busy putting forward a few different projects. What I've proposed with this concept hotel is fairly radical, and there's nothing like it on the market: an immersive experience at the 1930s Royal Spa Hotel, with costumes, music, food, decoration, and lots else from the era, backed up by state-of-the-art technology. To create a sense of being in that world, to conjure up an atmosphere that feels authentic, every single thing needs to be very specific. Getting it right is going to take the utmost precision and an unbelievable attention to detail, which is why I've hired two historians from University College London, and an independent film production company. The pilot is all about 1930s Belgium, but if this works well, we'll apply the concept to different geographies, cultures, and periods. Personally, I'd love to re-create a Persian caravanserai—a roadside inn along the Silk Road where travelers could rest, free from danger, and recover from their day's journey. Inside the walled exterior, small bedrooms—or not really rooms as such, more alcoves—were located off a central courtyard, and in the evenings meals were offered communally and people would talk, smoke, drink, and dance.

At the Gare de Bruxelles–Central I buy a box of Belgian truffles for my mother and some chocolate biscuits for the girls. I get a pair of socks for Dad; the truffles are meant to be shared with him, but I know he'll only get one, maximum, and Mum will scoff the rest. Her sweet tooth is insatiable, as Greg and I learned one Easter when I was ten and he was eight; we rewrapped our unfinished chocolate eggs in the purple foil, but while we were at school, she polished them off.

I board a smaller train, which chugs through the suburbs of Brussels and then Ghent and then Bruges, through people returning home from school and from work; shoes coming off, lamps and fires going on; children spreading out homework on kitchen tables, adults preparing dinner, steam from saucepans misting up the windows. Hotels are theatrical by nature, but homes are too—all those lighted interiors, framed by curtains. As a teenager, cycling slowly through the village on my way home from work, I used to glimpse into other people's houses and wonder what their lives were like. By the time I freewheeled into our yard it would be nearly dark. In my own home, everyone would be in separate rooms, Greg watching TV on his own, my father reading academic papers in his study, my mother marking schoolbooks in hers.

I take out the clear plastic wallet containing the palace details and read the estate agent's blurb. *Facing onto a beautiful wide beach, there is a horse-racing track next to the palace grounds and on the other side a busy thermal spa and open-air swimming pool. Nearby are several parks, a golf course, and a cinema.* A note in Trish's flamboyant handwriting says, *Location. Location. Location—perfect.*

There's no real need to check the building before I sign the papers—all that's been done by teams of surveyors, engineers, and architects—but I want to and Henri the Ostend lawyer thinks this is a splendid plan. Over the phone he says, "Of course you must—it's why you came. You can't go home without a tour!"

The long white palace stretches along the shore, fronted by two Royal Galleries—high colonnades with domed ceilings and beautifully tiled floors. It's eighty-five years old with all the old elegance of a grande dame. The proportions are spectacular—I feel my heart lift just to look at it. The winter sun, reflected off the walls and the white sand, is piercingly bright, strong enough to burn. Up close, there are signs of dilapidation and neglect; plaster is flaking like patches of dry skin and some of the tiles are cracked or missing. A cold wind blowing in from the North Sea has made sand drifts against the outer wall and is stirring up flurries of dry leaves around the Doric columns. Once upon a time I suppose there would have been someone to sweep up the sand and shoo away the leaves.

Henri has sent his secretary to meet me, a young girl called Ann with a blue wool coat and a neat brown bob who unlocks a side entrance, holds open the door, and says she will return in an hour unless I want her to stay. She clearly can't wait to be gone—I imagine there's a boyfriend to meet. I tell her two hours would be better. Ann looks delighted. The door clicks shut behind her.

I fish out the floor plan from my briefcase. It shows a T-shaped building, with banqueting halls and ballrooms named after members of the Belgian royal family past and present: King Baudouin and Queen Fabiola, the old Kings Leopold I, II, and III, the reigning King Albert and his Queen Mathilde, their children and grandchildren: Amedeo, Astrid, Aymeric, Emmanuel, Filip, Gabriel, Eleonore, Laetitia-Maria, Luisa-Maria, Maria-Hendrika, Maria-Laura, Maria-Theresea. A family mapped out in rooms. I think about which of them is alive today and wonder where they are and whether they're still together.

One hundred and eighty rooms over four floors, the largest of which, Albert, is seven hundred square meters with a ceiling height of nearly eight meters. The palace is empty, as Trish had said it would be, but I wasn't prepared for the echo of my heels tap-tapping along acres of tiled floors.

The space is breathtaking. Wood panels glow where the sun falls in great shafts through tall windows that look onto the beach at the front and gardens growing wild at the back. Shadows in corners and between windows make a tapestry of light and dark. Movement is generous—passages are broad and sunlit, with seats in them, and they are more or less continuous with the rooms themselves, so that as you walk around, the smell of perfume and cigars, the sound of glasses and laughter and conversation, a grand piano, a string quartet, can be felt, or imagined.

Seduced entirely, I want to explore hands-free. I leave my briefcase in a banqueting hall named Leopold II and discard the floor plan in the ballroom called Baudouin. I roam a wide and ample loop. Somewhere roughly in the middle the main staircase sweeps down and embraces the entrance hall. Not just a way of getting from one floor to another, the staircase is a space in itself: a volume, part of the building where action takes place, a stage.

Upstairs, the rooms and corridors feel like part of the same continuous fabric. I walk in and out of large suites with views out to sea and faded red velvet cushions in the window seats. In the crease under the seams I can see the scarlet they used to be. Despite being threadbare in places, the carpet muffles my footfall and the quiet draws attention to the emptiness, to all the people who aren't here.

I only realize I've entered a kind of dream when I hear my name being called.

"Kate? Kate! Where are you?"

I come out of the bedroom I've wandered into and see a man with white-gray hair that's been blown about by the wind. He is standing in the corridor holding my brown leather briefcase, which looks disproportionately small on him. He's in a navy suit, an apple-green tie, and camel overcoat; and despite being impressively big he's completely unthreatening, like a Saint Bernard rescue dog.

"Hello, Kate! I'm Henri. Ann called and said she was feeling unwell so she's taken the rest of the day off. I know she's exaggerating, but I don't mind—I was young once. How do you like the palace? Magnificent, isn't it?"

His eyes are bright and he must take lots of walks in the fresh sea air because his face is quite tanned, or maybe he's been skiing. I am so grateful for Henri's company that I immediately develop a crush on him despite the fact that he's slightly pear-shaped and about sixty.

"There's something downstairs I'd like to show you—part of the palace. Come on!" he says, and takes off back down the corridor, still carrying my briefcase.

Downstairs in Maria-Theresea, the smallest of the banqueting halls, Henri puts his ear to the wood paneling as if listening for a heartbeat and taps with his fingers.

"We have to find exactly the right place," he says. "Aha!" He gently pushes the wall with both hands. Nothing happens.

"The spring is a bit stiff these days," he says. He lays his shoulder against the wall and heaves and this time there's a creak and a rebound and the wall cracks open to reveal a hidden door.

"Wow!" I say.

"Wow indeed," says Henri, smiling widely. "Let's go!"

A narrow passageway leads along the inside of the wall. We use the light of our phone screens to see.

"Are we *in* the wall?" I ask, shuffling close behind Henri.

"Yes. We are like giant mice," he replies. After about fifteen meters the enclosed corridor opens out into a plain room with uneven flagstones and a window with small diamond-shaped panes. The glass is dirty and overgrown shrubs outside render the light greenish. The air feels heavy with damp. A wicker armchair is lying on its side near a heavy wooden door, mildewed. The room seems to hold all the abandonment of the rest of the building and there's something dangerously magnetic about the undisturbed sadness. Old cobwebs hang in soft gray droops from the ceiling; newer ones span the window, doorway, and corners and stretch between walls. The spiders have been industrious, but all they've caught is dust.

"I wonder if we can unlock that door," says Henri, taking a bunch of keys from his coat pocket, looking through them as if each one holds a message. He moves toward the door, breaking the Miss Havisham feeling as he goes, tries one key and another and another but none fit. Eventually he pulls the door in toward him and draws back the bolt. "Maybe it's not locked," he says, and shoves hard. The door bursts open and Henri spills out into the garden.

It's toasty warm in the café. The windows are all steamed up. There are lots of small red tables, very close, with people crammed around them, coats and scarves bundled over the backs of chairs, hats and gloves on tabletops or poking out of handbags. Our table is a bit rickety. A couple at the next table lean toward each other, foreheads and elbows nearly touching. The woman's hair is up in a chignon and a lock keeps falling across her face whereupon she twists it back into the knot. After this happens three or four times, her companion gently lifts the strand of hair and tucks it behind her ear, smoothing it down. He frames the side of her face with his hand and gazes at her and I feel bereft.

We order French onion soup and a small carafe of wine. Henri pushes the sugar bowl, salt, and pepper to the edge of the table and lays out the floor plan. He unbuttons his cuffs and rolls up his shirtsleeves.

"Can you read anything? I can't!" he says cheerfully, and dips into his jacket pocket for spectacles. He may be older but he has strong forearms and a sparkle in his eye and right now that's enough. The skinny waitress plonks down a basket of bread and pours the wine sloppily so that a fat drop lands on the map. Henri brushes it away and leaves a pale red streak on the paper. "*Excusez-moi, monsieur,*" says the waitress about the spillage.

"*Pas grave,*" replies Henri without looking up from the map.

"*C'est une carte au trésor?*" asks the waitress, craning for a look.

"*Oui, c'est ça.*"

"*Allez, bonne chance!*" and she wiggles off.

"The garden room is here and this double line indicates the hidden passageway, I think, but there's nothing to show the secret door. Here's Baudouin, here's Maria-Theresea, and here's Albert, adjoining—so it should be round about here," says Henri, his forefinger tapping the place, but I'm distracted again by all the names.

"Where are they all?" I say.

"Who?" replies Henri.

"Astrid, Albert, all the Marias—"

"Some are in Brussels, some live by a lake in a very large house, some are in the countryside near a forest—they're dotted all over the land."

"Are they happy?"

"It's a good question. Albert and Paola have lived separately for most of their marriage. He had a child with another woman—secretly—and there have been other rumors. So maybe they are happy separately but perhaps not together. As for the others, Baudouin always smiles in photographs. You never see him not smiling. The rest of them keep private lives—they only come out for weddings and funerals—so I don't know. I hope so."

"I hope so too," I say, leaning over the floor plan in order to hide my face, and I can tell he hears what I haven't said.

He raises his glass and says, "To happiness, wherever we may find it."

We toast, and I say, "We found the treasure, we don't need the map." Henri says I'm right and folds the floor plan away just before the waitress brings a tray with two wide bowls of hot soup topped with Gruyère melted onto toast. The onions are caramelized and soft and the soup is dark brown, salty, and delicious.

"Do you like being a lawyer?" I ask. "I used to want to be one." Adam always said I should have been a lawyer because of my natural pedantry.

"It's a good job and I do like it," says Henri, "but it wasn't my first love. What I really wanted to do was skate. I was really good at it—I made it to the Winter Olympics in Austria in 1976 but I didn't get a medal and so I became a lawyer. I had a deal with my parents about that. But I still like to skate. Last winter, one very cold afternoon, I was driving back from court and I saw this huge sheet of ice in a field. I took off my camel-hair coat and put on my skates. I was just in a suit jacket, on my skates. And I flew." His eyes are glowing, he laughs softly. "The wind was blowing in from the North Sea, like today. With the wind behind you, you can lay yourself into impossible angles that you never could walking or running. You lay yourself at a forty-five-degree angle, your elbows virtually touching the ice as you're in a turn. Incredible! You're breaking the bounds of gravity. Nobody was there. I could wheel and dive and turn—I was free as a bird. I was really happy. I'll do that until I die, I hope. Oh, I was free!" Each time he smiles the wrinkles disappear and his whole face seems to lift.

Over coffee, I show him a picture of the girls on my phone. It's one I took last autumn, an ordinary Sunday afternoon, the girls on their bikes on the common, Charlie waddling behind, Adam getting cross with the kite because there wasn't enough wind. To make up for the technical failure, I'd bought them huge ice creams with strawberry sauce and the photo shows Milla and Hester beaming down at their cones like two saints. As I look at their smiling faces I'm flooded with a mixture of pride and sadness. It's a powerful sensation. I don't quite know what to do with it.

"Beautiful children too," says Henri, and that "too" is the best compliment I've had for a long time.

Suddenly he says, "Come and live with me! I have a wife already but she won't mind. The kids will love it, there's so much for them to do—I'll teach them to skate!" He stops and adds, "My wife is a lovely woman. She loves children—ours have grown up and left. She's lost without them. Her name is Marcella."

I love how he says "the kids" as if he already knows them, and that he's loyal to his wife even if his enthusiasm got the better of him for a minute, and it's really good to know that my mini-crush has been reciprocated.

"And there'll be rainbows, and trampolines, and we'll finally know the truth," I say, smiling. Henri smiles back. There's a touch of regret—another time, another place—but the moment ends gracefully enough.

23

The night I return from Belgium I wake just after 4:00 a.m. and go downstairs. In the shadows I notice a few dark spatters on the floor. I turn on a light, the better to examine them, but am mystified until Charlie wheezes in his basket and coughs up little spots of fresh blood. "Poor old Charlie," I say. In dog years he is an octogenarian. His black fur has lost its sheen and turned white around his muzzle. His coat bunches under my hand as I stroke him; dogs get wrinkles too. I wipe the crust from his eyes and give him some milk to soothe his throat, though it probably doesn't make any difference. I start to wipe up the blood so that the children won't see it, and then stop because I realize they need to.

At 7:00 a.m. the girls examine the faint sprays around Charlie's basket: blood on the kitchen floor is impressive but they aren't convinced it's his.

"How do you *know* it's Charlie's?" says Milla.

"Because it's around his basket, and some of it is actually *in* his basket—see?—and because I saw him cough it up," I say.

"Is he going to die?" asks Hester.

"Well, he's very old for a dog, sweetheart. His body is all worn out."

"What about his medicine?"

"That won't save him, I'm afraid. We should probably say goodbye."

"Why are they crying?" asks my mother when she gets up.

"It's Charlie." I gesture toward Charlie's basket, where both girls are draped over him, weeping. They hug and kiss him while he coughs and splutters and trembles. I think he might give out on the spot.

"Oh, I see. Yes, that's upsetting for them, but it's very unhygienic, what they're doing."

"It is, Mum, but they need to say goodbye, so maybe you should just turn away."

"He smells terrible."

"Yes, I suppose he does," I say. "I'd stopped noticing."

On the phone, Adam suggests taking Charlie to his parents' house—he can't have a dog where he's staying, and I'm worried it will be really upsetting for the girls to watch Charlie getting slowly worse. We agree that he'll do this today and my mum and dad can be in charge of handing him over. I decide to take the girls to school myself: I should tell their teachers what's happened. We all cry a bit as we say goodbye to Charlie, and hug him even though he does stink.

The school is only a minute's walk from our front door, yet we still manage to be late at least once a week. Today, though, I make sure to get us there good and early. Hester runs into her classroom and hangs her coat on a peg labeled with her name and a picture of the sun she's colored in. She goes off to announce Charlie's imminent departure to her friends and I go off to announce it to her teacher. "Oh, dear, not that lovely dog that your husband brought in, with the chicken-liver toothpaste?" I explain the situation and then steel myself for a second telling.

Milla's teacher, Ms. Ashwani, crosses the playground to collect her class. I take her to one side. "There's a couple of things," I say. "Our family dog is leaving, so that might upset her—she's known him since she was a baby—and as well, her father and I have separated, rather suddenly. So all of that might have an effect on her at school."

"Actually, she's already told us about you and her dad."

"She has? When?"

"We had a sharing session. The children were invited to talk about their Christmases, and Milla stood up and shared with the class what happened."

"Oh, my goodness."

"The class were very supportive. And Milla was very strong. One boy stood up and told her, 'It's OK, my dad left in Year One.' Afterward, I hugged her because I was so proud of her—it was such a brave thing to do."

I nod, dumb.

24

On Monday, I'm due to see the therapist for the first time. I've taken the day as holiday but Trish calls me at 10:30 a.m. "There's a problem—I need you to come in right away." I pause for a moment to take stock. On the one hand, it's outrageous that Trish expects me to drop what I'm doing and go into work on my day off. On the other hand, I am in my house calling my estranged husband every hour to scream at him and the appointment with Elisabeth isn't until 3:00 p.m. I agree to go in.

The problem is that the cleaners in Los Angeles have walked out on strike and it's being reported globally. The catalyst was the death of a minor movie star in the Regal on Sunset Boulevard who killed himself in the penthouse suite. The cleaner who found him was traumatized, naturally enough, but hotel management sacked her a few days later for failing to clean the room properly and when challenged they said they hadn't realized it was the same woman. The union called a strike. "Their workforce are Latino. They depend on us, yet they think we all look the same—if they look at us at all!" shouts the union leader on Sky TV. "We are invisible to them, they don't care!"

"Damn them," says Trish, slamming her office door. "We've got to turn this around, Kate—we're getting crucified. What was the manager thinking? You can't clean a carpet when it's stained with blood—of course it won't come out! The whole carpet needs to come out!"

*

It's true that as a cleaner you become invisible. I remembered this from my first job, in a country hotel called the New Inn even though it was three hundred years old. They took me on as a weekend chambermaid. I never quite got used to knocking on the doors of vacant rooms to make sure they really were empty; the slight trepidation of unlocking and calling, "Housekeeping!" and the oddly lonely moment you confirm that yes, there's no one there.

Big Sue, the hotel manager, lived there with a rather pathetic husband called Leonard, who didn't do anything. But maybe he was that way because Sue was a force of nature. If she liked you, it was like having the wind on your side. Big Sue was great, but most of the guests ignored me. Many people don't acknowledge the cleaner, maybe because it makes them uncomfortable that this person is seeing all their mess; the skid marks they leave in the toilet, used condoms in the bin, period-stained towels, blobs of unguents around the sink.

I used to cycle to the New Inn on a road that stretched for miles across a high moor and then descended through green fields into the village. When I was old enough, Sue offered me extra hours behind the bar, and at the end of the night she'd lift my bike into the back of her estate car and drive me home. At first I was nervous about moving from cleaning rooms to what Sue called a "front-of-house" job, but fascinated too—I'd never thought of the hotel that way but it made complete sense: there were times you were in role and onstage, and times when you were backstage. Sue showed me how to pull a proper pint of ale and nice full measures of wine and spirits, and when the beer pumps bubbled and ran dry, it was Big Sue, not Leonard, who went down into the cellar and changed the barrel. As well as showing me what to do, Big Sue showed me how to be. She pointed out the rules of the world I'd just entered—she didn't try to justify them, just made sure I was aware of what I needed to know to get on. In the hotel bar, she showed me how to treat regulars and welcome newcomers, how to accept tips graciously and rebuff come-ons so that the drinkers stayed at arm's length. If ever any of them tried to get closer Sue herself would deal with them, physically if necessary—once she threw an old lech out the front door and banished him, told him never to return. I received six proposals of marriage in that job and Sue treated each one as a trophy on my behalf, each time telling me I could do better.

Sometimes people would ask for food late in the evening when the chef had gone home and Sue would send me off to the kitchens to warm up an apple pie or put together a ham-and-cheese sandwich. I loved to move around the big steel kitchen, so clean and orderly, and know just where to find things and where to put them back. I enjoyed being in the hotel much more than being at home because Sue was so different from my mother. Perhaps it was just that Sue was less busy, or that she had one son who was fourteen years old and not interested in the hotel, whereas I was interested in everything; I was her understudy, a hotel-swot from the start.

Modern hotel rooms are designed to take the least possible amount of time to clean—for the benefit of the company, not the cleaner. In thirty minutes four members of staff can do sixteen rooms between them. Not long, but it's set up that way: cupboards have doors to reduce the need for dusting, and if there's no bathtub it's because showers are quicker to clean. Every month there's a deep dive—eighteen to twenty minutes per room. But there's one thing that never gets cleaned: the TV remote.

Walk along the corridors of any hotel and you'll see a cleaning cart parked neatly by an open door, perhaps glimpse a figure bending over the bed shaking out the duvet or changing the pillowcases. There's a pile of wet towels on the floor, a collection of coffee cups, yesterday's paper, dirty plates on a room-service tray. Often the equipment is labeled so that the cleaners know whose is whose—once I saw a vacuum called *Valentina*, the letters handwritten in blue felt-tip, the label fixed with an abundance of tape. Such a lovely name, Valentina, and so un-British. I wondered where she was from, how she got here, and what she looked like, because although I saw her machine, I didn't see the woman.

Paltry pay and minuscule breaks don't help, and sometimes the workforce gets angry and walks out—like the cleaners in Los Angeles—or gets sloppy and cuts corners; you should always wash the cups in your room before you use them because some cleaners just wipe them with the same cloth they use on everything else. I can't really blame them; being overlooked is not good for people.

This same tumbleweed feeling blows through many lives; carers, hospital orderlies, street sweepers, and bin men know it. Parked wives know it. Mothers know it and so do many fathers, especially if they are at home a lot, because looking after a home and children, despite being difficult to do well, is low-status and the lack of recognition can sap self-esteem.

When Adam and I got together we were equals in the world's eyes and in our own, but when I stopped work to look after our babies there was a subtle shift. My main activity became wiping. Tables, floors, hands, mouths, cheeks, and bottoms. Feet after they'd been in the sandpit. Charlie's muddy paws, the television screen smudged with fingerprints, walls smeared by little hands dipped in yogurt. Cleaning is hard physical work. PHC once had a lawsuit from a cleaner claiming repetitive strain injury in the wrists. She lost.

Branton trots in, dapper in a new suit.

"The strike isn't legal. They can't actually do this," he says.

"They are actually doing it, though," I say, "and good for them. They're standing up for themselves and nobody else is doing that—least of all us, apparently. So, good for them."

"Well, I suppose you could look at it that way," replies Branton, taken aback.

"Kate was supposed to be on a day off, but Trish called her in," says Sam apologetically.

"But I have to go at three," I say. They both look at me, nodding and smiling, and I wonder what I am doing that's making people behave like grinning idiots.

The truth is, the cleaners are right and everyone feels a bit guilty. Just before 3:00, I go into Trish's office, where she is consulting with Branton, and tell them what I think.

"We made a mistake and we should own up to it," I say. "The poor woman who found the body should get time off and counseling—like train drivers when they hit someone—and we should make this a policy, not just a one-off. Housekeeping clean two rooms in the time it takes us lot in head office to tie our shoes. We should make this an opportunity to do something for all our staff, because that's the right thing to do."

"Weren't you supposed to be having a day off?" says Trish.

As I walk to the Tube, I realize I've left my hat and gloves on my desk but daren't go back after my outburst.

I call Adam. He doesn't pick up and I remember he has a job interview this afternoon; he's finally admitted that his business isn't viable, but instead of this being a relief it feels like discovering that the disease is worse than anyone thought. And yet I keep prodding and poking; I can't leave him alone. I hate him and I miss him and I still love him and it all courses through me, making my blood toxic, making my veins ache, making me sick. It's a horrible feeling, as though my cells are turning on themselves. I don't know what to call it, but whatever it is, I am riddled with it.

25

"It's grief," says the therapist, later that afternoon.

"Well, that's a relief, I thought it was cancer," I say, only half joking. I can tell right away that Elisabeth knows a lot more than I do about where I am. Even filling her in on the backstory seems to introduce a bit of perspective. I lose it as soon as I leave, but for a few minutes, sitting on the wide yellow armchair opposite Elisabeth, it felt better.

When I get home the girls are clingy and my parents are stiff and formal, which means they've had another row. Apparently, Your Father went out for a drink with Your Estranged Husband, and this did not go well.

"What did you *expect*?" I say to both of them, taking in the state of the kitchen. They've been staying with us twice a year for ten years and evidently still don't know where the pans go. The girls have had beans on toast and ask if they can watch TV. I say yes so that I can hear about Adam.

"What did you say to him?" I ask my father.

"I told him the problem wasn't so much that he'd been a lying shit, but that he'd been a weak man."

"And how did he take that?" I ask.

My mother rolls her eyes and I imagine Adam storming out of the pub.

"He didn't say anything."

I picture Adam sitting on a pub stool, chastened, and can't help feeling sorry for him.

"People do get over things like this," I say.

"They do," agrees my father. My mother remains silent.

We eat Indian food. If Adam were here he'd be fussing about turmeric staining the wood, but Adam's not here.

"Your Father and I think we should come and live nearby," says my mother, "to help."

"But what about your work?" I say, alarmed.

"I should retire soon and anyway you need help," she says. "I feel I ought to. It's my duty."

"Actually, Mum, I was going to ask Noreen," I say. "Why don't I go round after supper and see what she says? There might not be any need to uproot you and Dad."

Adam texts to say he's coming to collect some of his things. It's been nine days since he went away and although we've been on the phone a lot, I haven't actually seen him since that walk on the common. I think it's better if I avoid him this evening, especially if he's just had a row with my father, so I go to the supermarket.

Afterward I call in to see Noreen. Perhaps she sees in my face that something is wrong because she closes the door to the living room, where her husband is watching the news, sits me down at her kitchen table, makes tea, and gets the biscuit tin out. Noreen takes my hands and holds them while I tell her what's happened. Her hands are small and pale, dotted with age spots and very soft. She listens attentively, nodding to show she understands, and when I stumble on a difficult bit she squeezes my hands with surprising force, as if to pass some of her strength into me. I tell her everything. Occasionally she shakes her head, but she doesn't interrupt with questions or condemnations. Only when I finish does she say, "Oh, what a silly man—a lovely wife like you and two beautiful children. Of course I'll look after them, I'd love to."

Buoyed up by Noreen, I go to the bookshop before going home. It's closing time. I go over and ask the man for some empty boxes.

"Sure, how many?" he says.

"Ten."

He fetches a stack of flat cardboard boxes from the back of the shop, piles them up next to the till, and counts them. There are nine.

"Shall I get another one?" he asks.

"No, that should be fine. Thank you."

"That's a lot of boxes—are you moving?"

"No, but my husband is."

"Oh, right," he says.

To shorten the awkward silence I order a book, *Raising Happy Children*. The man is kind as he handles my order, or maybe he is just being careful.

"I'll give you a hand with the boxes if you like," he says.

"Oh! OK, thanks."

We leave the bookshop, he with a pile of flat boxes and me with several laden Sainsbury's bags. It's raining and cold and gray. Because of the boxes, he has to have his head over to one side, and it's on my side. We turn off the high street into my road.

"What's your name?" I ask him.

"Ben—as in Benedict," he says.

Benedict, as in a blessing. I don't know for sure, but I

think Ben is single. The basis for this assumption is that I saw him once, more than a year ago, walking along with an attractive blonde and have never seen him with her again. This of course doesn't mean anything, but I'm not interested in accuracy at this point. I wonder what else Ben does, because he's not in the shop every day. He seems light and watchful. I decide he must be a poet.

At that moment I realize that Adam will probably be leaving the house just as we get there.

"We might bump into him. My husband, I mean," I say.

"Oh. Right," says Ben.

The remaining minutes' walk is filled with silent horror on my part and, I am sure, his. We don't see Adam. Ben leans the boxes against the wall next to the front door. I thank him and he leaves. When I get inside, I call Jo and tell her that I've embarrassed myself thoroughly with the man from the bookshop and she reassures me that it isn't that bad. But it is.

At bedtime, the girls pull me into their bedroom and close the door.

"Why did Grandpa say that my daddy is a lying shit?" asks Milla.

"How did you hear that?" I'd closed the sitting-room door and the TV was on! "You weren't meant to hear that, I'm sorry. Grandpa is quite angry with Daddy."

"Why—because he ran away?" says Hester.

"Well, yes."

"But he wants to come back," says Hester.

"Does he?"

"Yes, he told us. And we want him to come back. We miss him," says Milla.

"I miss him too," I'm surprised to hear myself say, "but don't worry, you're seeing him this weekend—you're going for a sleepover. That will be fun, won't it?"

"Yeah," says Hester sadly.

26

The following evening, Trish calls, extremely agitated. Richard collapsed at work; suspected heart attack. Valerie had already gone home and nobody found him so he lay on the floor for several hours until one of the night cleaners on his rounds raised the alarm.

I leave the girls with my parents and rush back to the office. There were sirens wailing in the background during Trish's call; maybe they weren't to do with Richard but in any case by the time I get there, the ambulance has gone.

"He had a weak heart," says Trish as soon as I see her. "Apparently he was dead when they found him but they called an ambulance anyway because who else do you call?"

"The police!" says Valerie, incensed. "If I'd been here, this never would have happened. I sit right outside his door; I see everything. I know what kind of phone call he's having just by the way his eyebrows move. Moved."

"You mustn't blame yourself," says Trish.

Valerie looks at her, dumbfounded. "I don't blame myself—I blame you! You went to the shareholders behind his back, and you sent Don to tell Richard that you'd sold off the best thing this company had—apart from him—and you knew it would be like daggers in his heart!"

Since there's nothing I can do for Richard, I leave them fighting and go home.

I get to work early the next day. In the vast, shining lobby a few dark suits scuttle across the polished beige floor. Several more are coming down the escalator. When they reach the bottom they scatter like marbles. At the far end of the long glass reception desk there's the usual trussed-up, architectural arrangement of strange plants. I wilt slightly inside my coat. Richard was due to retire next Christmas, but this is so sudden. I don't know how we'll manage without him.

Trish says she has some good news that will distract everyone from our sad loss, and sends a company-wide email to announce that she and Don have secured the acquisition of the Ambassade hotels in the United States and Canada. A chain of fourteen luxury hotels that are a bit down at heel but certainly not concrete boxes, which is something, I suppose. Valerie tells anyone who'll listen that the shareholders backed Trish and Don over Richard, who had serious misgivings about the plan. "Sack seventy-five people," they'd instructed him, twenty years ago. "Sell a hotel," Richard had thrown back. And now they had: they sold the Regal on Park Lane to a Saudi oil baron in a private deal that Don and Trish had already lined up.

When this comes out, everyone feels sad about it—something about an old and grand institution being broken down, a loss of dignity, like sacking the royal nanny after she's brought up all the little princes and princesses. It may be true that she's no longer needed but she's given years of devoted service and should be honored. Selling her off like that—underhand, uncelebrated—and two trusted advisors betraying him, went against everything Richard stood for. People began to say that news of the sale broke his heart.

"There is no such thing as a broken heart," Trish declares. "The heart is a muscle, not a vase. Muscles can be weak or torn or strained but not broken—you never hear about a broken bicep, do you? You can break a fingernail, or a bone, but not a muscle. It was well known: he had a weak heart."

"He was not weak! His heart was strong, and true!" Valerie cries.

At lunchtime I escape with Gérard for an hour. We take the alley to get away from the usual office haunts. Peter is laying out his wares—today, mainly small electrical goods; a blender, two toasters, several hair dryers, a grilled-cheese sandwich maker, a waffle iron with drops of hardened batter stuck to the outside, and a handheld sander.

"Would you like a food processor?" I ask. "One extremely careful owner who upgraded to a newer model and palmed the old one off on me?"

"You don't want it?"

"Definitely not."

"I'll take it."

"What's all this?" says Gérard, looking at a table farther up the alley.

"Taxidermy!" Peter shouts. He seems to think this very funny, or else he's drunk. There is a row of dusty glass domes, one with a toad underneath, another with a lizard. "Look at the bat!" says Gérard, but Ronnie points instead to an open felt box displaying a fang. "See this?" he says. "Wolf's tooth! There used to be wolves in the British Isles, you know. There's a man in Scotland trying to bring them back."

Toto watches us from his cage.

"Parrots are supposed to talk, aren't they?" I say. Toto blinks, and sips his water dispenser.

"He's a quiet one," says Peter. Toto tilts his head to one side and looks down demurely.

"That parrot is a flirt," I say.

In the pub, we raise a glass to Richard. "Everyone is still in shock. But the numbness will wear off," says Gérard.

"And then it will get better?"

"Worse, probably," says Gérard. "In the beginning there's all the fuss and arrangements, and it takes time to sink in." He asks how things are going with me.

"Not great," I tell him. "I can't sleep, I can't eat, I can't stop thinking about him, and her, and the other her. I'm possessed."

"Are you getting any help?" asks Gérard delicately.

"My parents are staying at the moment, and that's tricky at times. But I've found someone to help me with the kids when they've gone—my neighbor Noreen, who used to be a childminder. And if you mean a therapist, I'm going to see one—slightly dreading it."

I remember what Gérard said when I first told him about Adam. "Tell me again how you get over something big," I ask.

"It takes time," says Gérard. "That's no secret. Everyone says so. But something they don't tell you is that it also takes work. You have to work things through—to understand and accept them. It's hard, but it's worth it, because this is how you find your own place, inside yourself. And once you have that, life's different. Better, in fact."

"How long does it take? I want this to be over as soon as possible."

"It takes a while," he answers. "Years, really."

"It hasn't even been two weeks yet," I say, dismal at the thought of what lies ahead; the effort required.

PART THREE

A thousand half-loves must be forsaken
to take one whole heart home.

—*Rumi*

27

I had to send my mother to collect *Raising Happy Children*. I saw Ben in the street a few times, and said an awkward hello as we passed each other. Meanwhile I was trying to raise happy children, seeing lawyers and mediators and financial advisors and estate agents as well as doing my job.

The weeks began to take a new shape. The girls stayed with Adam on Wednesday nights and every other weekend. On Mondays I took the girls to school and then went to see Elisabeth. The therapy sessions lasted fifty minutes and I spent most of those crying in the yellow armchair. I learned not to apply makeup until afterward but even then arrived at work blotchy. On Fridays I collected the girls and Noreen did the other days.

I shopped at lunchtimes in the big Sainsbury's near the office so that I didn't have to drag the girls round later. I was extremely busy by day, and by night I could not sleep because the children were disturbed and fretful and because I was also disturbed and fretful. The doctor gave me sleeping pills and a tranquilizer for daytime use. I took the sleeping pills but not the tranquilizers.

Elisabeth recommended *Facing Co-Dependency* and *Co-dependent No More*. While on Amazon I also ordered two volumes of poetry and a novel. I felt a pang of regret ordering the poetry; I was squandering an opportunity to show Ben that I was the kind of person who reads poetry even when not trying to impress him.

On Valentine's Day, Adam put a fat red card through the letterbox. Enclosed was a letter asking me to forgive him. I threw the card and letter away after the first reading; he had ripped my codependent heart out. I wanted to stab him.

The children rushed in after their swimming lesson.

"Mummy, did Daddy give you a Valentine's card?" said Milla.

"Ye-es," I said.

"Can we see it?" said Hester.

"I don't have it anymore."

"What! You mean you put it in the bin," said Milla.

"Um, yes, I did."

"Did you rip it up?" asked Hester.

"Yes, I did," I admitted.

"You shouldn't have done that, Mum," said Milla.

"I'm going to tell Daddy," said Hester.

Early the next morning the girls stood together on the window seat and watched as the bin men removed the bag containing the shreds of Valentine's card. They wailed and cried.

"Mum, you're rubbish!" said Hester.

I thought about taking a tranquilizer but it wasn't even 8:00 a.m. By 8:30 a.m. I had told them to Bloody Well Shut Up. I stomped off and sat in the kitchen, feeling guilty and hard done by. Hester came to look at me and went back to report on the situation.

"Yep, she's red in the face," I heard her say to Milla.

"She's going to cry," said Milla.

I thought it would be better if I didn't cry in front of them again, so I shoved the misery back inside and went to join them.

"I hate you, Mummy," said Hester.

I took them to school early because it was easier to wait in the cold, wet playground around huddles of other people than to be at home on our own.

As soon as I got to work I went on Amazon and ordered more books I didn't want to buy in the bookshop: *Trauma Through a Child's Eyes, Connection Parenting,* and *Parenting from the Inside Out: How a Deeper Self-Understanding Can Help You Raise Children Who Thrive.* I thought these books would feed into *Raising Happy Children,* a book I still had not read.

28

Don was duly appointed president. He promoted Trish and they both moved up to the eleventh floor. There was excitement and anxiety in the air. Anyone who worked directly for Don or Trish was pumped for information at every watercooler, coffee machine, and toilet in the building. What they all wanted to know was "Is it going to be all right?" The press reported Don's rise and excellent reputation and all hailed the new King of Hotels.

Trish's new office is four times as big as her old one, with a white leather sofa and a big postcard window.

"When the weather's fine, you can see Saint Paul's Cathedral," she says. I start toward the window to have a look but she cuts across with "It's not fine," so I sit down.

"I am promoting you," she says.

"Oh! What to?" I ask.

"I want you to take more responsibility in general. Among other things, I want you to break down the Guest Experience so we can build it back up in the same way, everywhere. I'm setting up project teams and you're in charge. I haven't thought of the job title yet. You can make one up, if you like."

"Thanks," I say, not sure if this is a good thing or a bad thing. As Trish talks I notice the painting on the wall behind her. It's of a bridge. Something about it strikes a chord. Trish is listing what she wants me to do, but it's apparent that she's already made her mind up about how it should be done. My eyes are drawn again to the painting. Something peaceful and quiet in it, the bridge arches elegantly over a river that looks like a summer meadow—perhaps it *is* a summer meadow. It looks familiar—the proportions maybe, or the style. The quality is unmistakable.

I burst out, "Wait a minute, is that—?"

I had been going to say "real," but Trish, melting into a gracious smile, replies, "A Monet. Yes."

"I had no idea!" I say, getting up to admire the painting. "I didn't know we owned art!"

"Lovely, isn't it? We recalled it from the National Gallery. Richard had loaned it out so that 'the public could enjoy it,' but what about us, the people at PHC?"

Not many people are going to see it if it's in your office, I think but don't say.

"There's more, actually—there's a Raphael in the boardroom until we decide where to put it, and one of David Hockney's swimming-pool pictures is coming back from Tate Britain."

Monet and Raphael! A shiver runs through me. Hockney, for goodness' sake! I know those pictures; they make me want to move to Los Angeles for the heat and the ripple of bodies moving through sunlit water.

Coming out of Trish's office, I glance across the pool of secretaries, heads bowed over their work. One of the chauffeurs is sitting back in an armchair reading a newspaper, his legs stretched out so that I can see his stripy socks.

The boardroom is empty, quiet as a church. A tall room with wide oak doors and a long, gleaming table. I slip inside and at first think Trish was having me on because the back wall is bare, but then to my left I see him, an angel, looking out from a dark green canvas, a young man with fair hair falling in loose ringlets to his shoulders and skin so smooth that even up close the brushwork is undetectable. How is it possible to paint skin like this, to account so perfectly for shape and shadow, bone structure and rounded, rose-gold cheek, the dimple at the corner of his mouth? His clear green eyes pick up the darker green background. Impossible to understand how even a great artist like Raphael could bestow such poise, the way the angel's hand rests lightly on his chest, the tilt of his face as he gazes out of the canvas, alive beyond the work yet resting in it—these matters are beyond angles and skill. Almost androgynous, his masculinity is assured by light but definite tawny sideburns, the musculature on his arms and shoulders.

So this is an angel. I've never seen a real one before, only those winged cherubs; fat little jokes that annoy me to hell. There's not much light in the room, but nevertheless the painting seems to shine. I hover in his limpid gaze, drinking in this feeling of somehow being touched by grace, and oh, but it's a deep, sad feeling and troubling.

29

"I don't have a job description anymore," I told Gérard.

"We're past job descriptions, Kate," he said. "Not quite in the danger zone, but definitely past job descriptions."

"What do you mean, danger zone?"

"Trish and Don, they're in the danger zone. At their level it's about behaving in a certain way, speaking in a certain way. It gets into how you think. It can take you over completely—unless you're strong, like Richard was. At a certain level, you're paid to drink the company Kool-Aid."

Nevertheless, the pay rise came just at the right time. Adam found a job, which helped, but we were running two households now. I told Adam that I needed to know that I could stand on my own two feet before deciding whether or not I could get over his affairs.

"Affair," he corrected.

"Whatever," I said. "The point is, I need to be properly independent. If we do get back together we both have to be sure it's because we want to."

Workmen came and took away Richard's huge oak desk and replaced it with Don's lighter, smaller one. The paintings arrived and got divvied up. Everyone expected the

Hockney swimming pool to go in Don's office since he enjoyed its glamour, but instead the workmen carried in Raphael's angel. "He'll need more than an angel," muttered Valerie.

Don embarked on a trip to all PHC regions around the globe, a territory-marking exercise that turned out to be wildly expensive, not just because of the first-class air tickets but because in order to curry favor, the regional heads had Valerie freight out his favorite beer from the Black Isle Brewery in Munlochy, a small village in northern Scotland. Crates were flown to the four corners of the world, the ale chilled and ready for his arrival in the penthouse suite and also in the limousine that picked him up from the airport.

"This is just money out of the till," said Valerie. "Richard would never have indulged in such behavior."

Valerie didn't come in the next day, or the one after that. People started to ask her whereabouts. "I have sent Valerie on compassionate leave," said Trish. "She's infecting the whole office. It's time we moved on."

"Do you mean 'affecting'?" I said, but it wasn't the only time Trish muddled her words. She wrote an all-staff email and sent it with "War Regards," and another signed "Beset Wishes."

Trish became obsessed with the Guest Experience even though this was now supposed to be my job. What she really seemed fixated on was breaking it down into small, replicable pieces. She commissioned an agency to design a sleep kit: lavender pillow spray, a roll-on blend of the essential oils of juniper, mallow, and mugwort to be applied to pulse points, a sachet of valerian-and-rose bath salts and some chamomile tea, all zipped into a small silk pouch branded with the company logo. In a development of the old chocolate-on-pillow tradition, PHC hotels started to give a Good Night's Sleep kit instead of confectionery. The cost was astronomical, so Trish added a toothbrush and a tiny tube of toothpaste and got Colgate to sponsor the whole thing.

Project teams went to speak to guests all over the world; I took France, Denmark, Spain, and Portugal. Travel is supposed to broaden the mind, but on those truncated trips I wasn't visiting with wide eyes and an open soul; I was focused entirely on the documents I needed to see and the people I needed to talk to—thirty guests of varied ages and nationalities—my mind directed on what I should be saying or taking away from meetings and getting home as fast as possible to see the girls. My itinerary went: airport, taxi, hotel, taxi, airport, out. I didn't set foot on the soil of the country I was in, didn't use their currency, didn't attempt one word of their language, because MasterCard and Visa and basic English are accepted everywhere. Travel like this is as impersonal as surgery. I was continually snubbing my host. The worst was the visit to Copenhagen; the hotel overlooked the Tivoli Gardens but I didn't cross the street to even stick my nose through the gate and smell the air.

30

The girls started creeping upstairs to my bed, which meant my nightly walkabout had to be very quiet. I limped around the house with shame and self-pity, the most unwelcome guests of all. At times I couldn't bear it. And so I started to throw things away.

I began in the kitchen, tackled the pile on top of the fridge: old vouchers from Sainsbury's, a reminder from the dentist, last year's family planner, the phone directory, coloring books three-quarters done. Next, the cupboards: Tupperware with lost lids, my favorite blue cup with the broken handle, an expired packet of dumpling mix, a jar of molasses, a shiny flan dish never used. Out, out, out, out, out.

Another night I sorted through my clothes, discovering my criteria as I went along: stained—out; frayed—out; misshapen—out. Out if it was stiff and uncomfortable. Out if I'd never liked it anyway. Out if it was too baggy, too tight, too dark, or too light. I deliberated over a cashmere jumper bought in last year's January sales; the fact of it being cashmere had trumped the fact of it being prawn pink. Seldom worn, I'd been keeping it because of the money spent, but that money was gone and now the jumper needed to go too. The relief was palpable! Old, gray knickers went, baggy bras, socks that fell down. The "out" pile was much, much bigger than the "in" pile.

At the back of the wardrobe was my wedding dress. I wouldn't wear it again and I couldn't imagine wanting, now, to pass it on to either of my daughters. It was probably sentimentality that made me go downstairs to fetch a brand-new bag from the roll of bin liners. I shook it open—wide, black, as deep and dark as a hole in the ground—and carefully placed inside my white wedding shoes and the white silk dress, which rustled and whispered as I tied the bag closed.

I stood for a moment wondering, what am I supposed to do now? I felt as though I'd just drowned a kitten. Abruptly, I decided I didn't like the clothes I'd worn yesterday so I bagged those, and then I noticed the pajamas I was wearing; I hated these pajamas! I stripped off, stuffed them into the bag, and tied it. I had spent three hours going through all my clothes and there I stood at the end of it, naked.

31

Hotel therapy. That's the kind I wanted. I thought I'd like to bring my girls and move into a hotel, where we would be looked after and kept warm. We could have a suite, or one big room with three beds. The girls would make friends of the staff, the whole hotel would be their playground—the lifts, the trollies, the free mints in the lobby, back of house with the staff room and the huge kitchens, where the chefs would give them special treats. We would have room service and clean towels every day, chocolates on our pillows every night, badminton lessons in the car park.

"But who puts them there?" asked Hester, about the pillow-chocolates.

"Maybe it's the tooth fairy's wicked sister," I said.

"Or maybe the tooth fairy puts them there herself so that people's teeth fall out quicker and she gets more," said Milla.

In real life, there were no chocolates on our pillows. The girls were staying up later and later, and when I put myself to bed it was like covering a car with a blanket, the engine still running. It didn't make any difference what time I turned off the light, how much or how little wine I drank—hot milk, hot toddies, herbal tinctures, aromatherapeutic bath suds—none of it made any difference. Even with the pills I would go to sleep with difficulty; you couldn't call it falling, more like a slow descent hanging on by fingertips. Eventually the drugs would kick in; the mechanics would stop whirring, the grip would loosen, I would sleep. And four hours later I would wake, as if some switch had been thrown. These night shifts left me frazzled, with the certain knowledge that I might drop or break things both literally and metaphorically, and so I operated with extreme caution, hazard lights flashing in the corner of my vision at all times, as if my life was a vehicle I had no license to drive.

Every day at 3:00 a.m. I'd sit up like a bolt drawn on a door, as if keeping an internal appointment—which I was, because every morning at 3:00 the same crowd of worries showed up; I spent hours each night walking around the house with them, listening to them, feeding them, clearing up after them.

My thoughts made rooms. There were rooms to suit each particular anxiety: huge chambers of fear for how this would affect Milla and Hester and for how I was going to get us through this, whether I even could. Long corridors of rage against Adam, worry for him too. Lower down, there was anger and pity for Louise, envy and spite for Judy Garland, and thoughts about my parents, especially my mother. I needed a hotel to accommodate them all. Trish often made an appearance. Money worries took up a lot of space. It was like having another job; by day an executive at PHC, by night running the Hotel Insomnia.

"How are you doing?" Yvette asked the girls.

"The kids are all right—the adults aren't," Milla said. She was right about the adults. For the first few weeks, I operated on autopilot: minimal functioning with erratic outbursts. I tried to uphold established routines, but sometimes the old bedtime stories would make me cry or I'd slip out of a trance and realize that I'd been stirring the soup for twenty minutes. Adam was a mess as well—unshaven, he looked drawn and shadowy, as though he were being hunted down by faceless horsemen with swirling cloaks. His friends were worried about him getting into some kind of trouble. He had a reputation for volatility.

One day Hester asked, "Mummy, what's a cunk?"

"I don't know—where did you hear it?"

"Daddy said it. We were crossing the road with him and a bike went in front of us really fast and Daddy shouted, 'You cunk!'"

But I didn't think the kids were all right. Milla started to leave notes. I'd be hovering in the middle distance and come round to find small folded pieces of paper strewn like white petals around my feet. Inside were little drawings—a unicorn, a fairy, a rainbow, a smiling sun—and little writings: *You are pretty*; *You are kind*; *You care for others*; *I love you*; *Best mummy ever*.

We were lost at sea on separate boats. Milla's notes were like messages in bottles thrown out in hope of finding land and being rescued, invocations to summon her mother back from the deep: I knew because I'd done more or less the same thing when my father's affair came to light and my own mother set sail without saying goodbye. In a way I lost her then; after the initial crisis passed, she started teaching. She never really came back.

As well as her little notes, Milla started to eavesdrop, another activity I was familiar with from childhood. With this inside knowledge I tried to stay one step ahead: I'd make absolutely sure she was asleep or watching television behind a closed door before making any personal calls, but often I'd be mid-outpour with Yvette or with Jo, and I'd look up and see her standing side-on in the shadows, pressed against a wall. I knew Milla was only trying to piece it all together, but I understood now a comment my mother had made when she caught me folded under the stairs, listening to one of her phone calls. "It's like living with the Gestapo," she said.

Hester stepped up her campaign to change her name and when I was steadfast in my refusal she retaliated by withdrawing the title "Mummy"—but only when she remembered, which wasn't very often. She followed her elder sister's example of message writing, only hers were the opposite of love letters. I would find notes propped against the kettle in cronky four-year-old handwriting: *To Kate. You are going to hav a chopt off hed and it is not a jok. Hat from Diego.* I understood that *jok* meant "joke" but sometimes her spelling foxed me. "Hat from Diego?" I asked, because Diego the cartoon character did in fact wear a sombrero. "Do you mean you want a hat like Diego's? Because that we can do."

"HATE, Mummy, it says HATE!"

A few days later she lost a tooth and when I looked under her pillow at 3:00 a.m. to retrieve the tooth and replace it with a coin there was more hate mail, this time for the tooth fairy: *If you don't giv my mune I will smash you.* I took the envelope down to the kitchen and wrote a reply using my left hand. *Maybe you could ask nicely? I am sure we can be friendly, xoxo.* I slid the envelope back under her pillow with the tooth still inside, no coin; I didn't need to consult *Raising Happy Children* or any of the other child-rearing manuals under my bed to know that the tooth fairy doesn't respond to threats.

32

On my way home from work one day I found Peter and Ronnie in conference, Toto looking on.

"You missed it, darling!" said Peter. "The police came to arrest us all—they took names and addresses, but in the end they didn't take us."

"The royal servant?" I asked.

"DVDs," said Ronnie. "They were pirate."

"We had some good ones—some children ones," said Peter.

"Disney, he means. Not wrong'uns, sweetheart," corrected Ronnie.

"No!" said Peter.

Ronnie picked up my shopping bags and carried them all the way to the Tube. "You know we all love you, darling, don't you?" he said. "Peter loves you. He'd never say it, but he does. If there's ever anything we can do for you, you just let us know, all right? We can come round. We'll carry your bags, paint the walls, dig the garden, beat someone up for you—we'll make sure he doesn't come back, you just give us the nod." He was probably exaggerating. Nevertheless I was quite glad they didn't know where we lived.

That Peter and Ronnie had worked out my situation wasn't surprising; I had been bringing them remnants of my household for weeks. But I must have been giving off some kind of vibe because one lunchtime while I was shopping in Sainsbury's a man approached me in the grocery section, where I was busy wondering if the girls would eat spinach if I disguised it in an omelette.

"Excuse me," he said. I didn't realize he was talking to me.

"Excuse me, miss," he repeated politely. I looked up from the green leafy vegetables to see who was calling me "miss." He was good-looking, with round, high cheeks and wavy black hair and he spoke with a posh accent.

"Excuse me, but I have to ask—are you single?"

"What?" I said, though I'd heard him.

"I'm really sorry to accost you like this in a supermarket of all places, but I saw you and I just had to ask whether you're single?"

"Ah . . . not really," I answered. I still had my wedding ring, but wasn't wearing it.

"Not really," he repeated, mulling it over. "Well, let me put it like this—are you single *enough* for me to ask you out for a drink sometime, or a coffee?"

"Oh!" I said. "Um . . ."

"My name's Abs," he said hurriedly. "What's yours?"

"Abs?" I said. "As in stomach muscles?"

"As in Absolem."

"Oh, right, of course—sorry. My name's Kate."

"No problem, Kate," said Abs. "So, how about a coffee?"

Still embarrassed about my mistake over his name, I found myself giving Abs my number. But I worried about it afterward. I couldn't stop thinking about Adam and whether I should tell him. I called Jo.

"It is a bit odd, being asked out in Sainsbury's," she said.

"But it could be quite good for you. It's just a coffee, and you're entitled to have coffee with whoever you want—you and Adam are separated, remember?"

Abs texted me the same afternoon to suggest we speak on the phone before meeting up. He referred to this as a pre-date, which I'd never heard of. We arranged to speak at 9:00 p.m. but he didn't call, so at 9:30 I started getting ready for bed. When I checked the phone later I saw that he had tried calling at 9:27 and sent a text at 9:31.

"I tried to reach you just after nine," he said when we did speak. Half past does not qualify as "just after," I thought but didn't say.

Abs said he'd planned a virtual date, as a surprise. It would take place on this phone call. I'd never heard of one of those either. He asked me what color dress I'd wear—the only question he did ask—and then proceeded to pick me up in an unspecified fancy car and drive me round "his" London, showing me the places he grew up and went to school, then on to the London Eye, where he had booked a private capsule with musicians, hors d'oeuvres, and prosecco.

"Prosecco?" I said. "If it's a virtual date couldn't we have champagne?"

After the London Eye, the fancy car took us to a one-room restaurant at the top of Battersea Power Station, which I could only imagine derelict, and then on to a flat overlooking the river, where there would be dancing.

"And now I'm going to do something really spontaneous," said Abs, after the first dance.

"Oh," I said.

"Can you guess what it is?"

"Not really," I said, though I had that sinking feeling.

"It's just a really spontaneous thing that I'm going to do, can't you think of it?"

"No!"

"Well, I'm going to kiss you."

"Oh."

"Is that it—'Oh'? Is that all you can say? You've been saying 'oh' for the whole date, apart from complaining about the drinks. Maybe you're stressed—or are you just tired?"

I had no idea what to say. I was of course deeply stressed and completely exhausted, but this was not the problem.

"Can't you say something to help the situation?" he said. "I was just trying to be spontaneous. I really don't know what to say now. Can't you say anything at all?"

"Do you do this all the time?" I said. "Pick people up in Sainsbury's?"

"No! Well, I won't lie—it's not the first time I've ever spoken to anyone."

"I think I'm going to go now," I said. "Bye."

Ten minutes later he sent a text: *Is this how you treat everyone who tries to be nice to you? What a waste of space . . .*

33

Jo adopted me as a project, of which she was the director. Every time I saw her she wrote a list of things I should do or buy.

— *A lipstick in Barbie pink (this season's color)*
— *Hair in a ponytail (makes you look younger)*
— *A new jacket fitted at the waist (sexy)*
— *Chicken, fish, or steak with veg—no carbs (stay thin!)*
— *Exercise, for fitness and relaxation—twenty minutes a day (will help you sleep)*

She was bossy, Jo, but her lists were loving.

I lost weight. Even my feet went down a size, which I still don't understand, unless the shock somehow made them arch more and then they just stayed that way. My bum shrank but so did my cheeks, which made me look older. Jo said I looked better than ever, though I worried she was humoring me. People say that at forty you have to choose between your arse and your face but they don't mention breasts; what happens to them—do they go with the bum or the face? Mine got even smaller. "You're not forty yet—don't think about it," said Jo, but if there'd been a book called *Your Arse or Your Face* I probably would have bought it.

34

In the cupboard under the stairs I found a box set of *The Sopranos*, which we used to watch together; Tony Soprano having a midlife crisis, suffocating under the weight of his triple life: waste-management consultant, strip-club owner, Mafia boss. Carmela incensed every time she found out about a new "gumah." Wife, kids, girlfriend, the Mob all making demands, Tony falling slowly apart. Perhaps all midlife crises are to do with the gap between who you wished to be and who you really are; the life you'd hoped for and the life you've actually got. You feel it as an ache, this gap, and the crisis happens when, in increasing desperation, you try to fill it—cars, motorbikes, handbags, and shoes—and not just any old ones; this is where branding and marketing get a foothold. Someone sees themselves on a Ducati; for someone else it's a Harley-Davidson, a VW camper van, a Porsche, or a Mercedes-Benz. Chanel handbags, Jimmy Choo shoes, Tiffany earrings. Younger lovers, older lovers, online lovers: any lover will do as long as they won't see us as we really are. Botox, detox, a new job, a new hairstyle, chocolates, gardens, grand pianos: you can throw ten thousand things into the gap; it will never close.

In the same box as *The Sopranos* were three sets of negatives from a weekend photography course at Central Saint

Martins that I'd given Adam for his birthday not long after his collapse. I thought it would help him to become absorbed in something and he'd always said he loved photography. I had a sense that Adam wasn't very proud of himself or where he was in his life. Outwardly he was doing fine but he had fallen short by his parents' estimation and, crucially, his own—hadn't lived up to the early promise of his brilliant youth, though nobody ever said so.

Most of the negatives were head-and-shoulders shots of a young woman, apparently also in the course. She looked vaguely uncomfortable, unsmiling, almost sulky, sitting side-on with a backward glance to the camera, long dark hair coming over a bare shoulder. Peering at the negatives, I thought at first she was wearing a camisole and then I remembered the course took place in high summer, so it must have been a sundress.

When he came home on the Sunday night, he said it had been great. He made no mention of anyone else in the course, but finding these portraits made sense of a cache of emails he'd written afterward to a woman called Janey in which he'd asked whether she wanted to meet up for a drink.

I'm not sure, maybe. Are the others going to be there? Janey had replied, sounding uncertain.

After I found Janey in the cupboard under the stairs, I asked Adam about her. He refused to discuss it, said it was nothing. I had the feeling I would stop finding things only when I stopped looking. He'd hidden so much—not just from me, from everyone—and he was still holding back, wanting to prevent things from coming fully out into the open, wanting to keep things hidden. Hiding was the main thing, I realized.

35

The instructions on the back of the Mr. Muscle drain cleaner read:

1. Pour the entire contents down the plughole
2. Allow to work for one hour
3. Flush with hot water

Exactly what I wanted to do, and not just with the contents of that bottle. The instructions made it sound so easy: all I had to do was open the bottle and like a genie the product would come out and do all the hard work; no scrubbing, brushing, scraping, or swilling necessary, in fact no effort whatsoever required on my part. All I had to do was open the bottle and wait.

The dejunking books had similarly clear instructions. When clearing out a drawer, for example:

1. Empty the drawer
2. Clean it thoroughly
3. Sort through contents throwing away anything broken, ugly, duplicate, or unused
4. Put the remainder neatly back into the clean drawer

A kind of madness seeped out from the small hours. My perception fell slightly out of step with reality. It was as though surreal was a color, like teal or cerulean blue, and everything took on its strange hue.

I lost my appetite; the only time I wanted to eat was after the night shift—a couple of digestive biscuits with a cup of tea at 6:30 a.m. Everything I ate tasted like cardboard, including the biscuits, but at least they were sweet cardboard.

I sorted meticulously through drawers and shelves. By 6:00 most mornings there were two bags by the door, rubbish and charity shop—but the charity shops didn't open until 10:00 so that bag went to Peter. A couple of times I had to book a taxi-van for things I couldn't carry on the Tube: an armchair, a small sofa, beanbags—the worst furniture idea ever—a large rug, a side table. Peter would often be outside his shop by 8:00 a.m., sweeping the street, setting up for the day, but if he wasn't I'd leave my offerings tucked in by the door.

36

The bulbs in the backyard had not fared well, due to the clay in the ground, I supposed. A few weaklings with limp, pale shoots were all they yielded, no flowers. One weekend our neighbor David came over with tulips—he and his partner Edward had a beautiful back garden, and a surfeit. Edward was still besotted with the younger man and though David had decided to bide his time and wait until the infatuation passed, that didn't seem to be happening very quickly. I told David about my emergency crush on Ben from the bookshop.

"I've got a massive crush on him too," said David. "Everyone has! It's the eye contact—he gives such good eye contact—you really feel like he's interested, like he really cares."

"Maybe he does," I said.

"Maybe he does," David conceded.

We dug out the dense, sodden mud and replaced it with sacks of soft, crumbling compost. It was immensely satisfying to bury the new plants in the earth, pat them down, water them in. You could feel the good it did.

"There should be a book on how gardening can heal your broken heart," I said.

"Oh, there is," said David. "Why do you think our garden is so gorgeous?"

*

On Amazon—so that Ben wouldn't see the kind of person I really was—I bought *Gardening for the Soul: Blossoming Again After Blight, Mend Your Broken Heart: How to Get from Hurt to Healing,* and *Get Over Your Breakup: How to Turn Devastating Loss into the Best Thing That Ever Happened to You.*

Embrace your newfound freedom, the books advised. Make a list of the things you can do now that you couldn't do before. Have fun. You can do whatever you want. Experiment, the authors encouraged—have your own ideas, see what feels right. I could eat all the things he didn't like, have cake for breakfast, spend as much money as I liked on a single bottle of wine, buy a cocktail shaker and take up martinis.

37

Muscle of the Month: The Heart. A large screen in the leisure center displayed a picture of the heart with its four chambers, main entrance and exit veins clearly labeled: vena cava, aorta, left ventricle and atrium, right ventricle and atrium. Very simple, very spacious—not how my heart felt at all.

"Try something else," the doctor had said, refusing to renew my prescription. "Swimming might be good, or a relaxation class—yoga, perhaps. You've got to get a good night's sleep on your own; you can't rely on these pills forever. If it doesn't work, you can come back in a month."

"Find a still place," said the yoga teacher. He meant a place inside. I did not feel still. There was a heaviness in my chest, a weight I felt but could not find. "Yoga is not competitive," said the teacher. "Focus your awareness on the subtle body—the invisible double of the physical body, the vehicle of the vital force. It's always there. You can't see it but you can feel it."

Never mind the subtle body; the actual bodies of the people in the room were something to behold. Apart from a few stragglers at the back like me, this class seemed to be where all the perfect people go. Dancing around on their mats in hot-pink shiny leggings and tiny weeny shorts designed to show off exquisitely rounded buttocks, they even had beautiful shoulder blades and backs of their necks.

It was like arriving in a country populated by off-duty ballerinas. I knew I shouldn't have been looking, but I wasn't the only one—the blonde in the fuchsia leggings glanced over at the redhead in a lime-green leotard to see how high her leg went, and both of them looked when the shorter, bouncier brunette lithe in her navy-blue bodysuit flipped like a pancake between handstand and back bend. Yoga may not be competitive, but people are.

The subtle body of the yoga class incorporated Scotland, Wales, Ireland, and the jungles and temples of Far East Asia. I'd never seen so many tattoos: twelve Celtic crosses, eleven Buddhas praying, ten tigers leaping, nine eagles soaring, eight dragons roaring, seven snakes a-coiling, six roses blooming, five "Om" symbols, four hummingbirds, three French hens, two turtle doves, and a dolphin in a blue sea. Many people had writing on their body: Chinese characters, phrases in scripts I could only guess at—Sanskrit, Hindi, Tibetan, perhaps. One guy in a baggy T-shirt at the back near me had *Love* and *Hate* tattooed on his knuckles, but I think perhaps he was in the wrong room.

Toward the end of the class the teacher told the regulars to start their closing sequence and the rest of us to wait for guidance.

"If you're waiting for instructions . . ." he said, and proceeded to tell us how to move into a shoulder stand. I was waiting for instructions. I wanted to be told the right thing to do and the right way to do it, the right way to live.

38

I went to buy a new swimsuit. I needed a new swimsuit because I didn't want to be reminded of Adam's comment every time I got into the pool. I picked out a couple to try on and there was one I liked; an updated 1920s style. When I put it on it was horribly baggy, especially round the crotch. I stepped out of the changing cubicle, went to find an assistant, and asked for a smaller size. A bikini across the shop caught my eye and I went over to flick through a whole new rail. There were not many other shoppers that morning, though I thought I saw a young woman look quickly away from me at one point. Eventually, the shop assistant returned. He looked embarrassed.

"I'm sorry, there are no other sizes in that style."

That style? What style? Oh, God. I was still wearing the swimsuit; no wonder the assistant looked uncomfortable. I darted back into the changing cubicle. At first, I felt as though I had woken from a familiar nightmare in which I had been walking down a crowded street in my underwear, and then I realized that I had actually just done this in real life and there was nothing to wake up from.

So I went somewhere else and bought a swimsuit and a sports bra, called a Determination bra; aptly named because you needed quite a lot of determination just to get it on. On the Tube home I saw someone reading a book called *The Escape Manifesto*. The blurb on the back said: *Have you spent your life jumping through hoops? Do*

*you try to please others by doing what's expected of you?
Do you wish for something more?*

Perhaps Adam wished for more, and didn't know
how to say that, even to me, his wife—especially to me,
perhaps—and didn't know where to find it. Maybe that
was why he constructed alter egos to hide behind: for
Louise he was Prince Charming, the kindly and experi-
enced older man; for Lorna his disguise involved a new
name, Adam Norton—it sounded pretty good. Over the
years, several people had told him he looked like the actor
Ed Norton. Anyone could have guessed the film-star ref-
erence, but what it meant that he used this name was
something only a wife would know, something to do with
his collapse on the sitting-room floor and why he never
threw anything away: he needed all those things to shore
up the leaks in his self-image like the boy at the dyke, but
he couldn't hold back that sea forever.

Perhaps it would have been better had I not seen him
fall to the floor in his suit and tie, though he'd done that
right in front of me. He needed a witness, but I also saw too
much. Poor Adam, he couldn't have known—neither of us
could—that being seen in despair was even more painful
than the despair itself. He couldn't endure me having seen
him as he really was. Seeking relief, he became Prince
Charming to Louise and another new man to Lorna. As Ed
Norton to her Judy Garland, his real life melted away—no
more mortgage, no money troubles, no wife and kids—and
he assumed film-star qualities: mysterious and un-pin-
down-able, loyal to his dog.

39

I read a review of a book written by a woman who had crossed the Atlantic on a windsurfer. I thought enough time had elapsed for me to go back to the bookshop. Instead of my usual sneaky walk-past check, I would enter the bookshop regardless of who was in that day. Ben was not in. I found the book and took it up to the till.

"That's a display copy, it's a bit dog-eared," said the nice woman. "I can order you a new one if you like—it'll be here tomorrow." So I ordered the book and while she was putting the details into the computer, I noticed some new paintings high up on the wall above the bookshelves; small landscapes and seascapes, one of a forest. I remarked on them.

"They're Ben's," said the woman.

"Oh!"

"He's just finished this series, so we thought we'd display them while he finds a gallery."

"They're really good," I said, and I meant it. I left the bookshop feeling elated; I was right! OK, so Ben was a painter and not a poet, but it's more or less the same thing, isn't it?

I went to collect the book the next day, paid, and then said, very fast, "I like your paintings especially this one this one and this one they are really good goodbye."

Ben said, "Thank—" but I was out the door before he could say "you."

*

The book about crossing the Atlantic on a windsurfer read like a thriller to me. The very idea was appalling—why would anybody in their right mind spend weeks alone atop a tiny board in the middle of a vast ocean? At night the sailor slept inside the specially designed board knowing that it was too small to be picked up by any ship's radar, so there was always the possibility of being run through and splintered by small- to medium-sized yachts and boats or completely submerged by huge vessels. Storms thundered over her, she was slapped and bruised by the water, her tins of food were dented, her sail ripped; but other nights she was lulled by the wind and waves, and watched the phosphorescence glow in the darkness, the stars bright overhead. Sometimes she raced with dolphins, swam in the Gulf Stream, was visited by whales. She began to feel the moon in the ebb and flow of the water, could tell tides without the tables, learned the positions of the stars: there are signs that we can learn, to place over the heavens, to read the sky, to predict the weather and how long it will last. She tested the old proverbs and found them true.

I liked what the sailor knew. When crossing an ocean aboard a small craft there are a great many things to be aware of. Learn to sort these things into three buckets and you will be a lot happier:

— *Things that require your immediate attention*
— *Things you need to keep an eye on*
— *Things you can't do a damn thing about*

40

One bedtime, Hester picked *We're Going on a Bear Hunt,* an old favorite because of the way the words rolled along and because the drawings were so appealing.

Uh-uh! A river!

A deep cold river.

We can't go over it.

We can't go under it.

Oh no!

We've got to go through it!

This could have been a mantra from one of my self-help books. "Girls," I said, "this book is exactly right—it's telling us how to deal with our situation, with Mummy and Daddy's separation. We can't go over it, we can't go under it, we've got to go through it."

"Shut up, Mummy! I just want a story!" said Hester.

"I don't want to listen to this," said Milla. She slid off the bed and locked herself in the bathroom.

On my insistence, Adam moved two carloads to store in the loft and garage at his parents' house, but many of his things were still in the house; there wasn't enough room where he was and besides, that arrangement was temporary. Three times I'd bagged up things of his and, remembering they were not mine to throw away, put them back.

*

There are signs that we can learn, the sailor said. How had I not noticed any change in Adam? Perhaps because there wasn't one; he hadn't fallen in love with her, he said, and there was no glow, no quickening, no new shine in his eyes, so perhaps his loyalties were not with another woman. But in any case he deserted us, and maybe he also deserted himself. I felt his absence like a closed-up, empty room but he denied it, didn't want to talk about it. So I allowed myself to be confused—here was his physical form walking the dog, making pasta, folding laundry at midnight, eventually coming to bed, and yet he was not present. There were signs; I ignored them.

The sailor carried very little, had only a few instruments: an almanac for celestial navigation—which got soaked and disintegrated early in the voyage—a compass, and a waterproof watch. She learned to pay attention to what she noticed, to use herself as an instrument. Mid-ocean, after many days and nights of being surrounded by sea and sun and stars, she noticed how serene she felt, despite her extreme vulnerability to the elements. This was not a false sense of security, she said, this was a secure sense of security. She realized the call-and-response nature of things. She had the feeling that something bigger than herself was including her—had been, all along. Greater Forces, and she didn't just mean the weather. She jettisoned everything that now seemed superfluous. It wasn't only that she didn't need them anymore; they were actually getting in the way. She dropped the watch in the sea, feeling only a brief regret as it sank quickly out of sight.

*

At 3:00 a.m. I went on Amazon and had a quick "Look inside" a few more books for tips. *Get Over Your Ex* advised meeting new people. For those who couldn't get out much, such as full-time working mothers like me, they recommended making online friends—insomniacs, presumably, or friends in different time zones. My 3:00 a.m. was 10:45 a.m. for someone in Western Australia, 10:00 p.m. for someone in La Paz, 7:30 a.m. in Gujarat. But I didn't want to find people online and it wasn't only Adam's Internet adventures that put me off; it seemed like a form of shopping and I didn't want to buy and sell people like that and I didn't want to be bought and sold.

Shuffling about in the near-dark so as not to wake my daughters, sleeping in my bed, I opened his wardrobe to look, yet again, at his clothes hanging there. Mostly shirts, suits, and jackets; smart clothes he didn't wear very often but looked so handsome in. A small white feather rested on the shoulder of one of his suits: such gentleness; I didn't disturb it. I smoothed his lapels, stroked his sleeve. The thing I'd been working very hard not to admit finally poked through. All my activity was a furious attempt to avoid it, bury it, deny it, but I'd known all along; hearts do break.

I let out a sigh and my breath lifted the feather up off Adam's suit shoulder to twirl slowly down to the ground, a reminder that there was such a thing as grace.

41

There were problems completing the purchase of the Ambassade chain. Someone, somewhere, had miscalculated PHC's buying power and that person was sacked, along with all of his team. Trish and Don went ahead with the deal regardless—they canceled the Immersion Hotel and resold the Belgian palace to help pay for it.

"Ostend really *isn't* a premier destination," said Trish. "Not from a global perspective."

"And the idea, while quite innovative, requires a great deal of seed money to get it off the ground. I think we'll stick with normal hotels for now," said Don.

"The return would have been much higher than for a 'normal hotel,'" I said. "And actually the initial layout was only twenty percent more than conversion to a straight hotel would have been."

"Well, we simply can't afford that right now," said Don.

I was really disappointed. Embarrassed too, when I had to stop the historians' research and pay off the film production company, and I noticed that Trish and Don didn't stop spending vast amounts of money on other things. In any case, I decided to work on something quieter, something that wouldn't cost much and therefore wouldn't be scrapped. In my original job description, one of the points I'd most warmed to was: "To be a passionate ambassador and focal point for ensuring intelligence from staff is used when developing new products, projects, and services."

Six hundred and thirty-three thousand people in a hundred countries: so much creative potential in PHC's human resource. Richard had always encouraged hotel staff at all levels to interact with guests, talk with them, find out what they liked and what they needed—what better way to gain insight into the Guest Experience than by asking the people who looked after them? I decided to set up a modern-day equivalent of a staff suggestion box—which did exist, physically, in some hotels. Suggestions tended to stay in the hotel, though, and sometimes they even just stayed in the box.

Working with Tyler from IT, we came up with a digital version; a hybrid between a suggestion box and a betting shop. We called it "The Ideas Fair": people could submit ideas and they could also place virtual tokens on the ones they thought were the best; there would be cash prizes for the best ideas and for betting correctly on them.

Trish's sign-off was needed before anything new could be launched. "Kate, the bottom line is conversion rate—is this ideas sweepstake going to get more people to book hotel stays? Because if not, and I highly doubt it, it's not worth it."

"But ideas can come from anywhere, and from any-one—we don't know what might come out of this because PHC has never had an effective outlet for people's views and ideas before. Most of the work has been done, and once you approve it we could have it up and running within a day."

Trish made two amendments before she agreed; ideas could only be submitted if the person's name, job title, and location were also given, and as well as tokens for the best ideas, she decreed that tokens should also be placed on the worst ideas.

"Green for good, red for bad," she said. "A traffic-light system."

"I thought there were no bad ideas?" said Sam, who was helping with branding.

"That's 'no stupid questions,'" I corrected.

"You're both wrong," said Trish. "There are plenty of bad ideas and no end of stupid questions. I hear them all the time."

After Trish's conditions and Sam's branding and Tyler's final tweaks, we launched it: *Global Ideas Derby—Back the Winning Horse!*

Along with many other business sectors, the hospitality industry was suffering from the global financial crisis. At PHC, bookings dropped by 40 percent and that's disaster territory because hotels are highly geared operations. Profits were down; stress was high. The weird thing was that profits were down in areas they really shouldn't have been: possibly something to do with the "informal economy" operating in the hotels, mainly illicit use of rooms—staff living temporarily in the hotels. Many lower-level employees are itinerant, students far away from home, migrant workers at varying levels of legality, ex-convicts with no fixed abode. Sometimes rooms are let for cash. The extent of it is not known but bits poke through here and there. The accountants unearth a bone or the IT people smell something funny.

Undeclared double-sell was one theory. Hotels double-sell rooms all the time; a good bookings agent can achieve

150 percent occupancy rate by selling rooms twice for the same date: meetings during the day (maintenance shove the bed in the bathroom and lock the door) and reconverting to bedrooms when the business day is done, or to an airline night crew followed swiftly by a day crew. The turnaround time between one bunch leaving and another arriving can be less than an hour, so the hotel has to be operating at a high level—front desk, maintenance, and cleaners all in communication with each other and fast. Cleaners say that even when they've stripped the linen and put new sheets on, sometimes the beds are still warm from the previous guest as the next is checking in downstairs.

42

"We need to change the mind-set," Trish said.

"Great!" I said. "So you want to make the culture more innovative, more entrepreneurial?"

"Less."

Trish and Don planned to script and choreograph as many jobs as possible, especially housekeeping. Their justification was efficiency; if all the cleaners did the same thing in the same order it would save time, which saves money. But that made no sense because even if the rooms are identical, each guest is different and they bring their world with them. Trish and Don seemed to want robots, but really, cleaners are more like anthropologists. Each time they unlock a door they dip into someone's reality: one guest pulls the furniture to the wall to clear space for prayer or exercise, another washes his clothes in the sink and leaves them to drip-dry all over the furniture, another has a bunch of bananas ripening in a sunny spot by the window. A good cleaner treats each guest as they are: individual.

In April, only four months after Richard died, they decided to sack Jean the cleaner, not for playing the piano but for sitting down too often while he was working.

"Routine footage of CCTV—" began Don.

"Wait a minute," I interrupted. "That's what you said last time, but something's just occurred to me—what's 'routine' about having CCTV cameras tracking the cleaners? We shouldn't be doing that, surely?"

"It's a gray area," said Don.

"I'm not sure I'm in full agreement with that statement, Don," I said.

"Don's absolutely right. Legally, it *is* a gray area," said Trish.

"The law may allow for interpretation but isn't it our responsibility to interpret it correctly? Fairly, I mean. And, with all due respect, many people would feel this to be . . . ahm, well . . . a bit unkind."

"It's too late to worry about that now," says Trish. "It's done."

Disgusted, I went to the Belgravia Palazzio anyway. Stanley, head of security, was there. "We'd better go in here so they don't see us," he said, opening a door into the old ballroom.

"What do you mean?" I said. "Spies?"

"Cameras." Stanley lifted down two chairs with velvet seats from a tall stack and went to make us a cup of tea. I waited for him in the abandoned ballroom. No more dancing now—the parquet flooring was in a terrible state, and at least half the room was filled with broken minibars.

"Too expensive to renovate," he told me. "They use it to store the dead fridges from all the London hotels, until a contractor picks up the job lot," he said.

Stanley told me what happened with Jean. "Three blokes turned up, and Don sent a personal message—a nasty touch, don't you think?"

"What about Jean's son?"

"We had a whip-round, raised enough for his airfare, and the aunt took him back to Brazil. Jean can't support them without work. It was unnecessary, the way they did it. Three of them, I ask you! Jean wouldn't have made any trouble—he wasn't going to *fight* them. One would have been enough. Don's message said that he'd been 'sitting down on the job,' and it was 'unacceptable,' and they took him away."

When I went in the following day, Trish had no lament for the minibar graveyard. "They're expensive to run and they don't last," she said. "We're phasing them out gradually. We plan to replace them with vending machines next to the ice dispensers located on every floor, and we're introducing a fee for the ice."

"But minibars are so good—they're so tempting," I protested. "I love minibars! One of the best things about coming into a new hotel room is opening them to see what's inside."

"They're outdated," said Trish. "And anyway, you cannot 'love' minibars, Kate. That's not love—that's nostalgia."

43

A room was laid out in the alley outside Peter's shop: a large red rug spread over the tarmac and on it a small sofa, two beanbags nestled against the wall, a brown armchair, and a side table with a horrible lamp. I found it disconcerting to see an inside on the outside and then realized this was because they were *my* insides: my rug, my sofa and beanbags, my armchair, my horrible lamp on my side table. I'd never liked these things, had dejunked them with gusto, but they'd been in my house for years, and confronted with them now like this, I felt eviscerated. Peter was smoking in the armchair, Toto's cage next to him, Ronnie reclining on the sofa drinking beer. They might as well have been sitting on my lungs and kidneys.

Ronnie asked if I'd seen the new Belgian café next to the Tube station. "You've got *moules*, and you've got *frites*. And you can have them for nine ninety-nine. And if you like a drink, you've got Belgian beers—you've got blond beer and brunette beer but no redheads." He laughed deeply and went on. "And you can have the beers for three ninety-nine each. Or if you like they do a meal-deal at lunchtime and you can have the whole lot for twelve ninety-nine, sweetheart. What do you think of that?"

Was this Ronnie asking me out?

"It sounds nice," I replied in a noncommittal way, wondering how to end this encounter with everyone's dignity intact. Then I saw Peter drink from my old blue cup with the broken handle; he'd glued it back together.

"You *mended* it," I said, as if mending was a new and revolutionary idea.

Not everything went to Peter or in the bin. I took the rest of the jewelry Adam had given me and distributed it down various drains across London: I let the gold earrings slide down a grating at the edge of Hyde Park, said goodbye to the silver bracelet as it plopped into a gutter by King's Cross station, and the river pearls I let go down a drain in a Pimlico side street.

44

Adam called, crying. "Charlie's dying," he heaved. It was
May. Charlie had lasted much longer than anyone pre-
dicted, but that was no consolation now. Milla and Hester
would be as distraught as Adam.

"I'm not there and I should be—I should be there with
him, to hold him."

"Then go," I said, hearing the pain in his voice.

"I won't make it in time, he suddenly got worse. He's
suffering. Mum said he can hardly breathe. Dad's taking
him to the vet this morning."

"Go right now, this minute, you might make it," I
said.

"The train takes two hours. It's too late," he said,
sobbing.

When he came to collect the girls later that week he stood
in the doorway, pale and haggard. I invited him in. He was
edgy, dancing about in the hallway like a boxer in the ring.
A surge of compassion rushed through me; it must have
been horrible, coming as a visitor to what had been his
home, unsure of his welcome. I laid my hand on his arm.
It was the first physical contact we'd had for months and
it startled both of us. He stopped jigging and looked at me,
full of sorrow. I could feel his regret, as complete and un-
equivocal as heat from the sun. I wasn't sure what he saw
in my eyes, but at that moment all I felt was sadness. I

moved toward him. We put our arms around each other and held each other tight.

Milla came downstairs. "Does this mean you're friends again?" she asked.

We moved apart again, but not very far. Adam waited for me to speak, an act of courtesy like holding the door open: I suppose he dared not confirm her hopes, or his own, or mine.

"I think it means we're trying to be friends," I said cautiously, but that was enough for Milla; she rushed forward and put us back into hug position as if she were arranging dolls.

"Please, Kate, let's try again," said Adam, and I wanted to— the books said it was possible, my own parents were living proof. I could hear Adam's suffering in every syllable, see it in the slight stoop in his shoulders, a flatness of step as though his arches had fallen, and I felt for him. After all, we were still married; we had our children to think of.

The mess we'd made affected Milla and Hester deeply. They brought home their annual school photo: the photographer had positioned their heads close together and buttoned up their collars; Milla smiled obediently for the camera, Hester gave a gappy grin. Their cheeks were chubby, their faces clean, soft hair brushed, but there was no shine around their eyes where their smiles should have reached.

"It's lovely," I said to them, and filled out the order form for two: one for me, one for Adam.

*

At 3:00 a.m., when the girls were sound asleep, I looked at their sad eyes in the school photograph and was able to cry. I didn't want sleep so much as a general anesthetic.

I knew how sorry Adam was, but sorry doesn't actually do anything—doesn't change things, doesn't make things un-happen or go away. Gérard was right; grief is slow. Incredibly, intolerably slow. A glacier crossing continents, its movement is imperceptible. And yet, something new was happening. I could feel it, bubbling, coming up from under.

45

Houses, like hotels, have different characters. It's easy to anthropomorphize a house: the front door can be the mouth, the two upstairs windows eyes, with lintels as eyebrows, and if there's a chimney pot with smoke rising, that can be a thought bubble; the house dreaming. Our house spoke to us: the bedroom doors creaked when I opened them first thing in the morning and afterward you could hear the occasional mutter as the wood eased into the day. The fridge hummed, the oven mumbled, and when the boiler started up at 5:00 a.m. it sounded like a stomach gurgling. It was like living with a kindly old person who was stiff on rising, slightly cranky at certain times of day.

I got to know our home better, simply because I was paying attention. After living there for ten years, I finally figured out the strange noise the bath made; it was the sound of water slowly leaking out because the plug was ever so slightly too small. Draining away, all these years. Once I realized, all it took was a quick trip to the hardware shop on the high street to buy a new one that fitted snugly.

The girls had taken the news of Charlie's death better than I thought they would, but I was worried. One night, after they had been quiet for a suspiciously long time in their room, I gently pushed the door open: they were sitting on the floor, Milla with the kitchen scissors, Hester with a pair of nail scissors, soft toys strewn around and a great deal of stuffing on the floor.

"At least you didn't cut each other's hair," I said.

"Only a bit," said Hester, turning her head to show a wide section missing at the back. "I want hair like Diego, but we thought you might get cross so we stopped and did the bears."

I gathered Hester's hair into a rather thin ponytail, which only partially hid the missing lump, and took her to the hairdresser with a picture of Diego.

"She's going to look like a boy with this haircut," the hairdresser warned.

"You mean I'm going to look like Diego!" Hester piped up.

And she did. Chubby as a cartoon character, she looked completely adorable with a crew cut and slicked-back fringe. The hairdresser gave us a lesson about how to re-create the look at home, and we bought some wax and gel and went home happy—or at least, Hester was 100 percent happy, Milla grumpy until I bought her a pirate comic, and I felt as though I'd dealt with the situation fairly well but that the situation itself was worrisome.

Their bears had had more than a haircut; the girls' room was a soft-toy abattoir. Some had been decapitated, some were amputees, anything they'd been holding—pink hearts, velvet rainbows—cut off and cast aside. Winnie-the-Pooh and Piglet looked the most beaten up: Piglet's ears had been severed, Pooh had lost his jar of honey, his red jumper hacked to pieces.

We spent most of the rest of that weekend putting the bears back together: Milla and Hester restuffed bodies, heads, and limbs and I stitched, although not very well—you could see the joins and things were a bit wonky. On Sunday afternoon we lined them up to review our work: terrible. The bears had gone from being round and gleaming to a bunch of down-and-out misfits.

"They look older," said Milla.

"They look ugly," said Hester.

"They look like Peter and Ronnie," I said. Hearing me mention men's names, the girls growled, so I added, "People I know from work. Well, near work."

Winnie-the-Pooh slipped over onto the floor. He was wearing a pink knitted cardigan belonging to another of their dolls, his cheeks were sunken, his famous and familiar potbelly visibly reduced. Almost a different bear. Hester picked him up.

"They're still cute though," she said, cuddling him.

For once, I wished my mother was there; she hated cooking but she'd have sewn the bears back together beautifully—I remember her darning the holes in the heels and toes of our socks and in the fingers of our gloves, something she'd learned from her mother. The world was different then; mending was an art. Nowadays, things are cheap. And not just that; women's place was different too—my mother's generation mended everything, saved everything, but I didn't properly learn domesticity because it was expected that I would go out into the world and work alongside the men, and my mother pushed me hard in that direction. I'd resented that, but now I was beginning to understand why; it's easier to be independent if you have your own money.

*

We decided to bake a cake. I looked up a recipe, we mixed the batter, and afterward the girls fought over who licked the bowl and who licked the spoon. While it was in the oven, they went upstairs to set up the teddy bears' picnic. I followed the instructions faithfully; checked the cake after thirty minutes as the recipe said. It had risen beautifully and smelled heavenly, but when I turned it out of the tin, a circle about the size of a ten-pence piece dropped from the middle in a splodge. I maneuvered the hot cake back into the hot tin, swearing, and burned my fingers on the molten cake lava as I put it back in. When I took it out a second time the sponge was golden and springy to the touch, cooked all the way through, but there was this small, puckered hole in the middle.

I slumped down into a chair feeling deflated: the cake was ruined; the children needed psychiatric help; I was a failure.

I called the girls, expecting them to be cross about the cake, or upset, or both, but in fact they were delighted. "It looks like a bum-hole!"

46

I began, slowly, to regain some weight, which everybody said was a good thing—except perhaps Jo. Consultation with Paul McKenna was vital. I went into the bookshop under cover of collecting another book and found him. His last Golden Rule: *Stop When You've Had Enough.*

Ben came over. I shoved Paul McKenna back on the shelf.

"Your book came in. We tried to call you, but the number didn't work," said Ben.

I checked the number; it was spectacularly wrong. I'd given that number in January when I ordered *Raising Happy Children.* I marveled at my state of mind back then and wrote down my real phone number. Ben said, "I was going to leave it one more day and come and knock on your door." I wasn't sure if this indicated compassion or attraction on his part, or neither, or both, but I wished fervently that I had waited one more day for that last Golden Rule.

One of the trashier self-help books stashed under my bed recommended the therapeutic value of revenge. Lady Sarah Graham-Moon's iconic acts were described in gleeful detail. At 3:00 one morning she poured five liters of white gloss paint over her husband's BMW, which was parked in the driveway of his mistress, cut off one sleeve of each of his thirty-two bespoke Savile Row suits, and distributed the contents of his wine cellar all around the village so that when they woke up in the morning, neighbors found £300 bottles of Chablis, Montrachet, and Château Latour next to their daily milk delivery. Lady Graham-Moon is often held up as an extreme example, but to my mind she simply did in one night what took me months and months; pinnacles of rage, depths of despair. Some nights I teetered and pulled back, other nights I reeled off and fell, flailing.

But at 6:00 a.m. I had to get ready for work and wake the children and get them dressed and breakfasted in time for school. My responsibilities meant that I couldn't allow myself to lose it completely, but the situation was precarious—these duties held me, not the other way around.

There were other tales: one wife, discovering her husband's affair while he was in Rome with the other woman, used his credit card to buy a new dress and heels and went to greet them at the airport. She looked so fantastically, glamorously expensive that the paparazzi mistook her for a celebrity and the whole thing ended up in *News of the World*. In another, more quotidian example, a woman said that she had made herself feel better by snipping off every single button from all her husband's shirts and jackets and placing them in a Tupperware box for him to sew back on himself.

I'd already damaged Adam's Ducati—not very badly, it turned out—and I didn't want to do it again, but a lot of his things were still around. In a recent row, I'd asked him to take them, but he pointed out that he still owned half of the house. I went upstairs with a pair of scissors and opened the wardrobe where his suits and jackets were hanging. I started on his blue corduroy jacket. I used to like him in that jacket. I cut off the four buttons from each sleeve and realized I was bored. This was not going to make me feel better. I put the eight buttons inside the jacket pocket. I felt really tired. *Stop when you've had enough.*

I had several more books on dejunking by now: *The Life Laundry, Dejunk Your Life, The Secrets to Decluttering.* Dejunking, the books promised, would get it all out of my system, renew my energy and zest for life, and make our home a nicer place to be. I threw away everything that wasn't useful or beautiful and many more things besides. In the evenings after I'd brought them home from Noreen's, the girls practiced forward rolls across the carpet in the empty sitting room. The kitchen felt empty too without Charlie circling his basket, lowering down with a sigh. There began to be fewer places for the night terrors to hide in, but still they came, 3:00 a.m. to 6:00 a.m., night after night, the same three-hour slot; a relentless schedule. But I needed those dark windows. Sifting through my life, I gradually began to reshape it. Bit by bit I discovered that I hadn't, in fact, shattered or dissolved, and I wasn't going to.

47

June. Birthday season arrived in our household: Hester was turning five. At her party, she came away crying from the games to find me: "Daddy's chasing everyone else more than me." I could have said the same, I thought as I comforted her, and later told Adam exactly this.

"We're not going to have an argument at the birthday party, are we?" he said.

"We don't have to argue, you could just agree with me because it's true—you did chase everyone else more than me."

He sighed, weary. I walked away. But at the end of the party when the other five-year-olds had gone home and we'd disposed of all the dead balloons and wrapping paper, swept up the broken crisps and cake crumbs and half-eaten sticks of cucumber, wiped puddles of Ribena off the floor and put away the bunting, Adam stayed because Hester wanted him to put them to bed. He bathed them and read a bedtime story and kissed them good night and then he left, went back to his bedsit. The girls got up to wave him goodbye at the door. They were upset after he'd gone, so I read them another story and tucked them up again. Six months in, none of us had got used to the situation—every time he left the house it felt as though our fourth limb had been amputated.

"Did you have a nice birthday?" I asked Hester before she went to sleep.

"Kind of," she said, but she looked sad.

"Will you and Daddy get back together?" asked Milla.

"I don't know, sweetheart, I really don't know."

"I hope you do," said Milla.

"I liked it better when our family was together," said Hester.

I went into the bookshop to buy her another *Jewel Fairies* book to make up for the dismal party.

"Do you still have the *Jewel Fairies* series?" I asked Ben.

He took me to the children's section, knelt down by the bottom shelf.

"Do you know which you want?"

"No, but this one looks fine," I said, and pulled out a green book about the Emerald fairy.

"Hang on," Ben said. "That cover's bent." He went through the line of thin, jewel-colored spines. His dark blue T-shirt was the same color as his Levi's. I noticed his vintage watch and unwashed hair, which for some reason made him even more attractive.

"How about this one?" He held out *India the Moonstone Fairy*. On the cover was a fairy dressed in gauzy white fabric wearing sparkly sandals, and moonstone is one of the birthstones for June.

Perfect.

Milla was turning seven. Her birthday was also a disaster. Perhaps because of Hester's party she decided not to have one; said she'd prefer a treat with each of her parents, separately. Adam took her to Madame Tussauds, where the waxworks freaked her out—"They look like dead people standing up." I took her to the London Aquarium and I don't know whether it was an optical illusion created by the incredibly thick, curved glass on the shark tank, or whether my coordination was addled from lack of sleep, or both, but when I swooped down to see what she was looking at I whacked my forehead really, really hard and swore.

"Don't say 'Fuck' in the Aquarium, Mummy!" whispered Milla loudly. Other families turned to stare, and Milla was so mortified that she marched six feet ahead of me, bony shoulders hunched up high, for the rest of the way round, which had the one advantage that she then couldn't see me trying not to cry.

Afterward I took her out for a gourmet burger, fries, and thick malted milkshake to make up for it. We arrived at the diner at the same time as a man with round spectacles and curly auburn hair who held the door open and came in behind us. The waitress picked up three menus and tried to seat us all at the same table.

"Oh, we're not together!" I exclaimed.

The waitress apologized and the man smiled and said quietly, "Shame." I felt myself blushing.

"Who was that, Mummy?" asked Milla, peering round.

48

By July, only three ideas had been submitted to the Ideas Derby. One was mine, one was for something the company was already doing, and the other was a toothless suggestion from someone on Don's team. Trish hadn't been keen on the project to begin with and at this point she lost interest entirely.

I paid a visit to the IT department, bearing gifts: a packet of ginger biscuits and some Yorkshire Gold tea bags—the stuff they provided in-house was so bland. Tea is supposed to help you to stand up, but if it's going to do that it has to be strong.

"After all the hard work you guys have already put in, not to mention Sam's hard work on the branding"—mentioning Sam was tactical; the IT guys *love* Sam—"I thought we could give it one more shot. I know it's probably really hard and complicated, and I know you guys are snowed under with work, so I really appreciate this. I just want to see if it can work."

"What do you want me to do?" said Tyler.

"Make it anonymous."

Tyler laughed. "That is so ridiculously easy," he said. "I could do it in the time it takes to make a cup of tea."

"Deal," I said, picking up his mug.

49

Every morning when I dropped off the girls, Noreen fed me compliments: "Doesn't Mummy look lovely today?" Or: "Goodness me, you're doing *so* well, Kate." Or: "You're very, very good at your job." She was good for the girls—cuddly and uncritical, always soothing—and she was good for me in exactly the same ways. She gave me more smiles and hugs than I can remember from all of my childhood. Day after day, Noreen steadily provided encouragement and solace. I'd known it would be like this. Right from the moment I sat in her kitchen and told her everything that had happened, I had a sense that I would get from Noreen what my own mother had never been able to give—warmth and a hug and a "Well done, Kate."

On the Tube one morning, my attention was caught by a passenger moving exceptionally slowly, a bunch of keys swinging from a blue lanyard round his neck. He emanated vulnerability. I couldn't help thinking he shouldn't have been out alone, and then I saw that the lanyard had *King's College Hospital* written on it, and that he wasn't in fact alone; there was a small group traveling together: two carers, three patients. One of the patients sat down next to me. She must have been in her fifties, very short, dressed in cherry red, and she had deep wrinkles running from her eyes. She too wore a blue hospital lanyard round her neck, also with keys, though not as many as the slow-moving man. She introduced herself as Angela, and asked my name, which I told her.

"You know my name, I know your name," she said, and rested her head on my shoulder. The smell of hospital corridors came off her mouse-brown hair. Some of the other passengers in the carriage stared; Angela had contravened commuter law by invading my personal space, but she made herself comfortable so quickly that in fact I felt vaguely honored that she'd chosen me. We sat in perfect harmony for three stops before her carer gently roused her. Before she got off, Angela leaned over and kissed my cheek.

"Goodbye, Angela, it was lovely to meet you," I said.

"I'd like to know you more, Kate," she replied. We waved goodbye through the window. The train hadn't even left the station when a man opposite leaned forward to speak to me.

"Looks like you made a new friend there," he said. Little did I know that I was about to make another: Alastair, for that was his name, lived in a village an hour and a half away from London, which turned out to be a very good thing, though perhaps not for the village. He was what magazines call a "silver fox"; one of those guys who get better-looking as they age. Within two stops he was sitting next to me, and after another two he had told me he was married and that his wife didn't understand him. Specifically what she didn't understand, or like, were his affairs, the first of which was with his secretary thirty years ago. This, he confided, was a beautiful affair, lasted six years, and would have lasted longer if the boss of the company hadn't found out and sacked him. His wife hadn't discovered the secretary but she knew about the ones after, including his current lover, a German girl twenty-four years his junior whom he met at a conference and was considering leaving his wife for, though the wife didn't know that.

Alastair asked if I would consider having lunch with him.

"So you want to make your life a bit more complicated by asking me out for lunch?" I said.

"Alastair's got a big appetite," said Alastair. "He loves women, absolutely adores them. But you're right, he's in a bit of a quandary about Heike and Marjorie . . ."

"Oh, my God," I said.

"What?" said Alastair, gold implant winking in one corner of a well-practiced and self-consciously gorgeous smile. It was bad enough that he was married, worse that he seemed to think he could recruit me as another lover, and even worse that he spoke about himself in the third person.

"This is my stop," I said, and fled.

I hailed a cab to the office. Never had the bland and sterile open-plan floor seemed safer. "Creep, creep, creep, creep, creep!" I muttered as I walked to my desk.

50

Peter set up a record player and two old speakers outside his shop and played an LP of Greek folk songs. He swayed and sashayed to the music, whiskey tumbler in hand. That day he was displaying an array of secondhand towels, basins, a couple of orthopedic shoes, and some crutches.

"Only used once, darling. NHS, they are. An old nurse gave them to me, the hospital doesn't need them anymore."

Beside them were some huge, rusty iron keys. I picked one up, just to feel the weight in my hand, and it was heavy.

"You want the keys to my castle, darling?" cackled Peter, rolling a cigarette.

"He's only messing, sweetheart—take no notice," said Ronnie.

"Take it! I give it to you!" said Peter, drunker than usual.

"WHISKEY," cried Toto, from his cage.

"Oh, my goodness—he's talking!" I said.

Ronnie shook his head. "Piped up about a week ago, sweetheart. Now we can't shut him up. We thought it was a silent parrot, but it opened its mouth—I mean beak—and you should have heard what it came out with—it was effin' this and effin' that and you effin' bastards, and that was just the start of it."

"WHISKEYFAGS," called Toto, remarkably clearly.

"Wow," I said, "that's amazing. I've never heard a parrot talk before. You didn't teach him to smoke, did you?" I said.

"No, darling, no—I would never do a thing like that," said Peter, lighting his fag.

"WHISKEYWHISKEYWHISKEYFAGSFAGSFAGS," shrieked Toto.

"Oh, my God, he's off on one," said Ronnie.

"YOUFUCKINGWAAANKERRR," shouted Toto.

"Blanket, Ronnie. Quick!" said Peter. Ronnie rummaged in one of the saggy cardboard boxes under the trestle table, pulled out an old gray blanket, and threw it over Toto's cage.

"Get him inside, Peter!" said Ronnie.

"I'm going, I'm going," said Peter, lifting the cage and shuffling into the shop. Ronnie shut the door behind him.

"FUCKINGASSHOLEBASTARDCAAAANT," came Toto's shriek from inside the shop.

"That's really loud," I said.

"It's a terrible parrot, his language is. We don't know what to do with him," said Ronnie. He changed the record, turned the volume up. "*Is that all there is?*" sang a gorgeous female voice. Ronnie crooned along.

"I love Peggy Lee, darling, don't you?" Ronnie said. As I walked down the alley, I could hear the mellifluous voice echoing after me. "*Is that all there is . . . ?*"

51

By September, the general feeling in head office seemed to be that the company had gone to the dogs, and that they had discovered that dogs can't run a company.

"We"—Trish paused after the majestic plural—"have reason to believe things are getting worse and we don't know why. That's a worry."

"We need to increase the margin," said Don. "And we need to do it fast."

"More upselling, that's one thing we should do," said Trish. "Induce people to spend more. When a guest asks for a coffee the waitress should say, 'The special?' because it's more expensive than bog-standard house coffee, and when a guest orders vodka the barman should reply, 'Absolut? A double?' because branded goods yield more profit than the no-name equivalent."

Simple enough in theory, but I had seen upselling in one of the London hotels and it worried me. A family of five came into the lobby just after 9:00 a.m. The father asked, "Do you have a room?" The receptionist and I looked at the screen and we both saw that, yes, there was a family room available.

"No, but let me see what I can do," said the receptionist, whose name was Karolina. "And in the meantime, why don't you go and have breakfast—I can give you a discount voucher." She gave them five vouchers and pointed them in the direction of the restaurant. The family thanked her and obediently trotted off. Karolina entered her commission on the breakfasts she'd just sold in the daily log. Twenty minutes later, while the family was sitting at their bacon and eggs, she went to tell them she had found a room.

"A perfect example of upselling," said Trish.

"But she lied!" I said.

"Look. The family wanted a room—they got a room," said Trish.

"But she could have given them the room straightaway. Instead, she sold them five breakfasts for fifty pounds, which she earned commission on!"

"Smart girl," said Trish.

"Five cooked breakfasts for fifty pounds is a good deal for London," said Don.

"That's not the point—" I started, but Gérard came in.

"I think Kate's just saying that this particular individual may have got it wrong."

"Perhaps, but we can't go on with these holes in our pockets," said Don.

In the lift, Gérard said, "I told you, they've drunk the company Kool-Aid."

Trish wanted to reduce the workforce—in numbers and also by making them less of a force. Inevitably, a company-wide reorganization was announced, but Trish also wanted to introduce Branded Behavior.

She'd just come back from Chicago, where they were setting up a Hotel Village—an "innovation" that she and Don came up with, though I didn't see what was so innovative; it was just four hotels within three blocks of each other—but anyway, Trish told us about something that had happened in Chicago. She was looking for the Magnificent Mile, where she'd parked her hire car, and as she was walking past the back of the Ritz-Carlton two chefs were outside smoking on their break, so she asked them if they knew where it was.

"Yes, ma'am, we'll walk you there," said the first chef.

"That's OK—just point me in the right direction," replied Trish.

"Oh, no, ma'am, we're Ritz-Carlton—we don't point, we walk you there."

"But I'm not even staying here," said Trish.

"It doesn't matter," said the second chef.

"So you see, it *is* possible," said Trish. "Those guys were on their *break*, for goodness' sake! They had no idea who I was, I wasn't even a guest in their hotel, but they walked me to my car because they were Ritz-Carlton!"

I preferred to think that the Ritz-Carlton chefs acted that way because they saw it as the right thing to do, because they were true hoteliers. The whole history of the hospitality industry is about providing care for strangers as they pass through. It is the host's duty to honor their guests no matter what time of night they arrive, no matter how muddy and wet, how exhausted their horses, how broken their carriage. Hospitality is about giving and providing, it's about taking care of someone; it has something to do with love, maybe only the outer reaches, but still.

And so they introduced rules that described how staff should behave. New Brand Standards for Behavior instructed hotel staff to speak only when spoken to, never to initiate eye contact, to incline the head as a mark of respect. They described not people but droids. The assault on individuality didn't end there. Admittedly, it was a mistake to tell Trish about my savage dejunking, because she latched on to the idea.

"I've already dejunked the staff—I expect that's the best place to start?"

She decreed that we were no longer to have any clutter or personal detritus on our desks, and when we didn't take enough notice of this she introduced an obligatory system of hot-desking.

Now that we weren't allowed to sit in the same spot for two days running, nobody knew where to find anybody else. All the enjoyable aspects of being in an office disappeared; conversations and banter were replaced entircly with emails as people traipsed about with huge bags, a vacancy behind their eyes, their own agency gradually being eroded.

Gérard refused to give up his wooden fruit bowl and the silver-framed photograph of him and his cousin, carried them faithfully in a bulging briefcase and set them out in each day's new location. But after a couple of weeks he switched to Tupperware and a light Perspex frame. In the diaspora, I sometimes saw Sam with her wish-board under her arm.

"I need to have it in sight all the time or it won't come true."

It became harder to tell your whereabouts, because without personal touches to go by—family photographs, Gérard's fruit bowl, Sam's wish-board, postcards, snow globes, and teddy bears—the office became a nightmare of white ceilings, glass walls, thin beige carpets, watercooler and coffee machine in exactly the same position on every floor, the same temperature everywhere.

Working off Trish's latest obsessions, I saw a chance for something I'd wanted to do ever since I'd visited the Belgravia Palazzio.

"I've dejunked that old ballroom," I told her. "Raised ten thousand pounds by selling the minibars, and I've found a community project that wants to come in and replace the parquet flooring, restore the wood paneling, fix up the chandeliers, and retouch the paintwork. The hotel really wants to upsell. They want to introduce ballroom-dancing evenings and host wedding parties, as they used to, and they only need another thirty grand, which is such a small amount compared to what we've spent on the brand refresh that I told them I was sure it would be fine with you. Is it?"

"Oh!" said Trish. "I suppose so."

52

"I've been asked out four times," I told Adam. I was counting Henri the Ostend lawyer, Abs—aka Mr. Sainsbury's—Alastair the silver fox, and Ronnie the old-age pensioner.

"Have you?" said Adam.

"You don't need to sound quite so surprised," I said, offended. I didn't mention my ongoing emergency crush on Ben, though I was still a regular visitor at the bookshop. I went in to buy *The Lost Rivers of London*. The title was already a revelation; I thought there was only one. Once part of the capital's daily life, many of these rivers still flowed underground; they hadn't petered out completely.

I couldn't find it on the shelf, so I asked Ben. While he was at the front of the shop he picked out another book to show me.

"Look at this—beautiful, isn't it? It's about wood." That made me smile, but there was no innuendo intended, I am sure. He handed me the book, a large white hardback with simple woodcuts of trees on the front, very high quality and tastefully done. Since things were going well, I also ordered *Love's Work*, a book of philosophy. I had already read it but it belonged to Yvette. I wanted my own copy, and besides, I thought it would make me look poetic and philosophical.

"It's out of print, I'm afraid. We can't get it, but you might get it on Amazon or from a bigger bookshop."

I blushed at the mention of Amazon, as though I'd been caught out. I bought *The Lost Rivers of London* and ordered *The Principles of Uncertainty* in order to demonstrate my loyalty.

My mother came. I had been putting her off, but Noreen encouraged me to welcome her so I did. The visit started badly.

"Where *is* everything?" she said, alarmed by the echo and the spaces where furniture, crockery, clothes had been.

"I've been having a clear-out," I said lightly, as if it were nothing. I had taken the day off work, regretted it already.

"But, Kate, the house is practically empty!"

"I know," I said. "Good, isn't it?"

"No," she said. "It's out of hand. I should have come before, but you keep saying you're OK. Clearly you're not."

"The house was so full of stuff, though," I said. "Adam was such a hoarder."

"So now you're getting rid of everything that reminds you of him, I suppose? What about the children?" she said. "Are you going to throw them away too?"

On the first night of her visit I had a conference call, which I took in the bedroom with the door closed, but I soon heard shouting and crying and doors slamming downstairs.

"Is someone in a market or a gym or something? There's a lot of noise in the background," complained Trish. I finished the call with a pillow wedged between the wall and my head to muffle the sounds of my household. When it was over I went downstairs to see what was going on and found my mother stormy and upright on a kitchen chair and the girls sitting cross-legged on the sitting-room floor, watching an episode of *Diego and Rosita*.

"What happened?" I asked the girls.

"Grandma snatched the remote out of Milla's hand," said Hester, not taking her eyes from the screen.

"What happened?" I asked my mother.

"They were fighting over the TV and when I tried to sort it out they wouldn't give me the remote. They're very disturbed, Kate."

"No, they're not! Well, maybe they are, but . . ."

"I've never been very good with small children," said my mother quietly.

The following night was a Wednesday and Adam had the girls, as usual.

"Let's get a takeaway," suggested Mum, even though the fridge was full of vegetables waiting to be cooked. "They'll wait another day. Make a big soup tomorrow. Come on, let's have a night off."

We sat waiting for Chinese food to arrive. My mother drummed her fingers on the table. The kitchen seemed too bright and too empty. It wasn't that there was nothing to say but that we couldn't seem to find a way to start saying it. I lit candles, opened some wine, turned off the bright lights. We talked about my brother and his family and their life in Boston; we talked about my dad's retirement; we talked about her school; we talked about Adam's new job; we talked about my job.

"Would you like me to come and look after the children, sometimes, when you go away?" she said.

"Thanks, but I've already set it up with Noreen and Adam."

I thought she looked a bit crestfallen, but the doorbell rang just at that moment.

With Mum staying I couldn't do my usual night rounds—she was a very light sleeper—so I leafed through *The Lost Rivers of London* and soon fell in love with the whole idea of these rivers, hidden underground like buried treasure. The Falcon and Fleet, the Tyburn, Ravensbourne and Westbourne, the rivers Effra and Peck, Stamford Brook, Walbrook, Wandle: I wanted to see these rivers with lyrical and faintly exotic names. The Effra apparently flowed somewhere underneath our house, and I wanted to tell the girls about that and about all of the other rivers and brooks and streams—especially the ones that sounded like pirates: Beverley Brook, Black Ditch, Parr's Ditch, Counter's Creek, the Neckinger.

A foldaway map showed all the lost rivers and how they connected with each other, and with the Thames or other overground rivers. I looked at all the places I habitually went in London; there were rivers under all of them.

That night I dreamed that I dropped jewels into drains that led not to sewers but to underground rivers with fabulous names: Wintersbourne, Sittingbourne, Snowdrop, and Flight.

53

Adam texted to ask if I would like to go out for a meal for my birthday. I told him I already had plans, and then hurriedly made some. I planned a dinner. My mother was still staying so I included her and invited Jo, Yvette, Gérard, David, and Edward. Edward didn't come.

"He's out with the younger man," said David, glum.

"Bastard," said Jo.

"You can't say that. He's not, actually. He's just in love with someone else," said David.

As he said it I realized I felt the same way—Adam had acted atrociously, but it hurt Milla and Hester to hear him condemned, and it wasn't just for their sakes that I refrained. I didn't yet want to go out for dinner with him, but I'd loved Adam enough to marry him; he was the father of my children and that still counted for something.

My mother, who had been sitting quietly, sipping her wine—rather quickly, I'd noticed—piped up: "Kate's father had an affair, years ago, and when it all came out I was angry with him—extremely, and hurt, of course—called him a few names myself, but it felt wrong. He was the father of my children, after all. Do you see what I mean?"

"I was just thinking *exactly* the same thing, Mum!" I said. "And you know what, it was brilliant that you never slagged him off. That would have been awful for me and Greg."

"Well, it's good to know I got one thing right," said Mum.

"You got more than one thing right," I said, and gave her a hug. She reciprocated by patting me with a flat hand.

"Oh, Mum," I said. A hard pat was the best she could do. I'd been so critical of her for so long that I'd lost sight of the fact that she'd struggled with the same overwhelming situation that I was now facing. She'd done her best. "You did really well," I told her, and this time she hugged me stiffly back.

"So are you, darling," she said.

"You need a bit of practice at hugging, though," I said, which made her cry a little.

Someone changed the subject to a topic safer than good mothers and unfaithful lovers. There was talk about finding a good dentist. "The most important thing is how he treats you," said Gérard. "Actually, that's not just for dentists, that's for lovers too," he added, and the conversation came back around.

After dinner, Yvette brought out a birthday cake.

"Bother. I should have thought of that," said Mum.

"It's OK, Mum. I'm thirty-nine now, you don't have to do cakes anymore."

When they sang "Happy Birthday" there was an echo in the kitchen. I felt self-conscious about the house being so empty and said so.

"You can borrow my piano, if you like," said Gérard. "I'm going to leave PHC. Things are getting worse there and I'm not enjoying it. I've always wanted to go to Australia, so I'm going."

"Oh, no! I won't survive without you," I said.

"Oh, wow!" said David. "I'm always so impressed

when people change their lives. Good for you, Gérard. I wish I could do something dramatic like that."

"You can," Gérard replied to David. "You will," he said to me.

Later, when they'd all gone home, Mum and I finished the wine and talked some more. I asked her how she forgave my father.

"I don't know really—it took a while, but eventually I understood his side of it. When I found out, he told me everything. He answered every single question I had—and I had many, as you can probably imagine. We sat at the kitchen table for hours—it was horrible, but necessary. I could see it pained him to tell me details, to admit the ways in which he'd lied, but he did because that's what I needed—to hear all of it; the whole truth. Eventually, we became friends again."

When she said that I felt sad, and scared—her way back couldn't be mine because it had never been like that with me and Adam. I hadn't married my friend; I'd married my lover.

54

Peter put a sign up outside his shop: EVERYTHING MUST GO.

"Where are you going?" I asked. "Are you retiring?"

"No, darling—it's not true, it's just to get the punters in."

"Oh, I see. Is it working?"

Peter shrugged. "Not really."

When Gérard handed in his notice, Trish had security escort him to the door. Sam and I managed to locate his Perspex-framed photograph, which I now knew wasn't of him and his cousin but of him and his partner who'd died.

Consultants from PricewaterhouseCoopers worked out an algorithm that told us how many times and in how many places and how many sizes we should place the brand so that it entered the guests' subconscious. They told us that a couple of the brands were tired. Don and Trish decided that the hotels needed a makeover, and at *huge* expense Pallazio hotels were given a youthful upbeat feel by adding accents of key-lime green and bubblegum pink to the decor. It was similarly decided to position the newly acquired Ambassade chain as a high-end choice and to refresh the brand through a new logo with curlicue lettering and a color scheme of burgundy and gold, the same colors as a European passport.

The plans sounded fine on paper but there were problems and the main one was that the Ambassade hotels weren't living up to their current five stars, never mind the new six-star standards Trish set them. The Ambassade Central Park West in New York was the biggest concern. Regularly slated on TripAdvisor, this one hotel risked the reputation of the whole estate.

Trish announced a Guest Experience conference to be held in the New Year, mainly for the brand and marketing teams, but HR and legal were also to be invited—she and Don had put the targets up again; they needed enforcers. The conference would be held at the Ambassade Central Park West.

"We need to check up on that hotel anyway—we can kill two birds with one stone," said Trish.

Don and Trish persisted in making poor business decisions. They formulated a plan to buy disused hospitals and turn them into hotels, starting with the former tuberculosis hospital in Johannesburg known as "The Hamlet"—TB or not TB—an abandoned hospital in Beirut and a derelict sanatorium in Lima, Ohio. This, it was felt, was a very bad idea: making a hotel out of an old monastery where guests imbibe some of the peacefulness ingrained in the building is one thing, but hotel guests sleeping in the same place as people who couldn't breathe, where patients lay sick and dying, is quite another. But Don and Trish didn't care about that; they just wanted bodies in beds.

55

The Lost Rivers of London told me that part of my daily commute followed the course of the Fleet, the largest and most important of the forgotten rivers. When I traveled that section I thought of the Fleet: trampled on and ignored until it shrank almost out of existence.

One day I sat next to a girl and her grandmother on the Tube. The girl, who can't have been more than five years old, knelt up on the carpeted seat next to me and tapped her finger against the window, saying, "No, you can't. No, you can't. No, you can't," to her own reflection, over and over again. I was quite disturbed by this; her grandmother didn't appear to notice. The girl kept looking at me, perhaps because she knew she had won my attention. After a few minutes of this, I looked her straight in the eye and said, "Yes, you can." She started to cry and I realized I had been a little too vehement. The grandmother glared at me so I got off at the next stop.

Being kicked out of the office without having to serve his notice meant Gérard could fly to Australia sooner than expected, which he did, and another thing that was unexpected was that David flew with him—I knew David had taken Gérard's number at my birthday meal but I hadn't known they'd started seeing each other until they announced their departure date. Every so often they sent Snapchats— Sydney Opera House, Melbourne, Adelaide—but I didn't see the sights, all I saw was their burgeoning romance and I wished I had one.

Getting Gérard's piano proved more complicated than I could have imagined. I used a local firm, recommended by the nice woman in the bookshop, and had a series of conversations with the owner, Stephan, who asked questions about the size of the piano, door widths, how many steps up to the front door, access through windows. The phone calls were always in the evening, since I couldn't easily call from work anymore, and I could hear domestic noises churning in the background—a washing machine spinning, a television, a child playing. Stephan was very patient—I hardly ever knew the answers and had to wait for Gérard's replies from Western Australia.

When all the details were collected, Stephan said, "This isn't very straightforward, I'm afraid. To get a piano that size out of that flat we'll have to use the window or take the doors off, but either way it's going to take four men, and since the flat is in Kilburn that's going to be expensive. I've had a better idea—I have a piano in storage just down the road, you can have that. You'll have to pay delivery but that'll only be about thirty quid and I'll give you the piano."

"You'll *give* me the piano?"

"Yes, why not? It's just sitting there."

I emailed Gérard to say I didn't need his piano anymore and received two replies.

Gérard: *Ask to see his piano before you accept.*

David: *A man is giving you a piano and you haven't even met? Very romantic.*

56

I took the girls to Spain for the last week of the school summer holiday. Milla decided she didn't want a tan and applied sunblock meticulously to every centimeter of her skinny seven-year-old body, whereas Hester writhed to get away from it.

On the beach, Hester bounded up with a perfectly round, brown stone.

"Look, Mummy, I found a stone like a burger—it's the same size and it has those kind of lines on it that burgers have."

"Flame-grilled," I said.

"What?"

"It's what they do to burgers that make those lines."

"I'm going to give it to Dad to keep on his desk."

"As a paperweight?"

"No, just as a burger."

One morning I was drinking coffee on the balcony outside our room, enjoying the sun on my face. Hester came to keep me company.

"Mum, have you got your booby-tucker on?"

"Not yet, I'm still in my pajamas. I'll get dressed soon."

"Can I see your boobies?" She pulled open my pajama top and peered down.

"Where are they? Where are they? I can't see them!"

"They're in there somewhere," I said. She looked again.

"Oh, yeah! Mine are even tinier," she said, lifting up her T-shirt. I hugged her.

"Mummy, I love you more than this bench."

After a week in the sun, my shoulders were like brown speckled eggs. When we got back home, Adam came to collect the girls.

"All your freckles have come out," he said.

"I think they're age spots," I said. It had been years since I'd tanned.

"No, they're not, they're freckles. You've always been freckly—like your mum."

You've always been freckly: just a little comment, but it pierced. All the sadness came rushing in. He knew my skin. He knew my body. He'd been there when I gave birth, seen things about how my body worked that even I hadn't; knew its quirks and imperfections, how I felt about my own lumpy bits; knew me, intimately. And he did it anyway. Hester came down the stairs with the burger-stone, which allowed me to escape to the kitchen to stop up my tears and drink some water to wash over the question lodged in my throat. When was it, how was it, that I became so unprecious?

57

I read *The Lost Rivers of London* as if it were a guide to the lost rivers of my life, and in a sense it was. I had favorites. There was the Ravensbourne, rising at a well in Keston, flowing through Bromley, Lewisham, and Greenwich, joined by several tributaries, among which was the Quaggy; and the Falcon, which burst out of the pavement in a street in Clapham Junction during national floods—the road is named after it. I felt sorry when I read the fate of Stamford Brook, once the confluence of three smaller streams, covered by 1900, now a sewer; and poor Peck, springing in East Dulwich, running through Peckham, enclosed in 1823. Enclosed, covered, diverted, polluted; how could a city do that to its rivers? Yet there was hope: a campaign to unearth the Effra; commuters sometimes see Counter's Creek from the westbound platform of West Brompton Tube station; and the Peck still flows, much diminished, on the west side of Peckham Rye Park.

One weekend in September, with nothing much else to do, I packed a lunch and kitted out the girls in wellington boots to go river-spotting. It had been raining heavily for two days; conditions were perfect.

In retrospect, it was bound to fail: I had spoken about the rivers as if they were tigers or snow leopards or some other endangered species, so when I knelt down at a grating to hear the flow of the Fleet the girls were not impressed, and when I stopped in the middle of Charterhouse Street to peer down a grid where we could actually see water, they protested loudly.

"Mummy, we're *children*—we shouldn't be stopping in the middle of a road, we might get run over!" said Hester.

"We aren't even on a crossing!" said Milla. "Bad parenting, Mum."

"This is the most boring trip you've ever taken us on," Hester said, and she was right. I thought it would be like a special day out I had with Adam, years ago, when we crossed all the bridges over the Thames in one day on the Ducati. It doesn't sound very exciting, but we were close then; everything was fun.

To make up for the most boring outing ever I bought the girls two bags of crisps and a bottle of apple juice each. They tried to negotiate an upgrade to Coca-Cola and a third bag, but you've got to draw the line somewhere.

On the way home, they sat apart from me on the Tube, trading crisp flavors, legs stuck straight out in front. I thought about the pieces of jewelry I had dropped down various grids and gratings around London and whether, after a heavy rain or at high tide, they had reached the underground rivers and been carried along to the Thames, eventually released into the sea.

When we got off the Tube, I realized there was a conspiracy.

"Mum, we really, really want another bag of crisps," said Hester.

"We think you should. We nearly got run over!" said Milla.

"We didn't, actually," I said, "but if you really, really want another bag, then OK."

"Thanks, Mum!" said Hester.

"You are actually a good parent," said Milla.

The trip ended happily after all from their point of view, but I saw, again, how difficult it was for me to hold a line. Milla's comments on my parenting made me wonder if she had been studying the child-rearing manuals that sat in squat piles under my bed along with the other self-help books, unopened except when delivered—I saw the Amazon guy at least as much as I visited the bookshop, though he was no rival to Ben. When new books arrived I flicked through them before placing them under the bed as though all of the advice and help they contained would rise up through the bed slats and mattress and get into me by osmosis. The real books, the ones from the bookshop, were stacked in a much taller pile beside my bed; I wasn't reading those either, except for *Lost Rivers*, which I didn't so much read as consume.

58

Aged forty-seven, Trish was prescribed glasses. The optician told her that after forty-five it was just a matter of time, and that's for everyone. She reported this lightly, but I could see it had wounded her—not so much having to wear glasses as being lumped in with everyone else. Perhaps Sam, in making the appointment, had neglected to mention Trish's power and influence or maybe the optician simply didn't care, but in any case, that somebody hadn't recognized her position seemed to have slightly weakened it. Her spectacles had slim designer frames of very pale tortoiseshell, a tiny gold insignia on the side. She carried them folded close to her chest, her thin wrist curling around, the glasses touching her sternum like a fan yet to be unfurled. She reminded me of Marie Antoinette, or a bird with a broken wing.

The shareholders were leaning hard on Don, breathing down his neck. They didn't give a shit about mitigating circumstances, they didn't care about the world's problems, they saw only the unbanked money, and insisted that Don did too—see it, find it, bank it.

Don grew leaner and meaner. He was first in and last out, paced the eleven floors like a man who could get no rest. A rumor started that the office was haunted, though it was most likely sightings of Don, eyes sunk deep in his skull, striding up and down the escalator at strange hours, talking to himself. The nightwatchman—Harman from Sierra Leone—and two of the office cleaners—Filipe and Ana, a Portuguese married couple who came at 5:00 every weekday morning—spoke barely any English, but they managed to communicate something to the daytime security guard—Brian from Liverpool—who passed it on to Ian the receptionist, and Ian told everyone who walked in the front door. Rumor also had it that Don had started shouting at people who weren't there.

"He sees the ghost," Sam said.

"No, no—he *is* the ghost," I said.

"What do you mean? Don's not a ghost," she said.

"I know—there is no ghost."

"But there is—Ian told me that Harman actually saw it."

"That was probably Don, though," I said.

59

When I next went down the alley, Peter was nowhere to be seen. Ronnie was astride a gleaming red mobility scooter, L-plates stuck on the front and back.

"Had a stroke, didn't I? My wife didn't think it was too clever when I fell down the stairs with it, cracked a couple of teeth out—" He grinned to show the gaps. "The old lady never called an ambulance, though, did she? Guess who she did call? Peter. He came so quick, it was like he flew there—now that's a real friend—he helped me up, he called the ambulance. She was just wailing in the background, the old girl was—useless! Now I'm on one of these things—" He slapped the side of his scooter as if it were a horse's neck. "And I've got the L-plates, see? Sixty-seven, sweetheart, and still a learner—I don't mind, I still come here every day, for the company. And the drink."

Ronnie was minding the shop because Peter was at the local police station.

"But don't worry, sweetheart, he'll be back."

Toto had been shouting profanities through the window and passersby assumed it was Peter yelling abuse.

At last I arranged to view the piano, which was stashed in a warehouse at the back of a cage alongside a quantity of sealed boxes. It was a very old, black upright with candle-holders either side of where the music sits, so you could play by candlelight. I thought it was lovely. We went in

Stephan's car. He told me about his divorce and his daughter, who lived with him because the ex-wife kept going on retreats. On the way back he asked me out for dinner, very casually, in such a way that it didn't sound like a date, just meeting up with a potential new friend, and proceeded to give me instructions about what to do with the piano when it arrived.

"Now when you first get it delivered, it's going to sound a bit tinny because it's been sitting in storage. You'll need to get it tuned—here's a number."

I booked the tuner to come the same day as the delivery, took a day off work to receive the piano, and by the time the girls were home from school it was all set up. Hester picked out "Three Blind Mice" with one finger, and Milla played "Jingle Bells," which she was learning on the recorder, and then they fought over whose turn it was.

Yvette taught the girls to play "Chopsticks," which my mother had banned in our house when we were growing up. Yvette was still visiting often, more than she ever used to. I began to wonder if we were her refuge, a bolt-hole from her own marriage, which didn't seem very happy. One weekend I took the girls to Brighton and the tension was so bad that Milla whispered, "Are Saul and Yvette going to get divorced?"

Later Yvette said, "It will get better. I just have to hang on and hope."

The girls played "Chopsticks" incessantly. They played it on the top notes, they played it on the bottom notes, they played it as a duet with both parts the same, they played it slowly, they played it fast, they played it in a combination of fast and slow, but mostly they played it very, very loudly.

" 'Piano' means soft, you know!" I shouted.

We'd been separated for nearly a year but were still in a kind of marital limbo so I told Adam that I was going to have dinner with Stephan at which news he shrugged bad-temperedly.

"Have you been seeing anyone?" I asked.

"No, not at all," he said.

"Online?"

"No, Kate—I don't do that anymore. I'm waiting for you, and you know that. I've been living like a monk."

"Monks don't have a consistent reputation throughout history," I said.

"Don't be pedantic, you know what I mean."

I needn't have worried. The dinner was fine but it was clear by the time the main course arrived that this was going to be a one-off. Points of connection were few. Perhaps because of this, Stephan drank three large glasses of red wine. Over dessert he criticized his ex-wife in detail. By coffee the conversation had moved on to the incredible usefulness of microwaves to the single parent. Nevertheless I was very grateful to Stephan for the piano despite the dreaded "Chopsticks," which I banned.

I found a piano teacher through the mums at school. Linda arrived with an armful of music and more in a bag, to find out what we wanted to play. The girls started on their favorite nursery rhymes and simplified pop songs. When it came to my lesson, I hadn't given a moment's thought to what I might like to play.

"How about one of these?" Linda said, leafing through *Modern Classic Songs for Our Time*. She stopped at a page. "How about 'Somewhere Over the Rainbow'—something you can sing along to?"

"I'm not keen on Judy Garland," I said. We settled on an easy waltz and an extremely simplified version of Bach's Siciliana in G minor, which I loved.

60

There were various legalities that still had to be ironed out to do with the Chicago Hotel Village and since she'd put it under the "innovation" banner, Trish appointed me to work on these with Branton. At his suggestion, we met for lunch at a brasserie near the office. I ordered salmon and spinach, but when our food arrived, Branton looked at mine and said, "You need chips." Without waiting for an answer, he flagged down a passing waiter.

Perhaps it's you who needs the chips, I thought.

When the basket of French fries came, he tipped the whole lot onto my plate and shook salt over them. "They're good for you," he said. Throughout lunch, he helped himself to chips from my plate. The assumed intimacy surprised me, but even more surprising was that I didn't mind.

That afternoon Branton sent a text to say he'd enjoyed lunch and the text had a kiss.

I didn't mention the chips, but I did tell Jo about the slightly awkward dinner with Stephan and the text-kiss from Branton; she told me it was time to buy new underwear and wrote down where I should go. The next day I walked into Rigby & Peller on the King's Road, supplier of brassieres to the Queen.

"Lean forward," said the sales assistant. "That's right, bend forward. You don't put the bra on; you put yourself into the bra." With two expert motions she smoothed round from my shoulder blades up into the cups.

"You mean the fat on my back can make me have bigger boobs?" I said.

"You just want everything you've got out in front." She tucked me in and tightened the straps. "There," she said. "See?"

61

I went back to the doctor to get more sleeping pills. Jo instructed me to use an upcoming flight as an excuse to get temazepam and diazepam.

"I don't know if I need them," I told her, though I still wasn't sleeping properly.

"Well, can you get them anyway? I know loads of people who want them—you're not the only one who doesn't sleep, you know. They'll pay you."

"Jo! I'm not a drug dealer!"

"OK, just give them free then," she said. "Keep what you want for yourself, obviously, and I'll take the rest."

"Don't they have doctors in Primrose Hill?" I said.

"The ones here are wise to all the tricks," said Jo. "They ask to see the flight confirmation."

The waiting room was crowded, people bent over in stained chairs wheezing, coughing, sneezing, more limping in every few minutes. If you weren't sick already, you soon would be. I'd been waiting for twenty minutes when a seat came free by the doctor's door. There was no phone signal in the surgery and I had already exhausted all of the available reading material—dog-eared magazines, months old—and wished I'd brought a book. My eyes happened upon the fire extinguisher. The instructions read, *Stand against wall, undo hooks, hold firmly, point at fire, press hard,* which for some reason made me think about sex—it had been almost a year since I'd had any. I suddenly realized I was ravenous. I left the surgery without waiting to see the doctor and went out for a second breakfast feeling jubilant: my appetites had started to come back.

They'd had a bit of a reorganization at the bookshop, changed the name of my favorite bookcase. It used to be called "Philosophy and Self-Help," but now the books were separated into two sections: "Philosophy and Psychology" and "Self-Help/Motivational." Paul McKenna was here.

I said hello to Ben and looked at the "Philosophy and Psychology" shelves: Aristotle, Plato, Jung, Freud, Nietzsche, Wittgenstein, Kierkegaard. A title by Jürgen Habermas caught my eye, *An Awareness of What Is Missing.* I ordered the books I'd come in for and bought the Habermas because the title evoked something in me, like a lyric to a long-forgotten song.

The next day, I received a phone call.

"Hello, it's Ben. From the bookshop."

"Oh! Hello!"

"Your books arrived today."

He only called about the books, I reasoned, but then again one of the others could have called, and he did, so maybe he does like me.

When I went to collect my books—*Wide Sargasso Sea, The Age of Innocence,* and *The Portrait of a Lady*—Ben said, "You read a lot, don't you?"

"Oh! I don't read them—I just put them in a pile," I said.

Ben laughed, but I wasn't joking, I really did put all my new books into a pile. It gave me pleasure to look at them and open them, but actually reading them was something I seldom got around to. This habit didn't seem at all strange to me; it didn't even seem like a habit until Ben said that. I remembered that there used to be almost nothing I liked better than to read in bed with a cup of tea. I remembered the agony of finishing a book that I was in love with. The first time this happened was when I was seven with *Ballet Shoes*. I read that book three times in a row and afterward I still didn't know who I wanted to be most—Pauline, Petrova, or Posy. It was rarer, as an adult, to find books I loved completely—but surely, I thought, looking at the three books in my hand, surely I will love at least one of these. Jean Rhys. Edith Wharton. Henry James, for goodness' sake! I put the books in my bag.

Ben had left the till and was now coming back. He was trying not to smile.

"We wanted to give you a gift, since you spend so much in here."

"Oh!"

He handed me a book. It was Paul McKenna's *I Can Make You Thin*.

"Oh, God," I said. "Rumbled."

"I noticed you looking at it quite a lot."

"How embarrassing," I said.

"Not at all, it's like flicking through *Hello!* magazine. Everybody does it. I read *Quit Smoking Today* cover to cover."

"And did you?" I asked.

"No. Well, not because of the book, anyway."

"Thanks," I said, looking down at the four titles I was holding. "I think I'll go and start reading one of them."

"You're not going to put them in a pile, then?"

"I'll read one and put the rest in the pile," I said.

"Which one are you going to read?"

"I don't know yet."

At home, I made tea and went to my pile of new books. It was like looking at treasure. I laid them out on my bed, so that I could appreciate them one by one, feeling the weight and the quality of the paper. I felt excited and a little bit frightened. Reading would be like paradise regained; how could I have forsaken it for so long? I got the self-help books out from under the bed and laid them out in the gaps. I wasn't sure what I should read first. A parenting book, perhaps? But I was getting on quite well with the kids now. Relationship book? God, no. I didn't even want to know what codependency was. There were five books on surviving infidelity, which I shoved back under the bed—I thought I was surviving pretty well. Paul McKenna? But I'd already read that in my not-so-sneaky bouts in the bookshop, and actually I was happy with my weight now. High literature, maybe? I was tempted to go for Henry James with some poetry alongside. I remembered my practice of having two or three books on the go; I'd have a main book and one or two others to dip into for different moods or weather. I decided on Henry James and Sylvia Plath, an old friend I wanted to look up again—these could make a great pair, although a bit heavy perhaps. I looked again at the books spread over the bed; lovely rectangles of varying color and size like a patchwork quilt. My eye happened upon something I'd bought on Amazon months ago, a book by Gok Wan, and I knew it had to make the trio. So here it was, my reading recipe: *The Portrait of a Lady*, *Ariel*, and *How to Look Good Naked*.

62

The Ideas Derby finally took off. I received an alert every time an idea came in, and not long after it became anonymous, I started to get three or four a day, then double, then triple. Pretty soon it was clear that it had gone in-house viral, but I didn't tell Trish because it wasn't only ideas and suggestions that were coming in, though there were plenty of those, but also an outpouring of complaints and concerns. Many in languages I couldn't understand. I tried Google Translate and when that didn't work I found people I could trust not to report; Carlo from the dry cleaner helped me with the Italian, Ana the cleaner with Portuguese, Tyler found people in IT and accounts who could read German, Spanish, Hindi, Mandarin, and Cantonese, and I could manage the French.

Many of the comments were about the way Trish and Don were ruining the company.

"They're factory farmers, not hoteliers," said one.

"The duty of the host is to make his guest feel at home; the duty of the guest is to remember that they are not," said another. "Respect on both sides, consideration on both sides." I thought that was a good description of any proper relationship, including employer–employee. But that was not the model Trish and Don used.

As the deluge continued, I began to feel like an unofficial agony aunt, or a doctor listening to a very long list of symptoms, or a priest in a digital confessional, only there were no sins. Except maybe one.

A tip-off arrived in the Ideas Derby inbox: Don and Trish had secretly instigated a time-and-motion study using CCTV to film in random hotels to see how often the workforce sat down on the job, and they were using the data to sack people or get them on zero-hours contracts. I was appalled, but not surprised. This was exactly what they'd done to Jean.

I researched the "gray area" Don had quoted. It's important to be clear and it's important to call things correctly. As far as I could tell, this practice was at best dodgy; and at worst, immoral and illegal.

I made a list of options:

1. *Do nothing*
2. *Confront them*
3. *Leave the company*
4. *Report it, then leave*
5. *Report it, and stay*

Doing nothing was the same as agreeing with Trish and Don, so I ruled that out. I'd already tried confronting them on various matters—that hadn't worked and I didn't fancy my chances issuing ultimatums. Leaving the company without taking any action was the same as doing nothing, so that was out too.

I started a job search and found out where to take it. The case officer at the Information Commissioner's Office was sympathetic, but not much help. "I'm afraid your employer is right," he said. "It is a legal gray area, and even though you and I may find the practice distasteful, companies are allowed to monitor the workforce and find ways to make them more efficient."

"Even at the expense of values?" I protested. "What about human dignity and respect?"

"I'm sorry," said the case officer. "It's just not serious enough."

63

The first Christmas was always going to be weird. I wanted to lie low, fold in on myself, acquiesce to a deep winter, but it was mild that year. We saw on the news that the hibernation of bears was disturbed. Berries were gone from the bushes but fish were not below ice so the bears got confused; some died due to lack of food and many did not sleep all winter.

Mid-December I bought a Christmas tree and dragged it home feeling incredibly male, like a lumberjack. With some difficulty, I maneuvered the tree into the stand, crawled underneath to fix it, and after much swearing crawled back out, pine needles sticking into my knees, back, and hair. The tree was tilted. We decorated it anyway.

I bought myself some perfume while Christmas shopping.

"Would you like it gift-wrapped?" asked the young shop assistant.

"No, thanks, it's for me," I answered.

"You're so lucky—treating yourself to perfume!" she said.

"If I don't, no one else will," I said, trying to sound cheery, but I couldn't keep the edge out of my voice and the other shop assistant, a woman in her mid- to late forties, flinched as if an old wound had been touched. She was wrapping perfume in pink crepe paper for another customer, a man. Her eyes found mine for a moment and she smiled. Nothing was said, but something was communicated. I wondered if something similar had happened in her life.

Next time he came round, Adam commented on the angle of the tree and said, "I'd have put that up for you. You should have asked me."

My parents came for the Christmas holidays.

"The tree's a bit wonky," said my mother when they arrived, pressing her cheek against mine. "But it still looks nice."

"I could have done that for you," said Dad.

The emergency crush on Ben had gone on too long and I needed to wean myself off. This I knew because he had mentioned his girlfriend. Just casually, in passing, but it was like having a bucket of ice water tipped over my head: I woke up extremely quickly to the fact that I'd been trailing around that bookshop for months with big eyes, perfumed, and wearing a little too much lip gloss.

I almost groaned with embarrassment right there in the shop. Instead I said, "I've been having a really weird time over the last year."

"Yeah, I thought so," said Ben, nodding.

"And I've been coming into the bookshop an awful lot," I said, feeling my face redden. This was my confession.

"It's always nice to see you," said Ben. I blushed deeper, aware that I'd seen him more as life raft than as man and now here he was being even better in real life.

"You've been very kind," I said.

And I think he knew what I meant because he said, "Not at all. I hope it all works out."

A few days before Christmas Adam called by with presents—he was going to his parents' house. He handed over a bag of brightly wrapped gifts and took something out of his jacket pocket; a small box from the fine jewelers in Soho and an envelope.

"Open it later," he said. "You don't have to wait for Christmas."

"Adam, do you know what day it is?" I said.

"Er . . . should I?" he asked, sensing he'd put his foot in something.

"It's a year ago today that I found those emails from Louise. Prince Charming, remember?"

That jolted him but he rallied quickly: "Right, well, maybe you should open it on Christmas Day then," he said, attempting a rakish smile, pulling it off completely.

On Christmas morning when the girls were playing with new toys in front of the fire, Mum watching them from the armchair with a glass of champagne, Dad in the kitchen peeling potatoes, I went up to my room and opened the pale blue envelope. The card showed a picture of two gray geese flying together across a snowy-white sky.

I love you, Adam had written inside. *I never stopped loving you and I never will.*

"But that's the problem, Adam—you didn't," I said, to the card. "You didn't love me enough not to start; you didn't love me enough to stop; and you didn't love me enough to tell me the truth afterward—I had to find it out for myself."

Inside the box was a beautiful silver bracelet—an elegant oval with a gap to slide it onto your wrist. I tried it on quite carefully because it looked delicate even though the silver was solid and wouldn't have bent easily. Adam didn't know the fate of the other pieces of jewelry he'd given me. It seemed too mean to tell him, and besides, the drain-drops were private acts, personal remedies I'd chosen to help myself. The new bracelet fitted closely, perfectly, the kind of thing I'd have chosen for myself.

64

What do you call it when you realize something bit by bit? It's an epiphany if it comes all at once in a rush, but what do you call it when you work something out over a period of time? There was no single deciding moment, no flash of realization; it was more like an archaeological dig—months and months of repetitive work, down in the dirt with a toothbrush, not sure if I would find anything and if I did, whether it would be worth it. Maybe at the beginning, or even before, I had seen a corner of something—or not seen it but other-sensed it, like a water diviner with a twitching rod. It took months and months of hard work to unearth it. But it was—worth it, I mean. Once I began to uncover this thing, I carried on the excavation, unswerving, because I knew this was it: the gold, long buried; the oasis; the lost river. It's what they were all on about—Gérard, the woman who sailed across the Atlantic, Henri ice-skating, the man who embroidered shoes high above the Hudson. Your own place, somewhere inside to think, to dream. A room of one's own but internal, as vital to life as your beating heart.

Just after Christmas it turned colder—on the day after Boxing Day the weatherman said there was a good chance of snow. In the afternoon, there were films for family viewing. "I hate this sort of thing," said my mother, and went off to another room with a box of chocolates and the crossword. I settled the girls with my dad on the sofa, one on either side of him, tucked them up with a blanket and some Quality Street, and put the box with the silver bracelet and my wedding ring into my bag.

As I walked toward the common I saw a taxi and hailed it—the Thames was more fitting than a drain for this last drop. I had the cab take me to the South Bank. It was surprisingly busy by the river. Families meandered by—bobble hats, mittens, and scooters; couples walking off Christmas dinners; dogged joggers, thighs red from the cold. I found a bench and waited for a lull. I took the box out of my pocket and looked at the silver bracelet lying in the cotton wool, the gold wedding ring nestling inside.

If you are betrayed and you really want to understand why, eventually you'll find the ways in which you betrayed yourself. I had blamed Adam for everything and that was wrong. It was true that I'd been blindsided, but it was also true that I'd seen signs and ignored them—I chose the blindness; I chose to trust him.

"It's snowing!" shouted a small boy to his mother.

I looked up; it was. Snowflakes landed in cold, light dots on my cheeks. One fell in my eye; I blinked it out and stood up—I wanted to get home as soon as possible. Last winter, before all this trouble hit, there was a heavy snowfall and the girls and I joined in a snowball fight on the common that had a life of its own—strangers hurling snow at each other, laughing, forming loose, random, changing teams, and when they went on their way, new people came and played. We stayed for ages and arrived home cold and wet, but happy.

Dropping the bracelet and my wedding ring into the river was not right; I knew what I needed to do and it wasn't this.

65

I arranged to meet Adam for a drink. It was hard to find somewhere locally that didn't have memories and associations. I felt it needed to be a new place, though now I'm not sure why. There was one pub we'd never been to, on account of it being painted neon purple and bright green on the outside; possibly a message to anyone over the age of twenty-five to stay away. Inside, the pub was fairly normal; a pool table in the middle with four young guys having a game, some slot machines, a few other drinkers. Adam put his leather jacket over the chair and went to get the drinks.

Our problems seemed so particular to us—and they were—but at the same time they were so predictable. Just like our drinks. A pint of lager for him, a glass of dry white wine for her, they could have been drinks for couples all over London, up and down the country. I watched Adam at the bar. Everything about him was familiar: the wide-legged stance, calf muscles thrust back, most of his weight in his heels; the way he reached into his front pocket to scoop out loose change, examined it in his cupped palm before picking out the right money to hand over; the flat patch of hair on the back of his head that I used to comb up with my fingers.

Many times I'd regretted the nature and extent of Adam's betrayal: if only he'd had the inappropriate friendship but not the affair, or if the affair had been shorter, or if he hadn't carried on lying even after I'd found out. But the facts stood, and eventually I realized that it had to be that big and that bad. I wouldn't have left him for anything less.

Waiting for him to come back to the table, I wondered, again, how I was going to tell him. I didn't know how to say it, what words to use, but in fact I didn't have to say anything. I took the jewelry box out of my handbag and when he sat down I slowly slid it over the table toward him and from that he knew.

Stricken, he paled. He rose immediately from his chair, looked at me while he put his wallet and keys back in his pocket and hauled on his jacket. He zipped it all the way up to his chin, snatched up the box, and crammed that in his pocket too. There were tears in his eyes, but he sounded angry when he said, "You were never going to, were you? You kept me hanging on, let me hope, but you were never going to."

"I tried, Adam," I said, but he'd already left.

66

Peter's alley was filled with white flowers. Shelves, tables, and chairs covered in bunches of daisies, dahlias, and carnations still wrapped in cellophane and a day or two past their best—petals browning, heads drooping—a job lot from a garage forecourt. Nothing to sell that day; just flowers and Peggy Lee singing from the record player.

Peter was arranging and rearranging bunches, fag in mouth, whiskey in hand. "We start early today, darling," he said, meaning the drink. "We are alcoholic today."

But there was no "we." Toto had been taken away from Peter for disturbing the peace. They put him in a vet's surgery, but he scared the cats and dogs, so they moved him to an old-age pensioners' home.

"As if old people don't swear, darling! I'm an old-age pensioner and I'm terrible!"

"And where's Ronnie?" I asked.

"He died." Peter's eyes filled with tears, which ran over his bony cheeks. I'd never noticed how deeply lined his skin was. "The flowers are for him. He had another stroke. This one killed him, so we say goodbye."

"I'm so sorry to hear this, Peter," I said, and I really was.

"Drink, darling?" He poured me one. I took it.

"To Ronnie," said Peter.

"To Ronnie," I said.

"*Is that all there is?*" sang Peggy.

"These flowers would look much nicer out of the wrapping. Can I help you?"

Peter and I shook the flowers loose, laid them criss-crossed to make a border either side of the alley, and blanketed the furniture. From deep inside the shop Peter dug out some stubby candle ends and a piece of chalk. He wrote on the wall *RIP Ronnie*; the thick white letters showed up well against the dark yellow bricks—old London stock, Ronnie once told me, like him.

"Guess how many children he had?" said Peter as we surveyed our work.

"I don't know—three? Four?"

"Twenty-two," said Peter. "Guess how many came to his funeral?"

"I don't know."

"One."

67

After I told Adam that I wanted a divorce, he and I had meetings. Actual meetings with agendas, more formal than the ones I was used to having at work, and much, much more formal than the ones I started having with Branton.

Soon after our lunch, Branton asked me out for a drink; suggested a wine bar nowhere near either of our offices, which fact I duly noted. He was there waiting for me at 7:00, and by closing time we'd had several large glasses of red wine and some tapas, talked about lots of things that we never would have normally, but not actually made any physical contact; I hadn't accidentally brushed past him on my way to the ladies', his fingers didn't touch mine when he set down my drink, not even our shoes bumped under the table. We were still work colleagues, out for a drink.

When we left the bar I remarked how late it was and said I had better get home. There was a zebra crossing, and on the other side one of those old-fashioned street-lamps giving off a subdued yellow glow. We started crossing side by side—two work colleagues—but halfway over the road he took my hand and as we reached the other side, he bent down and kissed me under the streetlight. I was surprised, even though I'd been expecting something to happen. The surprise was that it actually did.

"Do you *have* to go?" he said after we'd kissed a bit longer.

The children were at Adam's. That morning I'd put on my new Rigby & Peller underwear. I did not have to go.

In the cab on the way to his place, I had a rush of nerves. I hadn't slept with anyone except Adam for fifteen years, and not even him for the last twelve months.

"I haven't done this for a really long time," I said quietly to Branton as the taxi chuntered along.

Branton was still holding my hand. He listened as I spoke, looked at me and nodded.

"OK," he said. And it was.

I started doing what the breakup books recommended: living like a teenager, basically. On Wednesdays when Adam had the girls I would nip to Branton's from work and go straight to the office the next day, after morning sex and breakfast. Branton bought me a toothbrush and I'd use his shower gel and shampoo and deodorant so that on Thursdays I'd catch his scent on my skin and hair. Once, I forgot to bring a top so he loaned me a shirt and that became the norm. It felt fantastic to leave the office on Wednesday afternoon with only a pair of knickers in my handbag.

Every other weekend, when Adam had the girls, I would see Branton either at my place or his. At my house, I liked to see his big shoes lolling in the hall, his jacket on the banisters, a jersey hanging over the back of a chair.

Sometimes he bought little presents for the girls: Matchbox cars, WWE figures that they held wrestling bouts with on the kitchen table—boy stuff. The girls loved these unexpected gifts, so different from anything I ever bought them, and when they asked where they came from, I said "a friend from work," which wasn't a lie. I didn't tell them about Branton because I didn't think it would help them to know that Mummy had a lover. Even the word was age-inappropriate and I couldn't call him a boyfriend because he emphatically wasn't.

He knew my circumstances, didn't pry. Only once, in bed at his place, did he ask what happened with Adam. I choked up. Branton pulled me closer and said, "A really bad breakup, huh?" and kissed my hair.

The only thing that worried me was that I was much older than him. At a push, I thought he might possibly have been in his early thirties. We never spoke of this, but one night in the pub by his flat we saw a poster for a capoeira class and Branton couldn't read what it said. He told me he was short-sighted but too vain to wear glasses. After that I worried: Had he even noticed that I was nearly forty? Did he only fancy me because he couldn't see properly?

In the middle of the night, I asked him, "How old are you?"

"Guess," he said.

"Thirty-one?" I said optimistically.

"Lower."

"Thirty?"

He shook his head.

"Twenty-eight?"

"Nearly!"

"Twenty-seven?"

"Yep. How old are you?" he asked.

"Guess," I said.

"Twenty-seven?" I almost fell in love with him just for that.

68

The Guest Experience conference was put off and reduced like a cut-price piece of meat. Instead of January, it was held at the end of March; instead of four days it was two; and the number of delegates went down from two hundred to seventy-five. We were still getting complaints about the Ambassade Central Park West, so the plan was that I would go out on the Monday to investigate; Trish and Don would fly out on the Tuesday to check everything before going on to Chicago to finalize their Hotel Village deal and would return to New York on Wednesday evening in time for the conference.

I arranged for my mother to come for the five days I would be away. Things with Adam were going through a very frosty patch, which my solicitor said was normal but felt awkward and sad. Adam didn't make eye contact with me anymore, and shifted his glance to the floor whenever he addressed me. I knew from the girls that he was grumpier than usual, and prone to tears. On balance, I thought they'd be better off while I was away with a combination of my mother reinforced by Noreen, and I arranged it so that all Mum really had to do was breakfast and bedtime. Both the girls and my mother were enthusiastic about the idea, which I was pleased about but also slightly puzzled by until Hester let slip that Grandma had promised McDonald's or KFC every night plus a bag of Haribo if they were good.

✳

In order to acclimatize, my mother came for the weekend before I left. As soon as she arrived, she spied *Raising Happy Children* on top of the fridge.

"Why are you reading that? They're perfectly all right," my mother said rather unhelpfully in front of the girls, who giggled. I wished I hadn't left it out, but then she added, "Really, darling—you're managing very well. Much better than I did," and squeezed my hand.

That evening, Mum restuffed and restitched Winnie-the-Pooh and Piglet while the girls watched *Diego and Rosita*. When she'd finished she sat them on the kitchen table and we admired her handiwork—the toys looked much happier. I thanked her and openly admitted that I wasn't very good at sewing.

"That's OK, Mummy—you're good at other things," said Hester.

"You're good at putting us to bed," said Milla. "And Grandma's good at that now too. She didn't used to be, but she's got better."

My mother inclined her head gracefully to acknowledge the compliment.

"And you're good at having baths," said Hester.

"And practicing the piano."

"And shopping at Sainsbury's."

"And she's good at dejunking," said my mother, which was also true, but I was done with that now. I gave *Raising Happy Children* to the charity shop and I dejunked the dejunking books and all of their self-help friends.

69

The driver who picked me up at JFK airport was called Gloria. She greeted me with my name on a board, shook my hand, introduced herself, and insisted on wheeling my case and carrying my hand luggage.

"I really think I should carry it myself," I protested.

"Why—because we're both women? But I am the driver and you are the client, so let me. OK?" she said.

On the drive to Manhattan, we talked about work and family. Gloria was married with two children; her husband was also a taxi driver and they'd come over to America from Colombia seven years ago, leaving behind six siblings, three aging parents, and an ancient grandmother between them. I told Gloria I was in the middle of a divorce.

"That's tough, with two little kids to support. You're doing OK with it though, right?"

"I suppose so," I said.

"Yeah, you are, you're OK—you're healthy, you got your children, you got a job, you got a home."

"That's true," I said.

"I've got something for you," Gloria said. She opened up the glove compartment and reached back with a £5 note. "I had a fare who tipped British. When you get back to London, go out and buy yourself a cup of coffee and some cake, OK?"

"I will, thank you—I love cake!"

Before she dropped me at the hotel, Gloria asked, "Would you marry again?"

"Maybe, if the right person came along."

"Really? I wouldn't. I'd be free."

70

The hotel was sick. I felt this as soon as I walked through the front door. The doormat was curled up at the corners to reveal a rubber underbelly and the color had run out of the fake flowers at reception. They gave a lackluster welcome at the Ambassade Central Park West and they gave it several times over. Doorman, receptionist, lift operator, concierge, and porter all asked the same thing: "How was your flight?" I began to wonder if they knew something I didn't.

There was confusion at breakfast—I asked for boiled eggs but the waitress, whose plastic name tag read *Signia*, misheard. "Wild eggs? What is that?" she said.

The restaurant area was at the back of the ground floor. There were no windows and the daylight coming in from the front of the building didn't quite stretch that far, so the hotel had overcompensated with interrogation-strength lighting over the hot buffet. Signia was very young and very tall with straight blond hair in a long ponytail. I found out she was from Latvia and had only been at the Ambassade for two weeks.

A middle-aged couple were breakfasting at the neighboring table. The man's admiration for Signia was evident—he couldn't help eyeing up her slim legs, narrow hips, long neck. "I wonder what sport she does," he wondered aloud. His wife ignored him, but when Signia returned with my wild eggs, he asked her.

"Basketball," she told him. "When I was younger, I

was good. I was selected for the national squad when I was thirteen and I went to the capital—alone, no mother, no father. It was still very Russian then and we had a coach who was very strict. We did exercises to make us grow taller—to stretch our bones. It was a very hard training. After some months I had a break—" She stopped mid-sentence. I think the word was going to be "breakdown," but she censored herself and said, "I had health problems. I went home."

I unpacked. The bedrooms weren't too bad; a bit faded perhaps, a bit too close to the shabby end of the shabby-chic scale, but they were large with high ceilings, and mine had a big window overlooking Central Park and a very well-stocked minibar, so in fact I quite liked it.

When it came time to go down again, I decided to take the stairs. The landing between each floor was decorated with lots of tall vases containing thin branches sprayed white, a ghost of a forest. The lighting was dim—eco setting, no doubt. On the second-floor landing, amid the fake trees, was a small turd, such as could only have been laid by an animal.

I headed straight for the general manager. I needed to see him anyway and now to report the turd in the stairwell, which I was really shocked about—in all my years working in hospitality I'd never seen anything like that. The receptionist took me back of house and pointed me in the right direction, but when I reached his office the door was open and he wasn't there. I decided to look around—I'd been sent there as a kind of hotel doctor; I might as well examine the patient.

In the staff area an off-duty porter lounged on a dilapidated sofa, wearing headphones, eyes closed, moving his body in time to his music. A small square window giving onto an alley at the back of the hotel was propped open but the room reeked of stale cigarette smoke; there were yellow streaks on the walls and dark brown spots on the ceiling.

The kitchen was empty. Breakfast had long closed but someone must have been in the middle of preparing something because on one of the stainless-steel counters there was a pile of raw chopped meat and minced onion. Pale liquid streaked with blood was seeping out and running off the chopping board, collecting at the edge and bulging into a large, heavy drip.

Inside a freezer the size of a walk-in wardrobe were catering packs of plastic-wrapped bacon, butter the size of breeze blocks, and one shelf with nothing but single scoops of ice cream laid out in neat rows on greaseproof paper, ready for a rush on ice cream that I couldn't help feeling would never come.

71

The next morning, there was a small dropping on the second floor in the same spot as before, amid the white twigs. I went to find the general manager; again he was not there. I looked for him back of house. One of the internal walls looked as though it were bleeding, but it was just condensation running over a rusty nail.

Signia was serving breakfast. In one corner, a group of extremely tall young men had pushed several tables together, but they were still too big for the furniture—elbows and knees jutting out, broad shoulders sandwiched in.

"The Australian volleyball team," said Signia.

We looked at them: six six-footers tucking into their breakfast. One, with curly brown hair and freckles over his nose and cheeks, glanced up at Signia, blushed, and looked away.

"Much better than your usual fan club," I said approvingly. Signia reddened and smiled at the floor.

"You should tell him that you were on your national basketball team," I said.

I didn't want to be surrounded by pale mounds of scrambled eggs, vats of undercooked bacon, and the smell of a hundred sausages, so I asked Signia if it was all right for me to take my coffee into the lobby. "Yes, of course it is!"

*

Hotels are terribly intimate, like any other setting where you're thrown together with strangers. You see a family, the teenage daughter tucking in her mother's bra straps at the back, a couple coming down to breakfast with their fingers loosely intertwined, a single stranger standing in the lobby wondering where to go, a child trailing behind his parents humming a song from *The Lion King*. Bodies are porous; vulnerability slips through. Even hardened businessmen and -women, when they talk numbers, talk about loss. Despite all the armor and warpaint, humanity shows: a shirt button pops open exposing a soft, hairy belly; damp patches grow under arms or behind knees; a mottled blush rises from chest to throat; someone stammers. The business world can be brutal. Those at the top have usually had to fight a few battles to get there and you can see in their bodies the toll it's taken.

Don and Trish arrived. They looked awful. I hadn't seen Don for a while—he'd been touring the hotels of the Far East, evidently developed a rattling cough. They paused while he spat into a tissue and wiped his mouth; his cough was as deep as a well, judging by the spume and spittle he drew up. Trish looked frayed. Over the last few months she'd become increasingly snappish, her eyes brittle, her neck sinewy, shoulders tensed, her hair bleached so dry it looked as though it might break as she twisted it around her fingers. I waved; we greeted each other. Trish said they'd flown first class and that Angelina Jolie was on the next bed.

"Did you sleep?" I asked.

"Don't be silly," she replied. "Don slept and Angelina slept; I watched four movies, back-to-back."

Don had lost an amount of weight and maybe he had

started losing hair too, because he'd shaved his head. He had a scar on the back of his head, a shiny white line two centimeters long, half a centimeter wide. The shape of his skull was somehow unexpected, made him seem naked. The shareholders wanted his head on a platter; it was almost as if he were preparing it for them.

Don only stayed a couple of hours—evidently he couldn't wait to get to Chicago—and for the rest of the day, Trish was demanding and churlish. At lunch, the water was too warm, the bread too crusty, her steak too bloody, the crème brûlée too soft. After the last meeting of the afternoon, Trish wanted to go shopping. She asked me to go with her, but I had anticipated this and arranged to finalize the conference menus, an activity for which Trish wasn't needed. I put her in a cab for Fifth Avenue; only a fifteen-minute walk, but Trish didn't want to arrive at Dolce & Gabbana on foot.

I agreed to everything the French chef suggested: kir royale as an aperitif, the hors d'oeuvres, the amuse-bouches between courses. Forty-five minutes later I locked the door to my room, and after I had spoken to the girls I turned off my phone and ran a bath. At Heathrow, for a bit of luxury, I'd bought myself a new bathrobe—five-star soft and velvety. I removed my earrings and stayed in the warm water for a long time, floating, sloshing, becoming a little softer myself. Afterward I lay on the bed, listening to the sounds as the day outside ended and the evening began. I could hear cars in the street below, heels clacking along the pavement, a dog barking, someone shouting in the distance. Closer, I could hear someone walk down the carpeted corridor, the lift going up and down in the shaft, other gurgles in the building. I fell asleep for a couple of hours and awoke in the dark, hungry. The phone by the bed had one of those spiral wires like an umbilical cord. I ordered soup and fish pie with mashed potato, food that barely needed chewing, ate cross-legged on the bed, and afterward raided the minibar for expensive dark-chocolate pastilles and a small jar of milk-chocolate-covered roasted almonds. It was a padded existence in a womblike bubble, where I only had to think of food and it was there, everything I might need provided. I drifted off to sleep under a duvet of eiderdown, occasionally surfacing when a car cut through the night or a bottle crashed to a pavement, but these things didn't trouble my slumber, they were so far away.

4:10 a.m.
     Knocking.

Satisfaction at having slept past 3:00 a.m. was immediately superseded by irritation at having been woken. The knocking continued like a low-level headache. "Excuse me, Mrs. Kate! Wake up!" came an urgent whisper at the door. It was the night manager, bent with apology, very sorry to wake me, but he did not know what else he should do—it was Trish, she was unwell and could I please come? As I pulled on my dressing gown and shoved my feet into slippers the irritation gave way to dread: What state could Trish possibly be in that would warrant the night manager waking me to attend her? Then the irritation returned. She's probably stubbed her toe on the bed, I thought, or dropped her phone down the toilet.

We took the lift to the honeymoon/rock-star/executive suite on the top floor, named to suit the occasion. Trish appeared at the far end of the corridor, barefoot but thankfully wearing a nightgown, with a long silk dressing gown, unbelted, hair loose around her shoulders. In a pantomime gesture, the night manager put his finger to his lips. By now incredibly pissed off, thinking of the Good Night's Sleep I was missing, I wanted to shout, What the hell is this? Some kind of elaborate and very shit joke? But something about the stance of Trish's body stopped me; it was so weird— drifting skyward as if waiting to be beamed up. She let out a moan and then I understood: she was sleepwalking.

Never wake a sleepwalker: this is cardinal, the golden rule. I whispered this to the night manager, who accepted it without discussion, and frankly, it was a relief: bad enough witnessing the discharges of a disturbed psyche without having to wake it.

At breakfast, Signia brought a pot of steaming black coffee, which I drank as if it were an elixir. When Trish sat down at the table I still didn't know how to tell her, only that I must.

"How was your night?" I asked after she'd finished her first coffee, laced with hot milk.

"Terrible, as usual—I never feel rested. I've got some new pills from the doctor but they're giving me nightmares."

"You were sleepwalking," I blurted. "The night manager found you in the corridor and he woke me just after four. We watched over you until you went back to bed, which was just after five."

Trish blanched as I spoke, put down her cup, folded her napkin, pushed out her chair. "I shall have to go back to the doctor and get something stronger," she said.

72

A badly run hotel is like a marriage that's not being cared for: it might look all right to a casual observer, but there are signs. The ghost trees, the blood-streaked drip in the kitchen, the small turd in the stairwell: the Ambassade was a wrong choice. I tried to articulate this to Trish before she left to join Don in Chicago.

"Oh, don't worry," she replied. "Don't worry about the fading wallpaper, the silly white twigs, the animal droppings—these are all things that can be fixed or removed. Remember the top three criteria. Location. Location. Location. In the hotel world, location is everything and the Ambassade has it." She had a point.

At the end of the day, after all my meetings were done, I remembered not visiting the Tivoli Gardens, fetched my coat, and went out. As I crossed over Central Park West an advertisement on a passing cab shouted, *INSOMNIA COOKIES—fresh baked cookies delivered anywhere in Manhattan, all through the night,* which struck me as a wonderful idea. Instead of a couple of dry digestives from a packet, warm cookies with gooey middles, syrupy oats, melty chocolate chips. I started fantasizing: Insomnia Cookies London. All you needed was a large urban population with a bit of cash and a high percentage of students, parents of young children, and stressed-out executives with no work-life balance. It could work anywhere! Insomnia Cookies Bristol. Insomnia Cookies Birmingham. Des Biscuits d'Insomnie Paris. Galletas Insomnio Madrid. Kekse

Schlaflosigkeit Berlin. Biscotti Insonnia Rome. I could be the European president, the managing director of Insomnia.

By the time I looked up from my daydream I was in the middle of Central Park—it was green and open, all the horizons had changed, the skyscrapers shoved to the sides as if the city had dejunked a part of itself to clear a space for running, skating, freewheeling. I thought of Adam flying along on his motorbike. I'd believed he needed that time to feel free, but he'd used it instead to be with someone else—in fact, to *be* someone else. How is it that you can live with a person for ten years, see them every morning and every night, be familiar with the main coordinates of their life, and still not know what's really going on inside them? Then again, people don't always know the contents of their own hearts; we are such secrets, even from ourselves.

Back in the lobby, a crowd was slowly congregating around the lifts, which weren't working properly. In many hotels it's the lifts that keep everything moving, pumping people round—bedroom to bar, gym to breakfast, lobby to spa— all the vital circuits. The bellboy was apologizing. "This is an old hotel," I heard him say, but the Ambassade wasn't old, just middle-aged. People thronged in the lobby and stairwells, bags and cases piled outside rooms in the corridors, blocking passages. The hotel was having a heart attack. Guests started laboring up and down the stairs with their luggage, making very slow progress because they were not used to the exercise. I feared there could be a few actual heart attacks, so I took off my coat and joined the bellboy and concierge in helping guests shift luggage into taxis, up and down the stairs. It didn't take long; within thirty minutes everything was working smoothly again.

The last rays of sunshine were coming in through the windows, which could have done with a clean, but still. I would like to say I sank into the armchair, but it wasn't real leather so it was more of a slither and a slide. There were two photographs on the wall opposite, both of roads: freeways at dusk or dawn—I couldn't tell which—but low in the pinking sky was a huddle of small gray clouds; a soft-focus traffic light glowed emerald, and road lights twinkled like seven-pointed stars. A feeling of deep contentment came over me—uncomplicated, unexpected, and very, very welcome. I don't know quite what happened to bring it about: I know that I found the photographs magical, that I'd enjoyed helping the guests, and that when Signia saw me flopped out in the lobby and came over to ask if I'd like some coffee—decaf so as not to interfere with the possibility of sleep—she did so with real warmth. Experience is like the weather; moves in its own way, changeable, impossible to guarantee.

We were on some wrong path with the Guest Experience thing. You can't manufacture a true experience. You can't dismantle it into component parts. You can study and predict, arrange things just so, have consistent branding, color schemes, and logos, but it will never be more than a wager because experience doesn't live in concrete things. The paint can be fresh, the carpets vacuumed, the surfaces dust-free. Pillows plumped, duvet turned back. Pristine uniforms, fragrant flowers in the lobby, smooth, soundless elevators, clean windows—but the most important thing is how you're treated. Hospitality is the relationship between guest and host. It's a matter of kindness, care, and respect. No matter how fleeting, it's the relationship that really matters, and relationships require presence. They don't come flat-packed with instructions and you can't assemble them; you actually have to be there. Even if everything else is in place, if the staff are wearing smiles but not feeling them, if there's no real presence, the Guest Experience still won't be good.

I thought of Richard. He would have been proud of me and he would have done the same; rolled up his sleeves and carried people's bags, smiling and chatting and making everyone feel all right, I thought tenderly. I hadn't known Richard for long, yet he'd given me so much.

Signia brought the coffee and poured out a cup. Just then I was grateful: for Signia, for Richard, the pleather chair, the hot decaf, my job, my mother, Adam, my children—all of it.

73

I woke to a strange cry in the night—an owl perhaps, more likely a soul. It came again. I wondered if it was Trish; she and Don would be back by now, ready for the conference tomorrow. I wondered if I should go and look, in case she was sleepwalking in the corridors again and had hurt herself or terrified a guest, but she was with Don and he must have known her habits by now.

Since I couldn't get back to sleep I checked my inbox. The Ideas Derby was seething with discontent, as usual. There were twelve new items for me to read. I'd learned by now to follow the sailor's advice and sort them into three buckets:

— *Things that required my immediate attention*
— *Things I needed to keep an eye on*
— *Things I couldn't do a damn thing about*

The third category held the most items by far: I couldn't sort out the halitosis of the general manager of the Empire Express in Denver, Colorado, even if it was making guests physically recoil, and there was not much I could realistically do to intervene in the theft of lightbulbs and toiletries from the storeroom of the Palazzio in Düsseldorf.

I called Insomnia Cookies. The guy on the other end of the line sounded half-asleep, which was reasonable given the hour.

"Ma'am, d'you want the Cookie Box or the Deluxe Cookie Box?" he mumbled.

"What's in the Deluxe?" I asked.

"Triple Chocolate Chunk, Chocolate Peanut Butter Cup, Oatmeal Raisin, and Snickerdoodle."

"Isn't that a kind of dog?"

"Uh, excuse me?"

"The 'doodle' one—it sounds like a dog, but maybe that's just because it sounds like 'poodle.'"

"Actually, you're right—there is a breed called Labradoodle," said the cookie guy, sounding more alert now. "My aunt has one! But a Snickerdoodle is basically a cinnamon-sugar cookie. I guess maybe you don't have them in England, right? They're delicious, especially warm. They're all so good, the cookies here—I've gained, like, ten pounds since I started."

"How long have you worked there?"

"Four weeks."

"Oh dear, that does sound dangerous. I'm glad I don't live in New York, in that case, and since I won't be doing this again, I'll have the Deluxe."

"An excellent choice, ma'am. And I'll sneak an extra Snickerdoodle in there for you."

While I was ordering the cookies, another alert came in: a lengthy email describing in detail how PHC was actively colluding with two of the world's biggest booking websites, BookYourBestHotel.com and RitzyPackage.com. At last, something serious that required my immediate attention. Someone, somewhere, was accusing Don and Trish of price-fixing.

74

By 7:30 a.m. the breakfast area was overrun with PHC conference delegates; the Australian volleyball team were huddled in the same corner as before, Signia chatting to them. Mehmet and Doris, two legal colleagues from the London office, were taking plates of food back to their table.

"We're just having something to eat," said Doris. The term "something to eat" was very broad: Mehmet had a pile of scrambled eggs, two rashers of bacon, two slices of bread, three sausages, a big puddle of ketchup, and three pancakes with maple syrup; Doris had a croissant.

Outside the conference room, delegates gathered with their countrymen and -women, conducting conversations in their own languages. Walking around, I couldn't distinguish all of them—was that Portuguese or Russian, with those guttural noises and hard stops? And was that Dutch or possibly Afrikaans? Mandarin or Cantonese? Hindi or Panjabi? Norwegian, Swedish, or Danish? I recognized French, Italian, German, and Spanish. With these I slowed down, lingered if I heard a few words I could understand—like looking through the curtains of someone else's home.

Trish was nowhere to be seen. I texted her, I called her, I went downstairs to look for her, called her room from the lobby but there was no answer. I imagined she was having a hair crisis, unless the unthinkable had happened and she'd derailed. The conference began at 9:00 a.m. as planned, and because the morning sessions were all with external speakers, it was less obvious that Trish and Don hadn't even shown up yet.

During the midafternoon break, Doris and Mehmet came over to speak to me.

"We're very sorry but we won't be able to attend the conference this afternoon because there's something we need to deal with," said Mehmet.

"Something very bad has happened in one of our hotels," said Doris.

"We can't say which one," said Mehmet.

"What's happened?" I asked. They glanced at each other.

"A guest has been attacked," said Doris.

"Oh, no!" I said.

"And we may be liable. There's a bit of a gap."

"What do you mean, 'a bit of a gap'?" I said.

"Well, it happened in a public area—one of the back corridors, late last night—so the CCTV should have picked it up, but the cameras were trained . . . ahm, elsewhere, so the police may not be able to catch the perpetrator."

"The cameras were trained on the staff," I said.

"At that particular moment in time," said Doris. Mehmet nodded.

"Who was attacked?" I asked. "Were they badly hurt?"

"A female guest," said Mehmet.

"It was very bad. We can't really talk about it," said Doris.

"For legal reasons," said Mehmet.

"The good thing was that it wasn't one of our employees who did it. It was another guest," said Doris.

"Who *allegedly* did it," said Mehmet.

"What do you *mean*?" I said, frustrated by their obfuscation.

"It's a four-letter word," said Doris.

"It begins with 'R.' I'm afraid it's the 'R' word," said Mehmet.

"Oh, my God!" I said.

"We know," they said, nodding.

"A woman has been raped in one of our hotels—and *this* is how we talk about it?" I said, letting my disgust show. Doris and Mehmet looked at each other, puzzled.

"No," said Doris.

"We can't talk about it," said Mehmet.

Not *all* companies stupidize people, I told myself. Not all companies take soft, rounded humans and force them into straight lines and strange language. Not all bosses are myopically self- and profit-obsessed, borderline personality disordered, I thought as I looked, again, for mine.

We allowed this to happen, I realized; as a company, we were failing on every count. A host's duty is not only to provide food and shelter, but also to make sure that their guests do not come to harm.

I went back into the conference room, as big as an auditorium. Still no sign of Trish, but Don had arrived, head bent, shuffling through papers, preparing to give his address. The chairs swiveled and had a handle to lower and raise the seat, and the plastic arms could also go lower or higher and you could move them separately. People were playing with arm heights and seat heights, shifting their weight around in the chairs. Outside, the weather was unseasonably warm, more like May than March; there was birdsong, and sunlight and gentle air, but since Don was about to give a PowerPoint presentation the windows were closed and the blinds pulled down.

Don stood in the middle of the room, mumbling and then spluttering, delegates seated around him in a big circle. His cough was a channel that connected him to a very bad place. We waited for him to speak. Only the chairs made a sound, rocking and creaking like trees. A fly was shut in the room, zigzagging in a crazy circuit around the heat and light of the projector.

"Someone kill it," came a voice. It might have been Trish, but it was dark and there were seventy people in the room so I wasn't sure. Don started talking in a very low voice; only snippets came through, but we all heard when he said, "The company is in the hands of the receivers."

A moment of shock, then a voice piped up, "Richard would never have let this happen. We were in safe hands with him."

Don looked up as if to answer. He had visibly shifted from one state to another and was now entering a third. He said, "Many of us will lose our jobs. It could happen very quickly."

People started to rise, tutting and swearing.

"A couple of months; maybe weeks. I'm not giving in without a fight. I don't expect any of you to stay and fight with me, but I will fight." Don spoke more clearly now, stood more upright, as if finding something recognizable in himself at last.

I'd had enough. I needed to go home; to see my children, hold them, breathe in the smell of them, and not go away again like this. I was sick of Palazzio Hotel Corporation, sick of putting on my work face every morning, sick of the corporate code, and traveling for work all the time, missing whole days and nights at home. I was sick of being one of Trish's people, and sick of working for a company that kept getting it so wrong. Location is not the main thing; the top three criteria for hotels are the same as they are for dentists, as they are for any other relationship—friends, parents, employers, governments, spouses, and lovers:

1. *How they treat you*
2. *How they treat you*
3. *How they treat you*

I left the conference and walked downstairs. Sure enough, on the second-floor landing the daily turd had been delivered in the suggestion of a forest by the animal I hadn't seen. In the lobby, the bellboy was apologizing to some guests by the lifts, which were having another seizure.

I had three calls to make, all to London. The first was to the Office of Fair Trading, which was very interested in the alleged price-fixing. They explained it could be a long process but that from what I'd told them, they could launch an investigation. They asked if I had considered whether I was really willing to see this through and if so, when could I come in and see them to go through the allegation in more detail and start the paperwork. "Monday morning at nine," I said.

Next I called the Information Commissioner's Office again and told them how CCTV had missed recording a violent crime because it was being used to spy on staff.

"Is that serious enough for you?" I asked angrily.

"I'm very sorry it has come to this," the case officer said. "But yes, we can look at this now. As far as I know it's unprecedented, but there may well be a case."

The third call was to my mother.

"I'm quitting my job," I told Mum. "Well, actually, it may be quitting me, but either way I'm leaving."

"Isn't that a bit—*rash*?"

"It may seem rash but in fact I've been thinking about it for ages. I'm coming home right now—I'm on my way."

"But I thought your flight wasn't until tomorrow evening—"

"I'll get another one. Airplanes are like buses, Mum—you can just turn up and buy a ticket, you know."

"That's very extravagant, Kathryn. Can't you wait?"

I ignored that comment and said instead, "By the way, I've taken a lover. He's twelve years younger than me."

That shut her up.

PART FOUR

I keep following this sort of hidden river of my life, you know, whatever the topic or impulse which comes, I follow it along trustingly. And I don't have any sense of its coming to a kind of crescendo, or of its petering out either. It is just going steadily along.

—*William Stafford*

75

Where I work now—the Mythos Suites Hotel, a five-star forty-room boutique hotel on the South Bank—we have an arrangement with the homeless hostel down the road; any unoccupied rooms, we put people up for the night who have nowhere else to go. Two hostel workers come and help get people settled in. They have to come in the staff entrance and we take them to the rooms in the service lift because although the guests are pleased enough to know about such a scheme, they don't actually want to see—or smell, or hear—it in operation. We can't take the addicts, but we can take the working girls—give them the night off—and the young runaways, the bankrupt businessmen, the broken wives and their frightened children. It's not a lot, two or three rooms a night, because the hotel is popular, but it's something. Manos, the hotel owner, is a sixty-two-year-old Greek shipping magnate who left his home in the Peloponnese at the age of fourteen, arrived in Athens with a few drachmas and nowhere to stay. Manos built an empire, but he knows that most people in that situation do not; that many people end up enslaved in one. And that's if they're lucky.

I love being the hotel manager. Eleni, Julie, and Andy, my coworkers, are Greek as well and of course speak Greek when I'm not around; they switch to English for my benefit, but I've started learning the language so that I can join in with them a little bit. I'm also learning a simplified version of the aria from the Goldberg Variations. Even dumbed down, Bach is beautiful. Linda the piano teacher told me that Bach composed the Variations for the Russian ambassador Count Keyserling, who suffered from insomnia, and that Goldberg, a young music student in the count's employ, had to sleep in an antechamber and play the clavier to the count during his sleepless nights. It must have been very soothing for Count Keyserling to hear the music, less so for poor Goldberg to be roused in the middle of the night to play.

I knew it wouldn't last forever with Branton, though to begin with it felt as though it could. After the hormone high of the first few months wore off, he drifted back toward other interests, the chief of which was sports. He played, and if he wasn't playing he watched—rugby, football, athletics, tennis, golf, darts, whatever was going. Formula One was what I liked least—all those whining cars. To begin with, it was nice to cuddle up on the sofa and then after the game, race, bout, or match ended have sex, which was also nice to begin with, but slowly it dawned on me that for Branton sex was also a sport and he liked to watch himself perform it. I couldn't blame him, he was an Adonis, but I did start to lose interest when I realized it was his own arms he was caressing, his own chest he was admiring. When I started getting boredom headaches, I knew it was over.

Yvette seemed relieved when I told her I'd stopped seeing Branton. I think that my being single somehow consoled her about her own situation; as if being unhappily married was better than not being married at all. I tried to tell her:

the end of a relationship isn't a catastrophe and you don't need another in order to be all right, but she didn't want to hear it. I understood—people used to try telling me things about Adam but I shrugged them off.

I see Adam when he collects or drops off the girls; more often than either of us would choose, but we are still linked through our children. We fight sometimes, but mostly we manage. The girls say it's a good thing we divorced. I agree and point out that it was also a very good thing we married in the first place: How else would we have them? They get that. They get all of it really, and in fact I'm often slightly alarmed at how savvy and sophisticated they are. Milla despises boy bands; she likes punk rock. She was telling me all about emo and screamo music, style, and culture—completely foreign to me.

"How do you *know* these things?" I asked her.

"How do you *not* know?" Milla said, equally incredulous.

My sleep still has a few holes in it. It's like jet lag from a very long flight. I used to fret so much: I can't sleep, I'm not sleepy, I can't get to sleep. Sleep was always this thing that I had to strive for and reach, but it's slowly improving. I've learned that I don't have to be the active ingredient. In Greek you can say, "*Me perni o ipnos*"—Sleep is taking me over. I like that.

76

The cakes on the counter all look delicious: a Victoria sponge with generous amounts of jam and cream; a lemon-and-almond cake, shiny and deep yellow; a rich-looking plum cake, golden on top with amber edges, purple plums sunk deep in the dense pale base. I sit at one of the square, solid tables, order a pot of English Breakfast, extra strong, and a piece of the plum cake. "Buy yourself a cup of coffee and some cake on me," Gloria had said in the taxi once upon a time in New York. I didn't think she'd mind me switching to tea.

I let the tea stew until it's as brown as the Arizona desert and sample the cake. The first mouthful stops me in my tracks—vanilla, nutmeg, plum; this cake is *incredible*. I eat it bite by slow bite, cutting it with big sips of tea, looking at my plate so as to experience the cake fully—visually as well as its taste and texture, the weight of each mouthful on my fork, the delicious smell.

"This cake!" I say to the waitress.

"I know," she replies, with feeling. I ask her for the recipe, but she says it's a secret, so I buy three slices to go, one more for me and one each for the girls.

By the time I get home the cardboard box has gratifyingly wide grease spots on the bottom. I peer at the cake, studying its nature. The defining qualities are a large, soft golden crumb, vanilla sweetness, buttery moisture, the scent of nutmeg, and a puckering tartness of the heavy plums at the bottom.

Rising at 3:00 a.m., I search in my recipe books and online for "plum cake," "plum, nutmeg, vanilla cake," and "vanilla cake with plums and nutmeg," find several versions that look as though they could do the job, and take bits from each to make my own.

My night kitchen is clean and calm. I move quietly to match the stillness. The kitchen is at the back of the house, away from the street, private and sheltered. I grease a cake tin, line it with paper. In a beige ceramic mixing bowl I cream together butter and sugar with the back of a wooden spoon, add two teaspoons of vanilla extract, whisk three eggs, and add them too. In a small pan the plums bubble in a slow-cooking syrup of water, sugar, cinnamon, cardamom, and clove. I leave them to steep while I sift the flour, tapping the sieve against my palm rather than the side of the bowl, because it makes less noise. This is a quiet cake. I grate half an oval nutmeg onto a board, bringing the leftover piece up to my nose for the warm, woody spice, combine the nutmeg with the other dry ingredients, add them to the bowl, and tip in the plums, mixing well, then pour the batter into the prepared cake pan and slide it into the hot oven.

As I wait for the cake to bake I clear up, make tea, read a bit. Our house at night is a changed place; sounds magnified, shadows deepened, time slowed. Still rather empty, but we're used to that now and in fact we quite like it. Dejunking was not the answer to all of my problems, but clearing the space did help somehow, if only by making room to accommodate all of those thoughts and feelings—so perhaps those books weren't completely ridiculous, and perhaps I wasn't either.

When the cake is done the kitchen is warm from the oven and smells like heaven. I let it cool in the tin for half an hour, before turning it out on a plate. When I do this, I see I've burned the bottom, tut a bit, and slice off the charred layer, taking some blackened plum with it, then leave the cake to cool a little longer.

I stare out of the window at the changing light. It's nearly 5:00 a.m. I feel satisfied, and grateful—which may not be exactly the same thing as happy but must be part of it.

At 6:00 a.m., I inspect my work. The cake smells good and seems to have the right color and the right weight. Sampling it, I know I'm off. It doesn't quite have the depth of the original, but that's OK, it's my first attempt. I may be off but I'm very, very close.

77

It's nice and industrious in the bookshop today, like a library or a reading room. I've got a couple of cookbooks open on the shelf. Ben has four or five titles piled up by the till and he's reading the top one; there's a woman perusing the card selection and an au pair flicking through gardening books with her young charge standing placidly by, munching his way through a bag of cheese-and-onion crisps. None of the celebrity chefs have quite what I'm looking for but there's an untrendy book that looks as though it's been on the shelf for quite a while with a couple of recipes I like the sound of: Upside-Down Plum Cake and Sussex Plum Heavies. The Lardy Johns sound good too.

The little boy sends up a great wail. He's spilled his crisps all over the floor. His au pair says, "Oh, *Christopher*," in a cross tone. Christopher starts picking up the crisps and putting them back in the bag.

"You can't eat those now, they're dirty!" she scolds.

"Want!" Christopher retorts.

"No!" says the au pair. Christopher reaches down, grabs a little fistful of broken crisps from the floor, and crushes them into his mouth.

"Naughty!" says the au pair, and yanks him out of the shop.

*

"Poor Christopher," I say to Ben.

"He moved pretty fast—he was well within the five-second rule," says Ben.

"I thought it was the *ten*-second rule," I say, thinking of all the dropped biscuits I've let the girls pick up and eat—never from a pavement, but sometimes those biscuits stayed longer than ten seconds on the kitchen or sitting-room floors.

"That's something else, I think," says Ben.

The woman looking at cards has gone. Ben fetches a dustpan and brush, and while he sweeps up, I sneak a peek at his pile of books. The top one is open so I can't see the title but the others are: *500 Words You Should Know, The Way of Tenderness*, and *The Happiness Solution Project: The Ultimate Guide to Feeling Happy Now and Forever*. Despite my wide reading on the subject I hadn't come across that one. Most of the self-help books I'd read talked about Happiness as if it were a trophy or the pot of gold at the end of the rainbow, but surely the rainbow itself is the magical thing? Often, feelings arrive two or three together; mixed, brawling, but if you could get all those unruly feelings to line up, there would be a spectrum, each fading into the next. Green, blue, indigo, violet. Sadness, tenderness, gratitude, joy. You can't just select one and delete the rest.

"I don't think it's possible to be happy all the time," I say.

"No, I know," replies Ben. "I just thought I'd have a look though, see if there's any useful tips."

"What's the one you're reading?" I ask, pointing to the open book.

He closes it to show me the cover: *Suddenly Single: A Lifeline for Anyone Who Has Lost Love.*

"Oh! Ouch," I say. Feelings flood in. Red, orange, yellow. Shock, surprise, compassion.

"It's not too bad," he says. "We were coasting really, more out of habit than anything else."

Another feeling shows up. One that probably shouldn't be here, but I let it in anyway. I change the subject to hide my elation. "Of the five hundred words, what's your favorite so far?"

Ben thinks for a moment. "It's not in the book, but I like 'aver.' And I like 'windowsill.' And 'loop.'"

"Those are very good. I like 'plum.' In fact, I'm looking for a recipe for plum cake," I say, and tell him about the wondrous cake. Ben knows the café I'm talking about.

"Maybe we should loop round there sometime and have some plum cake," he says.

"By the windowsill," I say, playing along.

"Naturally," says Ben.

"OK, well, let me know if you want to do that," I say, doubting everything I just heard.

"I do want to do that," he avers.

"Oh! Well then, let me know *when* you'd like to do that," I say.

78

Hester went off Diego and grew her hair. Now she wants to be a doctor. For her birthday last week I gave her a first-aid kit and a real stethoscope and now she's asking everyone, "What's the worst injury you've ever had?"

"A sprained ankle," said my mother.

"Cut knees when I fell over when I was three," said Milla.

"A cyst behind my ear. I had an operation to remove it—you can still see the scar," said Dad.

"A broken elbow in a car accident—you could see right down to the bone," said the postman.

"Broken heart," I said.

"Oh, Mummy, you're all right now. Tell me another one, a *really* good one, with bones sticking out, and blood running all over the place so I might slip on it."

And it's true, it's mended very well, my heart. There's still an ache sometimes, but that's OK. Trish wasn't completely wrong—the heart is a muscle, after all, and muscles need to be used. They need care and attention, regular exercise to keep them in good condition. People say time heals, but I don't think that's quite right—time is an anesthetic; tenderness and gratitude are what truly heal.

The Mythos Suites Hotel is just a bus ride away, but some mornings I have to go in early and on these mornings I leave the girls to have breakfast and then Noreen comes by

to take them to school. The other day I noticed an empty
box in the recycling that I hadn't put in there and asked if
they'd had an Orange Maid for breakfast.

"Yeah," said Milla.

"But you can't have ice lollies for breakfast!" I said.
"There's nothing in them!"

"They're refreshing and there's vitamin C inside, actually. It says so on the packet," said Hester.

"But they're not very filling," I said.

"It's OK, Mum—we had three each," said Milla.

ACKNOWLEDGMENTS

Thanks to Noreen Smyth, Laura Wade-Gery, Allie Boddington, Carolyn Stalins, Nikki Kastner, Ed McGarry, Roy Butlin, Russell Hansen, Tom Williams, Linda Pearce, and Panagiotis Chrysostomou for stories and moments that helped me write this book.

Thanks to my publisher, Paul Baggaley, for his support, and the wonderful team at Picador, particularly Francesca Main, Emma Bravo, Francesca Pearce, Claire Gatzen, and Ansa Khan Khattak.

Thank you, Sarah Crichton, for spotting the sucker-punch moments I was holding back from.

Thank you, Nancy Rawlinson and Jenny Turner, for reading the manuscript and helpful feedback.

Thank you, Paul McDermott, for helping me when I got stuck with this book.

Thank you to my daughter Lola Linehan for saving us both from the embarrassment of a naff title.

Thank you, thank you, thank you to Kate Harvey and Georgia Garrett for so many insightful comments, precise observations, generosity, enthusiasm, and warmth.

And thanks to Shakespeare's Macbeth, of course.